She coul[d] ~~ for the tende~~ in his gaze.

With black piercing eyes, he ravaged every curve of her body. His muscular frame tightened beneath his dark suit, and he swallowed firm and hard. Mercy, he was every inch a man.

She felt as if the world stopped spinning and stood still around them. They were reduced to their rawest forms in nature, simply man and woman, held breathless and captivated by each other.

She gasped for breath, the muscles along her stomach quivering for release. Growing hot, she felt a shiver quake from her bosom all the way down into her legs until it raced back up and settled into her heart.

That's when the realization struck her, like a thunderbolt sent from Zeus.

She was still in love with this man.

She loved Wyatt with every exploding cell in her body. Oh, Lord, she'd never *stopped* loving him…!

Harlequin Historicals is delighted
to introduce author Kate Bridges
and her debut book
THE DOCTOR'S HOMECOMING

THE
Doctor's
Homecoming

KATE BRIDGES

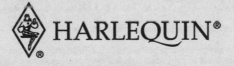

HARLEQUIN®

TORONTO • NEW YORK • LONDON
AMSTERDAM • PARIS • SYDNEY • HAMBURG
STOCKHOLM • ATHENS • TOKYO • MILAN • MADRID
PRAGUE • WARSAW • BUDAPEST • AUCKLAND

ISBN 0-373-29197-3

THE DOCTOR'S HOMECOMING

Copyright © 2002 by Katherine Haupt

This edition published by arrangement with Harlequin Books S.A.

® and TM are trademarks of the publisher. Trademarks indicated with
® are registered in the United States Patent and Trademark Office, the
Canadian Trade Marks Office and in other countries.

Visit us at www.eHarlequin.com

Printed in U.S.A.

Please address questions and book requests to:
Harlequin Reader Service
U.S.: 3010 Walden Ave., P.O. Box 1325, Buffalo, NY 14269
Canadian: P.O. Box 609, Fort Erie, Ont. L2A 5X3

For my husband, Gregory.
Thank you for helping to make the impossible possible.
With special thanks to my parents and in-laws.
To my agent, Charles Schlessiger, for believing in me.
To my editors Ann Leslie Tuttle and Tracy Farrell.
To my cousins, Bozica and Ivan,
I wish I could have written you a happy ending,
and to all the women in war-torn countries
who are fighting their own Barlows and Sinclairs.
And to you, for sharing my love of romance.

Chapter One

Montana Territory, 1882

He was a hard man to forget. Dr. Emma Sinclair took a deep breath, ignored the pounding of her heart and warned herself to stop thinking about him. With a skilled eye and a very steady hand, Emma threaded her needle.

Even after sixteen years, the thought of bumping into Wyatt Barlow during the last three days of her visit home made her pulse hammer and her stomach quiver. Would he still have the power to affect her? With those deep, riveting brown eyes and that warm, private smile that had always flushed her skin.

It didn't matter. He was the last man in Pine Creek she wanted to see. Now he was after her brother.

With hot afternoon sunshine blazing through the scrubbed windows and tiny Mrs. McCullough standing behind her just bursting to ask about Wyatt, Emma brushed aside her frivolous thoughts and concentrated on her young patient. She gently stitched the final suture in his arm.

"Are you feeling better, David?" She knew the morphine had taken hold.

Sitting on the rickety examination table, Mrs. McCullough's grandson raised his tear-streaked face to Emma's reassuring smile. "Yeah, I don't feel the pain no more."

She nodded and wrapped his arm with gauze. Her leg-of-mutton sleeves billowed up and down with her easy movements. She was itching to wipe the perspiration trickling down her neck beneath her braid, but her hands were occupied. A fresh, cool breeze rolled in from the window, scenting the air with pines and cedars from the valley.

To get a smile from David, she let him hold her shiny new pocket watch, last month's graduation present from her family, while she counted his pulse.

White-haired Mrs. McCullough, in a faded country dress, edged closer. "It's just our bad luck," she complained, "missin' Doc Brady on the one day he's outta town. You sure you know what you're doin'?"

Emma drew a breath at the insult, reminding herself the woman was her elder *and* the reverend's mother-in-law. "Yes, Mrs. McCullough," she said kindly, "I do. It might be my first time filling in, but I watched him do this all the time when I was growing up. And I got excellent grades in college."

She anchored a sling around David's arm. "Your grandson's going to be just fine." She was proud of her smooth stitching—and her quick response to her first emergency alone, although Mrs. McCullough didn't need to know that.

The woman's mind seemed to be on other things. "I bet your Ma's sorry you're headin' back to Philadelphia."

Emma shifted uneasily. The topic was changing to her personal life and that usually led to talk of Wyatt. "She's encouraging me to go. The training I'll get working alongside the surgeons is training I can't get here." Her bags were almost packed, her banking done.

She helped David off the wooden table to his steady feet. "We're all finished."

"Have you talked to Wyatt yet?"

Emma winced at the name. "No. Now, where did I put my soiled instruments?" She tried to keep her voice calm. Stepping to the wall of worn cupboards, she searched the sunny office, hoping the woman would take the hint. "I don't have much time to clean up, I promised to help my sister with dinner." She rambled on, "We're cooking turkey to celebrate my new job...I'm always the one who peels and mashes the potatoes."

The woman's face darkened. "Turkey dinners! Celebrations! What have you Sinclairs got to celebrate...?" She opened her mouth to say more, but the sound of children hollering and horses' hooves pounding the dirt distracted them both.

Someone—a child—a boy was screaming, "Doc Brady! Doc Brady!"

Emma jumped and ran to the door. Two white horses heaved to a stop in a flurry of dust. A single rider, a young boy, stood in the stirrups of one while holding the reins of the other, and screamed again, "Doc Brady! Doc Brady!"

She grabbed her medicine bag and ran. People dashed to him from all directions. Pain jabbed through her calf, just enough to annoy her. She kept moving, limping, sizing up the boy.

He seemed unhurt. Dressed in farm clothes, ten or eleven, he jumped off his horse, sobbing, "Doc Brady!"

Emma pushed her way toward him and dropped her heavy bag. "Doc Brady and his wife are in Levi Valley buying supplies."

The boy spun around. She peered into his eyes and froze. *Wyatt's son. Had to be. Same dark brows and piercing eyes.*

A honeybee whizzed by her ear at full speed. "What is it? Is it your father? Who needs help?"

"She's gonna die." He bent over and sobbed.

Not Melissa. Calming herself, Emma knelt and gripped the boy by the shoulders. "You're Tommy Barlow, aren't you?"

He looked up and nodded.

"I'm a doctor, my name's Emma. Tell me what's wrong."

Frowning, he glanced at her city-bought blouse, its fancy collar, the lace trim.

"Tell her boy," said someone, "she's a doctor."

"It's Melissa. The baby's not supposed to come for a long time." Tommy's voice broke. He clamped a hand over his eyes. "But my sister's screamin'...."

Terror seized her. "How long has she been screaming?"

"About an hour."

"Is she alone?"

"No, Pa won't leave her. Great-grandpa's there, too."

"They're at the ranch?"

"Yeah."

Thirty minutes away at full gallop. "Why do you think Melissa's dying?"

"I heard 'em say there's too much blood."

Heart pumping, she sprang to her feet. "How much blood?"

"I don't know, they said it was soakin' the bed."

"I'll get my supplies, you calm your horses."

Tommy nodded. Two men stepped forward to help him.

She raced back to the empty office and grabbed the obstetrical bag. Poor Melissa, she wasn't due for six weeks. Emma's stomach turned. The baby hardly had a chance.

And Doc Brady had said Melissa had a small pelvis. Reeling, Emma clawed through the bag for forceps. Doc

Brady should be going to help, he'd know exactly what to do. She'd send someone to get him. Her fingers wrapped cold metal. A short prayer burst from her lips. Her first delivery. Her first time with forceps.

She drove the fear down and flew to Tommy. He was gently tending to his mare. Her heart stirred. He'd lost his mother years before and now he was worried about his sister. It was more than any boy should have to think about. Should she add to his burden and tell him her last name was Sinclair?

No. It would upset him, more time wasted.

He glanced up as she hobbled down the stairs. Panicked, his gaze fixed on her walk. "What's the matter with your leg?"

"When I was a girl, I was bitten by a snake."

"A rattler?"

"Yes." Should she tell him his father was there when she got bitten?

His voice escalated. "You sure you can ride?"

"I'm sure." Neighbors' hands helped her mount her horse. She left word for Doc Brady and her brother, Cole, then tore off.

Wobbly and out of practice, she shifted in the saddle. She pressed with her knees. That was better.

The hot wind whirled around her blouse, drying her lips and ballooning her skirt. In rhythm to the gallop, her braid slapped against her back. She felt her blouse latch to the sweat of her spine. In a rumble of horses' hooves, Tommy appeared beside her. They cornered the general store.

She thought of Wyatt and her heart squeezed. He must be sick with fear. She whispered a prayer for Melissa and the baby. Did Wyatt have anyone he could turn to for comfort at a time like this?

She gulped air, trying to squelch the fluttering in her

stomach. The last time she'd seen him, through a crowd more than a year ago at Christmas, they'd pretended their eyes hadn't met. He'd ignored her completely.

What would she say when they came face-to-face? Words seemed so inadequate. *How are you, Wyatt? Please forgive my brother, he's so young. By the way, was there ever a solitary moment in the last sixteen years when you were sorry you didn't marry me?*

Nothing could ever persuade her to trust herself to Wyatt again. Not her. Never again.

"Hold on, darlin'," Wyatt whispered tenderly to Melissa, wondering if she could hear him as she slept. "Help's coming, Doc Brady's on his way."

The orange setting sun beat through the frilly bedroom curtains, across the flowered wallpaper, and blazed onto the half-dozen dolls lined along her dresser. He drew a trembling hand through his black hair and sighed. She cast a lonely figure, lying on the iron bed, a lacy sheet pulled over the womanly bulge of her stomach, while such youth shone in her face.

He wiped her forehead with a cool cloth and she moaned. Her wild auburn hair spilled about her, accentuating her paleness.

Ruth, gray-haired and hunched over, shuffled into the room with clean towels. Even with her poor eyesight, the old midwife had been a big help, coming quickly from the neighboring farm. Just having another woman around made him feel better.

She'd already changed the sheets. Thank God, Melissa's bleeding had stopped and things looked almost normal. The only remaining proof it'd happened were the scattered red drops on the legs of his denims.

"I've got everything set up for the doc," Ruth said.

''Clean towels, fresh water and a blanket for the baby, if we should need one.''

He glanced at Melissa's big belly and winced. The baby. Little girl or little boy?

Ruth placed a thin hand on his shoulder. ''Nothin' we can do now except wait. No doctor can stop what nature's intendin'. When they're this early...'' Her words caused his heart to spiral downward. She shook her head and wrung her hands into her apron. Leaving the room, she added, ''And poor Melissa, you should prepare yourself...''

No. Studying his daughter's sleeping face, his gaze traveled over her smooth cheeks to the freckles on her nose. He pulled in a shaky breath.

Was it that bad?

Melissa had lost an awful lot of blood, but maybe the worst was over. His gut tightened. Pulling the slat-back chair from the wall, he slid into it, grateful to anchor himself into something solid. It groaned under the weight of his muscled body.

He lifted Melissa's hand in his, delighting in its soft, familiar feel.

God, all they'd done for months was argue.

What a mess he'd made of everything, trying to be both mother and father to his children. What made him think he could raise them alone? Why hadn't he listened to everyone around him, telling him to marry again, at least for the sake of the children?

Because he wasn't very good at it.

He'd believed in love once, a long time ago, but he'd learned a lot since then, and romantic foolishness had been purged from his heart.

He was the one responsible for his wife's decline, and he shuddered at what the children had witnessed. The worst thing of all was that they were with him the night he found

Lillie, frozen in the storm. She was losing her mind with loneliness, she'd told him once. Even though he knew he'd done all he could to make the marriage work, to help her with her despair, in the end he couldn't help her.

And that had broken his heart.

Marry again? He shook his head. Not in a thousand years.

Melissa moaned and he nearly jumped. She fell back into a restful position as a name burned in his brain.

Cole Sinclair. What should he do about the boy? Food, shelter and clothing—Cole couldn't provide one of those necessities, let alone all three. What father could hand over a daughter and her newborn to such a helpless boy? When would Cole learn how to hold down a job?

God, if Melissa didn't make it through this—he clenched his jaw—he was going to skin Cole alive. And if she did make it through… Let there be no mistake. He would deal with Cole Sinclair.

Until then…

Kissing Melissa's hand, he placed it back at her side. He glanced at the clock on the dresser. What was keeping Doc Brady? Feeling so utterly useless, he had an urge to jump up and scream.

Blazes, he needed some air. He needed to move.

He got Ruth to sit with Melissa and stepped into the hall to peer out the bay window. With a good view of the valley from the second floor, he searched the dirt road nestled in the greenery. There was no trace of riders.

He stared at his horses galloping on the slopes. If he lost Melissa, nothing he'd worked so hard to achieve mattered. Not the house, not the ranch, not the three hundred horses.

If ever he needed the old doctor, it was now. Where were they? He felt an arm on his shoulder and he spun around.

Grandpa tried to smile but his forehead crinkled up with

concern, adding to the heavy wrinkles of his eighty-some years. His bushy brows drew together on his shiny bald head, his long gray hair fluffed around his ears. "Don't worry, boy, Doc's comin'. Ain't never disappointed us, no sirree."

Wyatt peered through the window again. What was that? On the horizon, a tiny swirl of dust.

Hallelujah, approaching riders. His heart sped. "It's them." He leaped down the stairs and out the door. Standing under the elm, he peered down the rutted road to where the hills split and the riders entered his valley. His anticipation mounted as he watched the cloud of dust twist and swell behind the two riders.

But…his eyes were playing tricks.

It took a moment for him to register what he was seeing. They were his Arabians, and he could make out Tommy. He squinted through the shimmering waves of heat, cupping a hand over his eyes. He tensed. Where was the doctor's head of white hair? And what was that? A skirt blowing in the wind? A woman?

Something about the rider seemed familiar. The angle of her head, the way she held her shoulders tight and leaned into the horse. As she turned the final border of trees, his breath caught.

"Emma."

His senses spun. Reeling back, his heart lurched and his gut slammed, as surely as if he'd been punched. Trying to right his balance, he rubbed his bristly cheek with his palm. Hell, he would have preferred a punch…a little blood, a few cuts, but at least he'd know in a day or two, he'd recover.

Emma. What the hell was she doing here? Coming to help Melissa? She sure as hell wasn't coming for him, not after how he'd treated her. He pushed aside his guilt as anger overtook him.

Now what? Was he supposed to let her help? After what her brother did? Dammit, was Wyatt supposed to quietly step aside and let Cole's sister deal with Melissa? Was that supposed to somehow clear the goddamn slate?

He rubbed a hand over his mouth and swore. He watched her, hypnotized, as she galloped straight toward him. He'd heard rumors she was visiting and that she'd finally graduated from the Women's College, a brand new doctor. He'd always believed she'd make a good one. *Was she?*

They thundered in. The mutts barked. He dashed out, reaching for the mare's reins before Emma could dismount. "Pa," Tommy shouted, jumping off his mount.

Wyatt's gut wrenched as he gazed up into her eyes. Her cheeks were flushed and she was out of breath.

His heart hammered against his chest with concern for Melissa. "Where's Doc Brady?"

"In Levi Valley buying supplies. How's Melissa? She still bleeding?"

He softened, letting the reins slacken between his fingers. "She's sleeping. Her bleeding stopped forty-five minutes ago."

Her shoulders dipped with relief. Sliding off the saddle, she touched the ground on tiptoe, standing a head below his large frame. "Any more contractions?"

"No."

Her cheeks grew pinker. "And the baby? Can you see movement in Melissa's belly?"

"Yeah. I almost jumped out of my skin when I saw the baby wiggling, clean through the sheet."

Her whole face brightened. Her eyes sparkled. "That's reassuring. Those are good signs. The best thing for Melissa is to let her sleep. There's nothing better we can do."

Maybe the worst *was* over. His daughter might be fine.

Emma's confidence made the clamp around his heart loosen. His hopes soared to the endless blue sky.

Tommy took the horses and led them to the watering trough. Wyatt couldn't help but beam at Emma. A smile trembled over her mouth, the pretty sight catching him off guard, causing his stomach to roll. He didn't want to be caught off guard. He suddenly realized their proximity, not two feet between them. Close enough to notice the clean scent of her sweat, the tiny drops of dew glistening above her upper lip.

She seemed to be affected, too, either by him or the hard ride. Face flushed, she pulled in a deep breath, her chest heaving and her pink lips quivering. Looking like she'd just been made love to.

Watching her was torture. He took a step back, tried to regain his composure, then his eyes found hers again.

"How are you, Emma?"

"Fine." She thrust out her chin. So she was still mad at him. Yet she'd come to help. And those big, greenish-brown eyes... Did they still flash more green than brown when she was angry? Yes, they did. He swallowed hard. Staring at her felt like an aching wound.

His probing gaze seemed to make her uneasy but she held her ground. Something about her was different. She was dusty from the ride, but in her starched city clothes and that fine braided twist of her glossy brown hair, she looked out of place. As out of place as a polished Easterner.

Hell, she *was* an Easterner now. She hadn't lived in Montana for years. She'd spent them working at her aunt and uncle's boardinghouse, paying for her studies as she could afford them, becoming a fine city girl in the process.

Another city girl, just like the one he'd married. People

and places he didn't understand. He shoved a hand into his pocket.

Tommy's boots crunched on the ground beside him. "Emma's a doctor," said the boy, "that's why I brought her."

"Please let me help, Wyatt." The huskiness of her voice as she said his name strummed through him. God, he'd missed that. "I'd like to examine Melissa," she said. "I won't disturb her, but I need to see her."

Before he could open his mouth, Grandpa stomped up from behind and blocked her path. "Landsake's girl, we're not lettin' a Sinclair through our door. Go back to that no-good brother of yours. We don't like Sinclairs around here. Every time we have something to do with your lot...even with your father, you know what happened—"

"Sir, it happened thirty years ago."

Tommy's head whipped up. "What! You're a Sinclair? Why didn't you tell me?"

Emma turned to the boy with sadness in her eyes, and Wyatt momentarily felt sorry for her. "It would have been a terrible burden for you to have to make that choice for your sister."

"But I trusted you—"

"You can still trust me," she assured him, her eyes moistening. "I took an oath to help people. Their last name's got nothing to do with it. And neither does mine," she said, directing the comment to Wyatt. Her chest rose and the lace around her buttons shifted. He jerked his gaze away from her chest.

"You're not gonna trust a Sinclair, are you Wyatt?"

He certainly was. His daughter was upstairs bleeding. "Melissa needs help, Grandpa, more than we can give her."

The old man propped his hands on his hips. "We can manage fine with Ruthie until Doc Brady gets here."

Emma reddened. "He may not get here till morning."

Wyatt's heart plunged.

Grandpa lost some of his color. "Not till mornin'?"

Emma's chin trembled but her hands remained steady, a good quality in a doctor, and that's what mattered to Wyatt. He stepped to her horse and untied her bags. "Come on in, Emma, and—" he paused, turning around to face her "—thank you for coming to check on Melissa. I'm grateful."

She flushed and nodded, averting her eyes, and glanced uneasily at Grandpa.

"You're playin' with fire," Grandpa muttered, but Wyatt could see mixed feelings churning in the old eyes. "Opening the door for her, yet slamming it in the face of her brother. You're playin' with fire, yes sirree."

Motioning to the stables, Wyatt tried to find some way to pacify the old man. "Please, Grandpa, the ranch hands have returned from fencing, ask them to wipe down the horses. Tommy, you did a good job going all the way to town by yourself and bringing back a doctor. Now help your Grandpa." The old man scowled and left with the boy.

Turning to Emma, Wyatt waved an arm to the big house. "Melissa's upstairs, follow me."

In five long strides, he reached the wide porch, carrying the heavy bags with ease. She trailed behind, flogging dust from her skirt.

When he turned and waited for her a second time, he saw her limping. A pang of guilt shot through him. She was trying to hide her discomfort as she climbed the porch steps.

"You all right?" he asked.

"I'm fine," she said, a little too quickly.

He frowned. "Your leg's bothering you."

"It's nothing. Blame it on new shoes." She looked away hastily as his eyes shot down to her feet. "Always takes me a week or two to break them in...."

Her scuffed, brown leather boots looked more worn than a week or two. She turned crimson and didn't meet his gaze, and he didn't question it further.

He yanked the screen door wide, fully intending to step back to give her space to pass, but he found himself rooted. As she brushed by him into the entry, her shoulder grazed his arm and a shiver of awareness rippled through his body. She inhaled sharply at their contact, blushing and blowing the moistened strands of silky hair away from her face.

What in heaven's name was he doing?

Chapter Two

The boy of nineteen had grown into quite a man.

A tingling wove its way through the pit of Emma's stomach as she glanced up to appraise Wyatt. His glistening black hair still brushed low against the back of his denim collar. His massive shoulders, now a yard wide, strained against fabric. The muscles playing under his work shirt were firmer, no doubt from roping and ranching all these years, and as he climbed the stairs, his thighs more lithe and muscular.

And Lord, he still moved the same. He'd always had a quiet power when he moved, a perfect harmony between every muscle and nerve in his body, whether he was riding a horse and roping a calf, or walking barefoot in the grass beside her.

That graceful, alluring stride.

A disturbing warmth rose through her legs and into her arms. She tore her gaze off his body and hiked the top step. Following along the hallway, she warned herself to ignore him. She must be tired and shocked to see him, that's why her body was responding. He was only a man, no better than any other, and certainly flawed at that.

They passed a rocking chair tucked into a bay window

and a wall of grayed photographs. Pictures of growing children, Tommy and Melissa she assumed. How lucky Wyatt was to have youngsters, to have a family of his own. At one time, she'd thought she'd be the mother of his children.

Well, what did it matter, really? After she'd left town, it'd taken him only a year to marry someone else.

The pinch in her calf grew numb. She knew she could manage the ache in her leg. As for the tear in her heart, the humiliation…

What did he remember of that hot, summer night, sixteen years ago? Did he remember how much they'd always liked to kiss? His soft lips fluttering along her neck, exploring her tender skin as far as she would let him? Did he remember how she'd opened her heart, telling him how deeply she felt for him, and what he'd said to her in return?

I don't love you.

She steadied herself, pressing a hand to her queasy stomach. She'd left him standing there by the creek, without saying another word. She'd never let him know how much he'd devastated her. What was it he found so unlovable about her? Other men, not all men, found her desirable. He'd found her appealing in some ways, obviously, but not enough to commit himself for a lifetime.

Her mind raced and she was unable to stop the flood of intimate thoughts. Where would they be now, if they'd remained together? What sort of lovers would they have become?

Would they still be such an eager couple, so intensely aware of each other? Would she still shiver at his feathery touch? Would her fervent kisses make his heart beat as wildly? Would their intimacy, their vitality, have developed into something even richer, something deeper as the years passed?

She wrenched herself away from her ridiculous thoughts.

Wiping her sweaty palms against her skirt, she reminded herself she was no longer a smitten girl of sixteen. She was here in his house for one reason only. To help Melissa.

They reached the bedroom door and Wyatt dipped his tall figure around the panels and smiled at someone he addressed as Ruth. The creases at his eyes when he smiled had aged him a little, she decided, but only added to the manly strength of his profile. An elderly woman stepped out to the hallway and Emma focused on her as Wyatt introduced them.

"No change in Melissa," Ruth whispered, her words comforting Emma. "I'll be in the next room if you need me."

Emma stepped past him as professionally as she could manage. For a fleeting moment, his rough hand brushed against her slender waist. The warmth of personal contact, his simple touch made her body shudder from head to toe. She swallowed hard and kept walking, ignoring how quickly he'd dropped his hand.

Her concern for Melissa pushed everything else from her mind. As she walked into the room, lace curtains billowed in the summer breeze and wind ruffled through her hair.

The auburn-haired girl was breathing easy in a loose cotton nightdress. Melissa's face was pale as she stirred and opened her eyes. Wyatt stepped beside his daughter, his bulky figure towering over the bed, and tenderly touched her hand. It touched Emma's heart, watching him. "How're you feeling, darlin'?"

"Better," she said weakly.

He heaved a sigh of relief and smiled. Glancing at Emma, he quickly withdrew his hand from his daughter's and slid it into his pocket. "Doc Brady's on his way, but there's someone else here to see you. This is Emma and she's a doctor."

"Oh, you're Cole's sister. Did you bring him?" Smiling, she scrambled up on her elbows and looked past Emma to the door. "I knew he'd come. I knew he would. Where is he?"

Emma's hopes fell in sympathy for Melissa. Realizing the truth, Melissa sank back into her pillow and lowered her misty lashes. Scowling, Wyatt folded his arms against his chest and circled to the foot of the bed, making Emma's nerves jittery.

"Cole doesn't know I'm here," Emma said, stepping closer and squeezing the girl's warm hand. "He doesn't know you've had trouble. I'm sure if he did, he'd be here."

Head bowed, Melissa nodded, choking back her tears. The girl must be terrified about her bleeding. Poor Cole, where was he? Had he heard yet? "It's a pleasure to meet you. Cole's told me a lot about you."

Lifting Melissa's hand, Emma checked her pulse. It was strong and steady. Then she reached under the bedsheet and pitted her finger into an ankle. No swelling.

She sank herself down at the foot of the bed, on the colorful quilt, noticing the jar of flowers by the window. "The blossoms smell heavenly."

"I picked them yesterday." Melissa looked up, her lashes clumped with moisture. "Cole's told me about you, too." She ran a hand through her tangled hair, a beautiful autumn color. "I must look a mess."

"You look wonderful, considering what you've been through." Emma smiled. "I'd like to do an examination. It won't hurt. Nothing internal. I don't want to trigger more contractions. Would that be all right?"

Melissa agreed and Emma stepped to the basin of water sitting on the dresser. As she washed her hands, she heard the soft thud of her medicine bag being placed on the foot of the bed. Wyatt lit the oil lamps and the room filled with a warm, golden glow, creating an intimacy among the three of them.

While scrubbing, Emma stole a glance at the slender girl. If her pelvic opening wasn't big enough to allow the baby's head to pass, not even forceps would help. What then?

She took a deep breath. *Cesarean surgery.*

But here, in the middle of nowhere? By herself?

She'd never performed surgery of any kind before. Like all new doctors, most of what she'd learned had come from books and lectures. She'd witnessed one birth, a healthy full-term delivery, but no Cesareans.

She'd read all about them, though, and was well aware that more than half of all women died from Cesareans.

Her breathing snagged as she dried her hands. She'd do whatever she had to, whatever she could. Surely Doc Brady would get here in time. Thank God in her new job in Philadelphia, she'd have supervision and help whenever she or the patient needed it, from the finest surgeons in the world.

Emma turned around. Both father and daughter were watching her. Melissa made no attempt to hide the fear in her eyes; Wyatt's was better hidden. But then, he'd always been good at hiding what he felt. Emma unbuckled her crisp medicine bag, and the smell of new leather wafted through the air.

"I'd like to stay while you examine Melissa," said Wyatt.

Pulling out her stethoscope, Emma nodded. He stepped to the window, turning his back.

Everything seemed fine until Emma checked the baby's positioning. She checked again with the same anxious results. The baby was lying across the womb instead of head down. If the head wasn't engaged into the pelvis and the water sac were to burst now, the cord might get compressed. The baby could die. She tried to smile calmly at

Melissa. There was no cause for alarm, Emma told herself, Melissa was not in labor. The baby had plenty of time to turn to the correct position during the last six weeks of gestation.

Emma pulled out a cloth measuring tape. "To measure your abdomen," she explained.

"Can I ask you a question?" Melissa asked.

"By all means."

"Even if it's about Cole?"

"This isn't the time to talk about Cole," Wyatt said in a gruff voice.

Melissa's face fell. "Why not?"

Emma laid the tape on Melissa's belly. For God's sake, Wyatt wasn't going to control the conversation. "We can talk about anything you like, as long as I see it's not upsetting you." She looked at the results of the measuring tape with some relief. Pelvic proportion might not be a problem.

"Talking about Cole never upsets me." Melissa smiled then caught sight of her father's stiffened spine. "Unless the conversation's with my pa." Her smile waned and her gaze flitted back to Emma, reminding her of an injured bird.

"I'm all done, Wyatt, you can turn around now."

Melissa stuttered. "Do you—do you know if Cole would prefer, would he prefer a little boy or little girl? He won't tell me." She lowered her brown lashes, running her hands over her big belly.

Emma turned her concerned gaze to Wyatt. The question obviously made him uncomfortable. He rubbed a hand over his bristly jaw and shook his head. The shadow of a beard gave him a rugged, unapproachable aura. His eyes met hers and her pulse rippled. When he looked back at his daughter, Emma noticed the red puffy circles under his eyes. At least she shared that with him, their concern for Melissa and her baby.

With an agitated sigh, Wyatt strode to the door. "I'll wait for you downstairs, Emma."

Emma stared behind him in shock. With a pained expression, Melissa glanced up at the closing door, then lowered her head. "My pa's ashamed of me."

Emma couldn't believe what he'd just done. Was he always this tough on his daughter? How could he be so cold? All Melissa wanted was some reassurance. Couldn't he give a kind response? What kind of person was he?

Proud and stubborn. Just like he'd been with Emma.

She reached for Melissa's hand. "Your pa is very proud of you. I must have passed ten pictures in the main hall of you and your brother."

"Those are old pictures. He hasn't told me he's proud of me for a very long time." She wiped her nose.

"Melissa, sweetheart, don't cry...."

"I don't think my pa loves me anymore."

"He loves you very much." Emma couldn't be sure of what Wyatt felt. She couldn't be sure of anything where he was concerned, but she had to find some way to comfort the girl.

"He's never told me."

"Some men can't talk about those feelings, but it doesn't mean they don't feel them. Your father loves you."

Melissa wiped her tears with the back of her hand. "I wish he'd talk to me more. We used to talk a lot. And dance. He's a good dancer, I taught him."

Emma smiled. "I can just imagine the two of you."

"Do you like to dance?"

"Oh...no, no..." She rolled down her sleeves.

"Why not?"

"It's not something I took to."

"Because of your leg?"

How did Melissa know?

"I know about your leg. Cole told me about it. You shouldn't let it stop you. When my grandma was alive, she used to dance the square dance, her and Grandpa every Saturday night, and she had a cane. I remember…"

Melissa went on about Granny and Emma silently finished her work. "Your condition has settled, honey, your baby's heartbeat is good and strong, just like your own. But I'm ordering you to stay in bed. No getting up for any reason. If you do, the pain may start again, and you'd be jeopardizing the baby. Do you understand?"

The girl's brown eyes, almost black like her father's, were solemn. "Yes, ma'am."

"One more thing. I have to tell you I'm very excited."

Melissa's head jerked up. "Excited?"

Emma smiled warmly and patted the girl's arm. "This little baby you're carrying is going to be my newest little niece or nephew. I'm very proud of you."

"Oh…" Melissa's voice caught. Smiling, she wiped another tear and gazed at Emma. "It's so lonely here. Will you stay awhile? Will you stay the night, in case I need you?"

The words triggered a wave of loneliness in Emma. She knew what being alone was like. When she wasn't at the hospital, she spent most of her time alone, despite the occasional charity event, or night out with her aunt and uncle. "I'd like to. At least until Doc Brady gets here. I'll speak to your father."

"Please convince him. Doc Brady's nice enough and all, but he's so old. I'm embarrassed when he examines me. I'd rather have you. Please say you'll stay."

What would Wyatt have to say about it? What could he say? "Okay, I'll stay awhile."

"Thank you." Taking a breath and fingering the buttons on her nightdress, the girl blurted, "When you were my age, did you ever argue—and I mean a lot—with your pa?"

Emma placed the tape inside her bag, suddenly saddened at the memories. "I'll tell you a secret. When I was your age, my father and I used to argue from sunup to sundown." *About Wyatt,* she added silently.

Melissa's eyes twinkled. "I can't imagine you, a doctor, arguin' with your pa."

"We did. I made a lot of mistakes with my Pa and I never got a chance—I mean I never took the time, to say I was sorry." She hadn't been as good a daughter as she should have. She was so sure her father had misjudged Wyatt, ignoring his strengths, exaggerating his flaws. But looking at it now, maybe her father hadn't been wrong at all.

Melissa grew quiet.

"Promise me no matter how bad the arguing gets with your pa, you'll talk to someone else about your feelings. Someone older than you, another woman."

"Can I come to you? Can I talk to you?"

Her pleading eyes made Emma feel a little guilty. "Well, no, honey, I'll be leaving for Philadelphia. Could you talk to one of your aunts? You have three or four that live nearby."

Sighing, Melissa drew her arms to her sides. "Sure." She gave a shallow smile, but the sparkle in her eyes dulled. "Yeah. I'll talk to one of my aunts." She fell against her pillow and turned her drawn face toward the ceiling.

Emma stared at the crestfallen face.

The girl was awfully unhappy. What was going on in this house? Did Wyatt know the extent of her unhappiness?

Someone sure had to tell him.

She would. Right now. Whether they argued or whether

he'd be reasonable, she had to make it clear Melissa needed friends and family, especially Cole. Blazes, Cole *wanted* to be involved, and Wyatt was doing no good standing in their way.

Emma packed up her things and said an uneasy goodnight. "I'll send Ruth in now. Try to get some rest, honey." Melissa only nodded.

With a tight ball in her stomach, Emma lifted her bag and left the room. It was lucky she'd come when she did. Someone had to be Melissa's advocate.

As for Emma personally, she was fortunate to be here, too. Sometimes she was afraid to go to sleep, his image was so vivid, her response so real.... The tingling of her skin when he bent to kiss her throat, the way her bones melted just looking into his deep brown eyes, the heat rising and dipping between them.... It was always a relief when she finally awoke.

She was sick of her dreams, and sick of Wyatt invading them. It was because she'd dreamed about him a week before she was going to marry Jonathon that she'd called off the wedding.

By seeing Wyatt's harsher, colder side, her silly childhood infatuation with him was rapidly fading.

Maybe he'd be leaving her dreams sooner than she thought.

What was keeping Emma? How bad off could Melissa be?

In a clean white shirt and corded pants, Wyatt spooned a heap of potatoes onto Tommy's plate. Did Melissa's bleeding start again? If *anything* should happen to her—

The stairway creaked beyond the kitchen door and Wyatt, startled, knocked a glass of water on its side.

The three of them worked fast. Grandpa threw a kitchen

towel in Wyatt's direction, Tommy scrambled to lift his plate out of the flow of water and Wyatt mopped the spill. The door swung open, and they peered up as Emma entered. She glanced timidly around the room and settled her cool gaze on Wyatt.

"How's Melissa?" Wyatt cupped the dripping towel in his large hands. He studied her closely, his gut clenched. He didn't want her to hold back any information.

"She's settled and quiet. Ruth's with her. It looks like she'll be fine." An air of confidence settled over her pretty features, and he relaxed.

Then realizing he was dripping water onto the floor with Emma standing there, assessing him with those clear observant eyes, a hint of amusement dimpling her cheek, he indicated a chair. "Have a seat. Are you hungry?"

Her expression changed; she looked worried. She slid her medicine bag onto the chair and wiped her palms against her skirt. "I'd like to speak with you in private."

His stomach dropped. "Oh, God, how bad is she?"

With a surprised exclamation, her braid shifted against her shoulder. Her full lips softened. "Sorry, I didn't mean to suggest—it's not about her health. It's about her circumstances. I need to speak with you."

For a moment, Wyatt's burning eyes held hers. Lord help him, her eyes still shimmered and swirled like bourbon in cut crystal. It was damn unsettling to know how much he'd missed them. And you bet she wanted to speak to him, but it came sooner than he thought. If he guessed right, she wanted to talk about Cole, to get her damn brother through the door as quick as possible.

He stepped to the counter and threw the wet towel into the dish basin. "If you don't mind, could it wait until after supper? Tommy's had a tough day. I'd like to get him ready for bed. We can talk then."

He walked over to the table and pulled a chair out for her, smiling innocently, waiting for her to take it.

She folded her arms across her chest, a lovely chest, and glared at the chair he was offering. "It's important we talk."

"Right after supper." He motioned for her to sit down.

Wavering, she glanced from Tommy to him. With an angry flounce of her long skirt, she lowered her bottom, a lovely bottom, onto the chair. He tucked it in underneath her. He tried to avert his gaze from her womanly curves, but how could he? Her shapely bosom and narrow waist beckoned to him.

"I've forgotten how well-mannered you are," she said.

Smiling at her rebuke, he tried to keep the laughter from his voice. "Thank you. Speaking of manners, Tommy, it's rude to eat before you offer your guests."

"I don't think she's stayin' long," hollered Grandpa from the other end of the table. "I mean, now that Melissa's settled. You know what happened the last time we trusted—"

"That was thirty years ago, sir," Emma said, her chest rising and her cheeks flushing. "It was an accident. A horrible one, but still an accident."

Grandpa squinted through his spectacles. "So your Pa kept insistin'."

"The judge agreed and cleared him of the charges. The team of horses simply got away from him—"

"And trampled my young niece. Why, she wasn't much older than Melissa, with a young baby of her own. Remember, Wyatt?"

Watching the crimson flood her skin, Wyatt's shoulders wound with tension. How could he forget the incident that started it all? His young aunt was killed, leaving behind a newborn baby, now a fully grown man. His cousin Jim.

And Jim never let anyone forget how much he hated Sinclairs. But Jim was another story, and he didn't live in this house.

Grandpa stiffened. "If Jim were here, he'd wouldn't stand for—"

"Well, he's not here," Wyatt interrupted. It took guts for Emma to show up at the ranch, and Wyatt admired her for it. "Let's not talk about it now, Grandpa. Emma's here for Melissa. Please, have a bite to eat. Tommy, pass the bread."

The boy did as he was told. Taking a deep breath, Emma took it. She eyed the cluttered table, strewn with pots and pans, and Wyatt suddenly realized how untidy it was. In the city, she likely never helped herself from a pot, like they did most nights. She and her aunt and uncle likely dined on fine china, every meal. Normally he wouldn't give a hoot, but at this moment…he rubbed the back of his tight neck.

Grandpa and Tommy helped themselves to pie. As Wyatt frantically searched the cupboard for a pie plate for her with no cracks or chips, he saw her press a hand over her long skirt and rub the muscles of her calf.

It was bothering her again. She'd rubbed it earlier. And if he knew her at all, she wouldn't make a fuss and wouldn't ask for help. So darn stubborn.

While they ate, he asked about Melissa's condition.

"She needs to rest."

"Do you think—will the baby make it?" He could barely say the words for the anguish in his throat.

"Well, the bleeding's stopped. Melissa's abdomen is soft, which tells me her placenta hasn't detached—"

"I don't understand medical mumbo jumbo," said Grandpa, shooing a moth away from his face. "Tell us straight. The baby gonna live or not?" Grandpa's bark was always worse than his bite, but Wyatt wished he'd tone it down.

"I'd say yes, Mr. Barlow, the baby should be fine as long as the bleeding doesn't start again. But you've got to keep Melissa calm and rested."

Wyatt would do whatever it took to make his daughter well. On Emma's instructions, he ran a bowl of soup to Melissa's room and was back in no time.

"When are you leaving for Philadelphia?" he asked.

"Day after tomorrow."

An uncomfortable feeling, a flash of something from the past, shivered through him. His eyes flickered, he glanced away.

"Hope you're packed 'n ready," said Grandpa. Wyatt cocked an eyebrow at Grandpa's rudeness. Grandpa scowled back at him.

Emma caught the interplay and her eyes twinkled at Wyatt, making him catch his breath. So she hadn't lost her sense of humor. He lowered his eyes and shoved another forkful of pie into his mouth.

"I've got the stagecoach tickets and I'm packed."

"Good," said Grandpa. "Don't wanna miss that coach. Never know when the next one's gonna be comin'."

"It comes every two weeks." She sipped on water as Wyatt leaned back in his chair, recalling the last time he'd seen her, Christmas before last. He'd heard then she'd just broken off her engagement. Why? He couldn't ask her why, or anything else about her private life. He knew he'd given up that privilege with the last harsh words he'd said to her.

She tilted the jug of water and refilled her glass. Loose tendrils of hair softened her face. Her braid dipped over her shoulder, brushing close to the table. Wyatt watched her slip the silky braid to her back. His muscles tightened. Her rope of tumbled hair glistened under the warm light of the lamp, which swung above the table, back and forth, back and forth. The last time he'd woven his fingers through its softness, he'd buried his face in it. He still recalled the scent.

The thought stirred a heat in him he was unprepared for. *Enough of that.* He sprang out of his chair and reached for the coffee.

Accepting a cup, Emma pulled a medical book from her bag and searched through the pages.

Grandpa sat taller. "What's that, missie?"

"A book of emergency medicine."

"Whad'dya need it for?"

Emma propped it on the table. "There's a good chapter on labor. I want to give you instructions for the night."

"Man alive! She's readin' it from a book! Doc Brady never reads from a book!"

Wyatt squirmed in his chair. She knew what she was doing, didn't she? "When do you expect Doc Brady will get here?"

Her round brown eyes glistened with hurt pride. As her slender hands drifted from the book and into her lap, he regretted asking so bluntly. "Just before dawn," she said, "if they find him tonight."

"Why wouldn't they find him?" said Grandpa.

"The doctor and his wife are spending the night at his sister's. It's his sister's eightieth birthday, and he's liable to take her out dining, or visiting." Ignoring Wyatt, who was now wondering if and how he should apologize, she continued reading.

Grandpa rolled up his sleeves and gathered the dirty plates. The red rash on his arm caught her attention.

"What's that rash on your elbow?"

"Never you mind, girl."

"May I look at it?"

"No." The old man yanked back so fast his spectacles almost fell.

"Maybe I can help."

"No female doctor's ever comin' near me. You women worry too much about everything. It don't make sense, a woman bein' a doctor. You'd have the whole town laid up for something—"

"Maybe I've got a cream—"

"No. It ain't nothin' but a few red dots." He rolled his sleeve back down. "Next thing you know, you'll be advisin' amputation. Yes sirree, goddamn amputation. I bet you even got a nice diagram there. How to saw off a limb in three easy steps." He stalked off with a pile of dishes.

She clamped her mouth shut, looking like she wanted to fling her book at Grandpa.

Wyatt almost laughed out loud. "Grandpa's a handful."

She pushed a fallen strand of hair from her face, and her eyes brimmed with emotion. "Isn't it important we try to get along? That the Barlows and Sinclairs bury their differences, for your daughter's sake?" She captured his eyes with hers.

Her words, softly spoken, slid straight to his heart. He didn't know how to respond. Of course it was important, but there were so many problems between them, beginning and ending with her brother Cole.

Tommy slurped the last chunk of berry pie off his plate. He'd been watching Emma all evening with something on his mind. "Did it hurt?" he asked her.

"Did what hurt?"

"You know, when you got bit by the rattler?"

Wyatt's pulse rushed. He leaned forward in his chair. "That's none of your concern. Wash up and get ready for bed." Lord, that was the last thing they needed to talk about.

A blush crept to Emma's cheeks. "It didn't hurt much. My leg went numb very quickly."

Wyatt nudged his son on the shoulder blades with a large, firm hand. "You've had a long day. It's time for bed."

"Did anyone suck out the venom?"

"Yes," she breathed softly, glancing at Wyatt, sending his stomach rolling. He jumped up and yanked Tommy out of his chair. "Let's go."

"Who saved ya?" the boy continued.

"A friend."

Heartstrings pulled in Wyatt but he couldn't look at her.

"I wanna hear the story," Tommy pleaded as Wyatt scrubbed his face with a wet napkin.

Grandpa banged the pots from across the room. "It's a sad story, one that doesn't need retellin'."

Oh, no, thought Wyatt, shaking his head, here it comes.

"It's sad because she got bit?" said Tommy. "Owww, you're gettin' the cloth in my mouth."

"Because they blamed your pa for what happened next," said the old man.

"*Pa? My pa?* You were there?"

"Yes, he was. First your pa saved her," lamented Grandpa, "then they blamed him for ruining her leg."

What's the point of bringing it all up? thought Wyatt. What could it possibly accomplish? Unable to stop himself, he finally met Emma's gaze.

Her eyes were misty and gentle. "Not everyone blamed you."

"All the Sinclairs except one."

"And that one didn't matter to you."

That wasn't true and his heart trembled.

With an air of resolve, she pressed her palms against the table, rose stiffly and stacked the remaining dishes. The past still bothered her, and it troubled him to know he'd hurt her badly. She had mattered. Looking at her, he had an urge to trap her in his arms and explain, but instead, he ran a hand over his bristly cheeks and silently cursed himself. He'd tried to explain it to her once before, but she wouldn't listen then, either.

"Come on, Tommy, let's get you to bed," said Grandpa. "Good night, missie. I take it you'll be leavin' soon?"

"Well, no, I'd like to spend the night."

Grandpa glared at her, then muttered under his breath as he left the room with Tommy.

Swallowing hard, Wyatt stood up and helped clear the table. "I appreciate that you're staying. Grandpa does too, the old man just won't admit it."

She paced to the counter with the platters, her back turned. "You're welcome."

His throat tightened, watching how guarded she was. He collected her books and bag. "Come, I'll show you to your room. I don't intend on leaving Melissa alone, so I'll take a bedroll to her floor. You can take my bed."

"No." She swung around and stumbled. "Don't you have a spare room?"

Did she dislike the thought of his bed that much? "I do but it's for Ruth. Don't take it personal, but she doesn't trust Melissa to anyone except the old doc. She's staying until he arrives. You'll be sleeping in my room."

She swiped her palms against her skirt. "I could sleep in the parlor," she said in a frantic tone, "or how about here, in the kitchen?"

"No," he said with a taut jerk of his head. "I'd like to ensure the doctor tending to my daughter gets a good night's rest on a mattress. Just in case you're needed again." It had nothing to do with the fact that she'd be lying in his bed, he told himself. Taking three long strides to the door, he shoved it open with a casual hand. Was she coming?

When he swung back, she was eyeing the door leading to the yard, looking ready to bolt. Did she hate him that much?

Who could blame her? After what he'd said to her that night, all those years ago, when she'd whispered those wonderful things in his ear, and he'd returned her honesty with a knife to her heart.

"Did you change your mind about staying?"

She squared her stance. "No."

"Follow me, then."

She raised her chin with a cold stare. "We still need to talk."

"We can talk when we get there. I'll set up a bath if you like. Seems to me your leg's troubling you more than you care to admit. It must have been difficult for you to come."

She stood motionless for a moment. Her mouth quivered as she spoke. "I wanted to help Melissa."

He pulled his shoulders back. Of course she did. She was a doctor. He had no right to think she might have been curious to see him.

Chapter Three

Emma couldn't believe she was here, all alone with Wyatt in his private bedroom. What decent woman would be caught in her shoes?

Her fingers fluttered to her neck as she regarded him through trembling lashes. Inclining his dark head, he leaned over the bedside lamp and struck a match. Soft illumination danced on his supple cheeks and curved jaw. His biceps flexed under strained cloth, and her pulse skipped.

With an air of rugged command, he strode to the book-shelves and lit the other lamp. Her eyes couldn't help but stray to the four-poster cherry bed. She gulped.

Firelight spilled over the rumpled pillows and wrinkled, creamy cotton sheets. It looked like a man's bed, no frills, no lace, the sheets askew as if he'd dashed to make it this morning, and yet, somehow appealing.

"Come in, make yourself comfortable," he said, as if entertaining a woman in his bedroom were a common occurrence.

Was it? Did he have a woman? Someone steady?

She didn't care. Dropping her hands to her sides, she stepped deeper into the room and scrambled to find neutral territory to look at.

Nothing was safe. Everything sent her nerves fluttering. The tantalizing smell of his shaving gear sitting on the dresser, the pile of laundered shirts, even the leather-bound book by the bed ignited a vision of Wyatt, reading half-naked.

There was a restless energy about his movements as he straightened the bedcovers. Trying to maintain her distance, she reminded herself he wasn't interested in her. He'd married another woman. Lillie Anderson from San Francisco, someone she'd never even met, a family friend who'd visited one summer with his California cousins.

It felt odd to be here with him, thinking about Lillie, how sad it was her life had ended. She'd heard Lillie was a nice woman, that they were happy for a while, until her sickness took over. Doc Brady had said it wasn't the first time he'd seen a woman go mad from isolation in the West, and probably not the last. In a way, Emma understood.

Back then, the smaller house was just two rooms, the ranch was just a fraction of its size with no hired help to keep Lillie company, the neighbors sparse. Winters were brutal and a far cry from the liveliness of San Francisco. Emma was in Philadelphia when she'd heard the horrible news of Lillie's death, and although she'd never known her, Emma had wept with sorrow. Death to someone young was always tragic.

Wyatt must have been grief-stricken. How did he get through it? How did he help Melissa and Tommy through it?

She straightened, toughening her resolve not to wonder about Wyatt's personal life. Getting hurt again wasn't in her plans.

His tall figure turned up at her. He quirked a dark brown in concern. "You sure you don't care for a bath?"

She shook her head quickly and moistened her dry lips.

"No, thanks." What was it about Wyatt's proximity that made her so blatantly aware of her imperfect leg? In the city, she often went days without thinking about it. "I've got Epsom salts in my bag. A foot basin would help, and tooth powder and a hairbrush, if it's not too much trouble."

"No trouble at all." He straightened to full height.

She felt an unwelcome heat rise through her limbs. Her mind raced for a safe topic. "You have a lovely home." She smothered her own groan. What a silly thing to say to a man in his bedroom.

A smile tugged at his mouth and his brown eyes twinkled. "Glad you like it."

Heat burned her face.

He laughed softly. "I'll get you the things you need," he said, stepping to the corner armoire and opening its doors.

She rolled her eyes heavenward. Glancing around the room, her gaze stumbled on the open book propped on the leather chair by the fireplace. Another book. So he still loved to read. She strained to read the title but the book was too far away.

Wyatt returned with fresh sheets, walking toward the bed. Her pulse leaped. "I'll change the sheets," she blurted. She stepped forward and slid the bedding from his grip. Their pulsing fingers grazed, their warm eyes met and she nearly dropped the whole bundle.

Pulling back her shoulders in a dignified manner, she tossed the sheets to the bed as calmly as she could. "I'll change the bed later, on my own."

"Suit yourself." He unlatched the balcony doors. "You can let some fresh air in, if you like, while I go get you a hairbrush. Help yourself to one of my clean shirts in the pile. Melissa doesn't have any spare maternal nightgowns, and I doubt her other tiny ones will fit you."

"Thank you," she croaked, knowing she'd never touch one of his shirts. She'd make do with her own clothes.

He left and she hungered for cool air. Stepping out to the ornate iron balcony, she breathed in the sweet night air. Crickets chirped in the grounds below. Slivers of light from the full, watery moon glimmered over the pines and the rooftops of the stables. She gazed at the solitary moon and heard a single owl's hoot.

Was there anyone out there for her? Would she always be alone?

She sagged against the rail and gazed out at Wyatt's domain. He must have worked painfully hard these past years to accomplish this much. The grit, the long hours, the two young children. She noticed he'd placed his bedroom at the front of the house, facing the valley, like a sentry post watching over his family.

What would it feel like, to be married to a man who protected his family with such devotion?

She'd never felt devotion like that, not even with Jonathon. With him, it'd been more of a friendship between two colleagues.

The only time a man had *ever* fought for her was the day Wyatt had saved her life. She was twelve years old, chasing field mice in the school yard with her other friends, forbidden by her father to even speak to Wyatt...

"Mouse!" someone yelled

"He's here! I've got him!" She laughed and started running after him through the golden weeds. She remembered the deep-blue shimmering sky, how warm the autumn sun was, tingling against her face. How good it felt to be alive.

Then she heard the rattle.

Rattlesnake.

She slammed to a stop. Her heart pounded. The serpent, thick and tall, was close enough to spit on.

Don't touch me. He didn't. A mouse raced by and the snake lunged after it. She nearly dropped with relief.

Then her left leg stabbed with pain. She looked down. Another mottled rattler, half the size, was quietly pumping its jaws into her calf. It slithered away before she could even scream.

She closed her eyes, felt the knifing pain. Over and over and over, until she couldn't feel her leg anymore. She didn't remember when she fell. Her eyelids tingled, her lips went numb. Her vision spun with blue sky and wispy strands of white. A jumble of screams around her.

"Get help!"

"Let's get outta here, in case there's more snakes!"

"Who's gonna help Emma?"

"I don't know, she might be lyin' in a nest of snakes! Lord almighty, look at her leg, it's all blown up already! Let's get the teacher! Run!"

Her friends left her.

She tried to focus on the clouds. Threads of white being pushed into shapes by the wind.

Then fifteen-year-old Wyatt Barlow had entered her curve of vision. A blur of black hair and black eyes.

She tried to talk but her jaw was numb.

"Shhh…Emma, don't talk…keep calm. The venom won't work as fast." He lifted her with strong arms. She felt protected. "It's safer in the clearing by the trees."

Her mind wouldn't focus. His shirt smelled clean. What would Pa think? She was forbidden to speak to a Barlow.

She'd heard her father say, *The Barlows are bad people. They got no capacity for forgiveness.* Pa would say, *Why won't they forgive me? They're cold, mean, bad people.*

Wyatt's voice didn't seem bad to her. He sounded clear and good and truthful. "I have to get the poison out, and

I'll be real gentle. My Pa used to say every good rancher's got to know how to save a man from a rattler."

She nodded. Her eyelids, too heavy, wouldn't open. He set her on the ground and something hard poked her shoulder. A rock or tree root, or maybe a lump of grass.

What was he tying above her knee? She heard the snap of a pocketknife, but felt nothing. She heard him spit out.

He's suckin' out the poison. Why can't I feel my leg?

He's touchin' my bare skin. What will Pa say? Where are my stockings? And then everything fell dark....

An owl hooted and flapped its wings. Emma sighed at the balcony, peering over the valley. That day had changed her whole life, in more ways than one. It'd opened her heart to medicine, and opened her heart to Wyatt.

She spent hours in Doc Brady's office, searching his books for cures to ease the scarring and atrophy of her calf. She never found one, but at some point, she forgot about herself and started watching him with his patients. She started helping. And, she became best friends with the boy who'd saved her life.

How could she have been so wrong about Wyatt?

He'd never promised to marry her, he'd never promised to love her. Not in words, but hadn't he promised in other ways? The way he'd touched her, the intimate glimmer in his eyes, the way he'd shared everything in his life with her.

She gazed up at the golden moon, shadowed in blue. An empty feeling swirled inside her, one that seemed to come too often lately.

Where did she belong? Where was her home? In Montana or Philadelphia? She'd tried to keep in touch with her friends in Pine Creek, but somehow over the years... And her friends in the city went about their busy lives, sometimes inviting her along, sometime forgetting all about her....

What was it again that that bubbly young woman at the one party had asked her?

Did Emma consider herself a woman first, or a doctor?

The question had left her speechless. Even now. Is that how people perceived her? Not even as a woman? She lowered her lashes, felt her throat squeeze. Didn't she have the same desires and needs and disappointments as every woman?

"Sorry it took me a while, I was checking up on Melissa."

Wyatt's boots padded onto the balcony, and Emma spun around to face him, her pulse quickening. "Is she all right?"

"Mmm-hmm, she's sleeping."

"Good. Rest will strengthen her and the baby." A breeze whispered over her skin. She gripped the metal handrail harder as she peered up at him, standing a breath away. He stood with his hands in his pockets, moonlight dipping across the handsome planes and angles of his face.

Uncomfortable with the sensuous flame tugging at her, Emma spun around and peered to the grounds below. She said the first thing that came to mind. "The iron flower boxes in your windows remind me of the ones I've seen abroad. In Paris." She let her thick braid slide over her shoulder.

"I heard you were there last summer. How was Paris?" He stepped beside her and leaned over the rail, much too close.

"It was beautiful," she said with a tremor, pulling her shoulder away, wishing he'd been there like he'd promised.

"I'm glad one of us was able to go." His husky voice

rippled through her. "Was it everything we—*you*—dreamed of?"

She pressed her lips together. It should have been Wyatt strolling beside her, not a group of strangers on a tour. She stared out at the dark silhouette of the hills. "The ocean was rough when we crossed, but seeing Paris was worth it."

He dipped closer, his shoulder grazing hers, his heat searing through her skin. "Tell me. What was it like?"

She tried to ignore the rush of fire inside her. "Paris is alive with people and culture. Cafés and outdoor tables bustling with faces from all over the world."

Move away, she commanded herself, but her body disobeyed.

She tilted her head to look at him. His eyes raked her face. His lips were firm and sensual. "Did you finally get to see a Monet in person?"

She swallowed. "I did."

"And the Notre Dame?"

Her mouth quivered. "I heard the choir sing in Latin."

They stood in potent silence. "Must have been quite a voyage." His eyes flickered in the moonlight. "Did you walk along the Seine?"

She swiveled away, twisting her hands. Didn't he remember *their* dreams of walking along the Seine together? Didn't he feel anything? How could he talk about Paris, like a stranger talking about the weather?

Because they *were* strangers. How easily she'd been fooled, listening to his promises. She'd never listen to his promises again. "I saw the usual things a tourist sees." She hugged her arms in the gusty chill. "I forgot how cool Montana nights can be." She turned on her heel and walked inside.

Scanning the room, she noticed he'd placed the toiletries

on the bedside table, but his book was gone. Her gaze raced across the room for the other book. He'd put that away, too.

Funny, wasn't it? There was a time when he couldn't wait to tell her about a new adventure story his cousins from California had sent him, or when he'd been deep in the thick of *Hamlet,* and couldn't understand a word. He used to love to share his books with her. Now he rushed to hide them.

She heard him latch the balcony doors, a loud click in the cold silence. "Good night."

"Please, wait." They still had to talk about Melissa.

His looming figure turned in midstride. "Something else you need?" He motioned to the foot basin. "I brought a pot of heated water and poured it in already."

She swayed closer until she was standing in front of him. She had to do this tactfully, without anger, without blame. "I'd like to talk about Melissa and Cole." *They* were the reasons she was here.

His mouth thinned. "There's not much I care to say. And I don't want to argue with you, not tonight when you've been kind enough to come and help."

She furrowed her brows. "But it's important."

His posture tensed. He took a step back and thrust a hand into his pocket. "What can I say about your brother? He doesn't have the capacity to look after Melissa, plain and simple. He can't even look after himself."

Emma's fingers curled into her skirt. "He's my brother," she beseeched him, "and with our help—"

"Melissa doesn't need a boy who needs help." His mouth twisted. "She needs a man capable of looking after her." He shook his head in that maddening, dismissive way. "I'm leaving now and I don't want to hear any more about it."

The man had the nerve to spin away. She raised her voice. "Well, you've got to hear it and you'll hear it from me."

Taking a loud, deep breath, he swung back, his expression icy. "What can you possibly say to help your brother?"

"This year's been difficult for him, for all of us, losing my father."

His eyes shimmered and his cheek twitched in the warm lamplight. "I'm sorry for the loss of your father."

She raised a brow. "Are you?"

"Yes," he snapped, looking angered that she'd questioned it. They eyed each other for a moment, then he sighed. Crossing his arms, he leaned against the low dresser and planted one booted foot over the other. "All right, let's talk about Cole. Might as well get it over with. While Melissa's lying here helpless and bleeding, how's he doing? How long has he been working at the livery stables now? Two whole weeks?"

Emma colored. Her skirts shifted. "He's trying hard."

"How much does pitching manure pay these days?"

She thrust out her chin. "He does a lot more than pitch manure. He's tending to the new horses, helping to break them in. Cole's young, he's learning."

"This is his third job this year, and it's only June. Do you think he'll learn to keep this one?"

"He hasn't found what he likes to do yet, but he's young, that's all. You were young once."

His voice dropped dangerously low. "What's that supposed to mean?"

She ran her hand along the bedpost. The truth was, in seeing Melissa today, the girl reminded Emma of herself at that tender age, the passion a young girl is capable of...and even though Emma didn't get the boy of her dreams, she desperately wanted to ensure Melissa did. "Are you sure you don't want Cole to have what—" she forced herself to face him "—what we once couldn't? A relationship between a Barlow and a Sinclair?"

A muscle pulled in his jaw. His swirling eyes narrowed. "I would never treat Cole the way your father treated me. And I was more responsible at twelve than Cole is at seventeen."

She couldn't deny it. As the eldest, Wyatt, at twelve, had fended for his family when his father had passed away. Irritated that he had a point, Emma tried another approach. "Look at it from Melissa's point of view. She thinks you're not proud of her anymore. She thinks you don't love her—"

"That's between her and me—"

"She's lonely," Emma pleaded, not caring if she hurt his pride. He had to hear this. "She's got no one to talk to."

"That's ridiculous. She's surrounded by family." He waved an arm in frustration. "She's got cousins and aunts dropping by almost every day to see her. She's *not* lonely."

"Like Lillie wasn't?" As soon as the words were out, she felt her cheeks flash with shame. She clamped her lips shut. She didn't mean to say it aloud.

He stepped back as if he'd been struck. His tough expression slackened and his eyes glistened.

"Wyatt, I'm sorry." Her voice quavered. She stepped forward with an outstretched hand but he ignored it. "I shouldn't have said that. As a doctor I'm concerned—"

His gaze sharpened. "You're right, you shouldn't have said it, you don't know anything about it."

"Just look at it from a woman's point of view—"

"You won't let up, will you?" The tension in his voice intensified. "Just as stubborn as you always were, won't listen to anyone. Well, I've come to a decision about your brother, one that's very simple.''

He paced to the door. ''When Cole can prove he's able to provide food, clothing and shelter for Melissa—all by himself, without the help of his dear old mother—then he'll be considered a potential husband. I don't think that's too much to ask, do you? Until then, he can damn well stay away.''

What? That would take too long for Cole to prove. Weeks, months, a year? The words smacked like a slap to her face. Cole had to stay away until then?

Anxiety spurted through her. Her chest tightened, gazing into impassive eyes. ''But my mother, my sister at the store, we'd like to help Cole. We're not rich, but if we can't help each other in time of need, then what's family for?''

''A man's got to learn to rely on his own resources.'' He gave her a cold nod. ''You won't always be around to help Cole, neither will I. He's got to prove himself, by himself. No one wants that more than me.''

Her jaw dropped, and with that, he left.

With a shaky arm, she lowered herself to the bed. As she listened to his boots thudding down the hall, she wondered what'd become of the hero she used to know.

She slid her head to her hands and massaged the pounding temples. No wonder Melissa seemed so defeated. What could Emma do now? She wasn't about to give up on getting the young couple together, but how was she going to do it with only two days left? What could she do to force Wyatt's hand?

''I got good Kentucky bourbon,'' said Grandpa, pulling out a bottle from his private stash in the library, the one hidden in the pine cabinet. ''Wanna join me for a change?''

Nothing would feel better to Wyatt at this moment than

the burn of good whiskey. He knew Grandpa didn't offer his best whiskey lightly, and the effort he'd been putting out for the last three hours to cheer Wyatt didn't go unnoticed. But Wyatt's pulse was still hammering thinking about Emma. She'd gone to Paris without him. Likely hadn't given him a second thought.

He shoved up from the rawhide chair and paced to the unlit, stone fireplace. A drink would only cloud his mind. "No, thanks."

Grandpa held up a finger-smudged glass. "You sure? Whiskey's good for the nerves, Doc Brady says."

"No wonder you like him so much. You go ahead. I'd like to remain clearheaded for Melissa's sake."

"I'll just take myself one shot." The old man poured himself a generous measure.

With a hand propped on the mantel, Wyatt stared at the mound of ashes. Was Emma right about Melissa being like Lillie?

No. She was dead wrong. Melissa's personality wasn't anything like Lillie's. Melissa was born and raised in the Territory, happy riding horses, happy with the simpler things of country life. She'd come back to herself.

Who did Emma think she was, reminding him about his failures with Lillie? He didn't need to be reminded of his inadequacies as a husband.

He damn well knew how inadequate he was.

What business was it of Emma's?

Curses fell from his mouth. He grabbed the dustpan and scooped ashes into a bucket. He'd been busy erecting the new fence, he hadn't had time to clean the fireplace or do much else around the house. That included giving Melissa the attention *she* needed. He clenched his teeth. The way things were going, he wasn't much of a father, either.

Well, then, he'd change it. He'd spend more time with

Melissa. No more arguments. The time for blaming her was past.

A jumble of nerves, he tidied the reading table. He rolled up the maps of Montana Territory Tommy had been looking at, and snapped Melissa's compass shut. He pulled out a stool, then thought better of it.

"I'm going for a walk," he said, striding to the door. "I'll be on the front porch if you need me. Melissa's side window is open. I'll hear if any commotion starts."

"Get some fresh air, good idea." Grandpa straightened his spectacles. "I'll be sittin' right here, next to the whiskey, in case anyone's needin' *me*."

The screen door slammed behind Wyatt. The rustle of wind on his face as he left the confines of the house resurged his spirit. He filled his lungs with fresh air and soothed his soul. Moonlight lit his path through the shrubs and trees as his boots crunched their way to the front yard.

He glanced up at Melissa's open window. She'd finally settled. Wyatt thanked God.

He wasn't a praying type of man, but he'd done a lot of praying today. He vowed to be a better father, to be consistent and firm, like he should have been when he first realized she was seeing that boy. From now on, Wyatt would decide what was best. Obviously, she needed his guidance, and she'd get it, no matter how stubbornly she insisted she was all grown-up.

An owl's hoot and the flutter of wings relaxed him. The wind gently hissed through prairie grass. He loved this land. How could anyone live anywhere else?

Leaning against the porch, he gazed up at the glittering stars. Montana was a tough land created for tough people. Many didn't make it. He'd seen them with their hopes dashed—drifters, settlers from the East, even ones who'd been here for years—starving, or through sheer bad luck, freezing to death in the blizzards.

Montana was a land of great potential for those willing to work hard, and work hard he did. But it was a land for men, not for boys like Cole Sinclair.

How did Cole figure he'd look after Melissa and the baby?

Wyatt, like any man in his right mind, wanted the two to marry. Half of him wanted to march into town tonight and haul Cole back by the scruff of the neck. But then what?

Most of Wyatt's family had married well and they were happy, unlike he'd been, unlike his sister Mary was. He supposed eight out of ten children was a pretty good ratio of happiness, but what if Melissa wound up deserted like Mary? Alone with four children, a husband who took off on her, the twins still in diaper cloths.

And damn if Cole didn't remind him of Mary's deserting husband. Young and irresponsible. Cole and Melissa had only been going together sporadically for a year. As soon as he found an excuse to leave, he'd be gone, too. Gone to search for gold, or some other lame excuse.

Mary's little place down the road didn't cost Wyatt much, and he was downright proud he now had the means to help out. It was her busted pride that got to him, and he didn't want Melissa suffering like that.

Wyatt would be fair; he'd give Cole a chance to prove himself. He hoped like hell the boy *would* prove himself. It'd be the best solution for everyone. But he knew, the boy, no matter what his surname, just couldn't cut it.

Then there was Emma.

Sighing, he slid a hand into his back pocket and watched the moonlight skim across the trees in the upper valley. Hell, how was he going to deal with her?

He rubbed a hand along his jaw. He didn't have to. She was going back to Philadelphia, and that was fine with him. He didn't need her, or want her, poking around in his decisions.

The flutter of birds in the elm tree made him glance up.

Emma. Standing there on the balcony, half in shadow, half in moonlight. His breath caught in the vision.

She didn't see him. Staring off into the distance, she leaned over the railing, blanket loose around her swaying hips. Couldn't she sleep, either? Her blouse was pulled out of her skirt, clinging softly to her breasts and spanning the swell of her hips. Her rich brown hair swirled loose around her shoulders, framing her soft face, entrancing him.

He thought he'd forgotten about every curvaceous inch of Emma Sinclair. But every time he stood near her, he still fought his desire for the fulfillment of making love to her.

His heart beat foolishly and he glanced away. He no longer wanted anything to do with her, he reminded himself. On top of all the problems her brother was causing, they came from two different worlds now. He didn't know her anymore.

Besides, what right did he have to look at her? He was the one who'd walked away. He was the one who'd stared into her eyes and lied when he'd said he didn't love her.

His stomach clenched. He'd tried to explain it to her once, a year before that horrible night, but she wouldn't hear any of it. So he'd kept his reasons to himself and did what he had to do.

It'd been easy to let her believe he'd left because of her father. Blazes, the way the man had treated Wyatt…

Wyatt was half expecting Mr. Sinclair to thank him for saving Emma, but instead, the old man stood in the middle of the street, shaking his fist, hollering, with poor young Emma on her wobbly crutches trembling right beside him.

"You ruined my daughter's leg! If you'd left it for Doc Brady, he would've made a smaller cut. Instead, you whittled the knife so deep, you spoiled the muscles."

"No!" Emma had shouted. "That's not true!"

"That's not how it happened, sir," Wyatt anxiously tried to explain.

Mr. Sinclair looked him straight in the eye and spit. He spit right beside Wyatt's dirty old boot. "You an expert? How do you know you never cut too deep?"

"Well...I did it the best I could."

"Your best ruined my daughter's leg! She's maimed because of you!"

"No..." Emma sobbed.

Wyatt's insides twisted. Maybe the old man was right. Maybe Wyatt had ruined her leg.

Emma shook her head, pulling herself together. "No, Wyatt. Don't go believin' you ruined my leg. You saved my life. Pa, you're wrong."

It took two years for her to persuade Wyatt it wasn't his fault. No matter how loud her father's accusations got, her refusals got louder. She was the most stubborn, intelligent, and the fairest, kindest person Wyatt had ever met.

They became good friends, stealing chunks of time together whenever he came to town to get supplies or talk to the blacksmith.

He taught her how to ride a horse. She taught him how to sew a button onto his shirt. He smiled, remembering the only way she got his attention for that was by stripping down to her chemise, lying on a pile of hay.

Her father's anger didn't diminish, though. It took Wyatt two years to realize her father was simply a good man who'd gone sour. Wyatt's family had never forgiven Mr. Sinclair for the death of one of their own, and Mr. Sinclair had never forgiven himself. He took his pain and anger out on Wyatt. Mr. Sinclair was suffering, but Wyatt never mouthed back. Sad thing was, Wyatt hardly even remembered his dead aunt anymore, and he didn't understand why everyone kept arguing about her.

Emma continued to argue with her Pa that her limp was caused by the venom, not the depth of Wyatt's cuts. She brought Wyatt an article from a medical journal she'd found, God knows where, indicating the proper way to handle a snakebite. He read it word for word, and it proved him right. Emma stuck by him like no one had ever stuck by him before.

Wyatt studied her on the balcony. He took a deep steadying breath. Poor Emma, always expecting the best in people, always getting the worst. First her father, then Wyatt, now her brother.

Wyatt shook his head in disgust at the whole lot of them. He didn't blame her for wanting to leave town. What reason would she have to stay? Not for him. At one time, maybe, but not anymore.

He knew it'd ended with Emma the day he married Lillie.

His heart trembled with guilt. There must have been something more he could have done for Lillie. When he'd first realized the trouble, he'd tried to coax her back to her native San Francisco for a spell, promising he'd go with her, but by then it'd been too late and she didn't want to go. He blamed himself for tying her to a life she wasn't made to lead. She was never happy in the country, always talking about the city.

He'd married her for the simple reason he thought he loved her. Not like he'd loved Emma, but he thought he'd never see Emma again.

And he hadn't. It'd taken him just a few hard months

after she'd left to realize she'd never be coming back. So he went on with his life as best he could.

Emma didn't even look the same anymore. She was poised and cultured, ripe for what the world had to offer. *A doctor*. Traveling to Paris, for cripe's sake.

They'd part again, and he'd watch her go.

She straightened at the railing and disappeared through the doors. His skin felt cool. Time he went in, too.

In the darkness, he heard a strange noise, one he couldn't decipher. He frowned, grappling to make sense of it. A slow whimper, like an injured cat.

His heart slammed against his chest wall. *Melissa*.

Chapter Four

Emma jumped when she heard the screams and was the first to Melissa's bedside. In a painful contraction, the girl was holding her breath, clutching her belly. She turned to Emma with crazed, pleading eyes, sending tremors down Emma's spine.

"Don't push down," said Emma, "let me check you first. I won't leave your side, I'll stay with you."

The words seemed to calm Melissa. The madness left her eyes. The contraction ended and she relaxed. Emma discovered her water sac had burst, and she was three-quarters dilated.

"The baby's coming tonight, honey. We'll all be here to help you. Don't push until I say. The birth canal has to fully dilate or else you'll tear." She pressed a comforting hand to Melissa's forehead. "There's no fresh bleeding, and that's very good news."

But the baby was still lying across the womb instead of head down. Emma gulped, more shaken than she cared to admit. She steadied her hands as she began laying out her instruments. Cesarean surgery was out; she'd do her best with forceps. It was too late to hope for Doc Brady's help.

Frantic footsteps pounded up the stairs, getting louder,

mimicking the hammering of her heart. Wyatt burst in, pale and disheveled, followed by Grandpa and a sleepy Ruth.

"Melissa?" Wyatt dashed to her side.

"Labor's starting," Emma explained, trying to keep the waver from her voice.

Ruth squinted. "Any fresh bleedin'?"

"No."

Wyatt, clutching Melissa's hand and stroking her sweaty face, whispered soothing words to his daughter. "We'll get through this together, darlin', shhh...."

Emma swallowed at the tender sight. Ruth weaved her way to Melissa's other side, holding out her hands to avoid bumping into anything. She'd be a bigger help if she could see, but even so, her presence calmed Emma.

Working quickly, Emma draped the mattress with a wad of towels. Grandpa swung his lamp onto the dresser and illuminated the lower half of the bed.

Melissa moaned with another passing contraction. A minute later, from behind the closed door, Tommy called out in a shaken whisper. "Is Melissa gonna be all right?"

Wyatt's stricken gaze flew to Emma. A soft gasp escaped her. They'd forgotten about Tommy, everyone assumed he was still in bed, sleeping.

Grandpa responded first. "Yes, boy, she's fine." Leaving the room, he said to the others, "I'll stay with him."

"Don't worry, Tommy," Wyatt spoke up, gazing at Emma with uncertainty in his dark eyes, "your sister's having the baby. Screaming is normal." Emma gave him a reassuring nod and soft smile, finding comfort in the warmth of his returning gaze. They were in this together, no matter what their differences.

Ruth shuffled beside Emma and spoke in a suffocated whisper, "She fully dilated yet?"

"Almost."

"You got everything? The string for the cord, the mucous bulb?"

"Yes."

"You know, I delivered thirty-two babies myself. Helped Doc Brady with another eight."

"I'm glad you're here. I can use your help."

Ruth nodded proudly, and Emma felt the woman's resistance toward her slip. Ruth slid more towels underneath Melissa and did her own check over Melissa's belly. She returned to Emma. "You do know what you're doin', don't ya girl? You know you need more than forceps."

"It's not time yet. We'll give the baby a chance to turn on its own." It was hot in the room. Emma took a deep breath and brushed the beads of perspiration from her brow. Her nervous gaze met with Wyatt's. He searched her face, probing her with silent questions, but allowing her to continue. Melissa moaned. He focused on his daughter, slid into a chair and grasped her hand.

An hour passed. Melissa became fully dilated, her contractions regular, but the baby still hadn't turned. Now the baby was in danger, and Emma had to do something.

They still had some time, but seeing that Melissa was unmarried, with no husband to make the legal decision, the decision rested with Wyatt. Emma pulled him into the hallway. With a panicked gaze, he towered above her, hungry for every word. Grandpa saw them from Tommy's room and joined them.

Emma's breathing hushed as she looked into Wyatt's tense face. "Melissa's having problems. I have to do a version."

His shoulders sprang up, his voice caught. "What's that?"

"The baby's stuck. Instead of coming out headfirst, it's

lying crossways. I need to go in there and turn the baby around.''

"With your instruments?"

"With my hands."

His face went grim. "Won't that hurt?"

She blinked and swallowed. "Extremely." Poor Melissa, she didn't know how much agony she was in for.

His mouth curved with sorrow. "Can't we wait? Maybe the baby will turn around on its own."

She had to be direct. "If we wait too long, the contractions will put strain on the baby. The baby might die."

He moaned. Looking suddenly weary, he brought a large hand to his raspy cheek and rubbed it.

"There's no time," she said, glumly. "Melissa's in full labor. The sooner we do this, the better for the baby."

Wyatt's eyes glistened as if struck with a new thought. He leaned forward. "Forgetting the baby for a moment, would it be easier on Melissa if we wait?"

"My book says—"

"Your book—?" said Grandpa.

"Let her speak."

"My book says the baby would be stillborn if we wait too long, and…" She fiddled with the hem of her blouse, struggling to find the easiest words. She'd lay it all out, let him decide. "…and Melissa will have to go through a version, sooner or later. Because alive or dead, the baby has to be delivered."

Wyatt drained of color. He seemed to lose his footing as he momentarily swung away.

"Wait a minute," muttered Grandpa. He walked to Melissa's door and yanked Ruth into the hall. "If Doc Brady were here, is this what he'd be doin'? A version?"

"Most likely."

"Have you ever done one?"

"No, but I seen him do one. Remember, Katy Ivanich with her third child?"

Grandpa paled. His mouth dropped. "Lordie, lordie. Both Katy and her baby died during that delivery."

Emma's heart stilled. Her eyes tenderly found Wyatt's.

Ruth touched Grandpa's shoulder. "Katy's husband wouldn't allow us to do the version soon enough. Not until two days had already passed."

"All right," Wyatt said, springing forward, "Let's not wait. Do it now, Emma. I'll take Tommy downstairs where it's quieter. Grandpa, you can join us. Ruth, I'd appreciate if you'd stay and help Emma." He turned to go.

Emma reached out and grabbed him by the elbow. She let her fingers linger, gaining strength from the heated touch. "Wait, Wyatt," she said as kindly as she could. "Could you stay? Please?"

Groaning, he scrutinized her face with an agonized expression. "I don't think I could sit beside my little girl another moment and watch her go through this torture."

She braced herself and simply said it. "Melissa will fight this. I need you to hold her down. You and Grandpa both. By her shoulders, you'll have to pin her down for me."

His mouth trembled. He didn't speak, as if she'd knocked the wind out of him.

"Lordie, lordie," said Grandpa, pacing down the hall.

Emma turned to Ruth. "Please take Tommy downstairs to the kitchen and shut all the doors along the way."

Turning back to Wyatt, she noticed he wasn't moving. She was deeply touched by his anguish. "We'll get through this together. I'll do everything I can to help her." When he looked down at her and nodded, she reached out and slid her warm hand into his clammy one, and led him back into the room. A bond of friendship.

Angels, we need you.

Wyatt gave Melissa her worn rag doll to hold on to, and for the next twenty excruciating minutes, Emma was sure Melissa's screams were heard for miles into the valley. The rotation worked. The baby's head crowned quickly. Five more contractions and the baby slid into Emma's waiting hands.

A tiny baby boy. Blue, limp, not breathing.

Sliding him onto the towel, she tied the cord and cut it.

No sound. With a bulb syringe, she sucked mucous from the back of his throat. He cried then. Weak at first, then louder still. He pinked up and she guessed his weight at five pounds.

Wrapping him in another towel, he squawked again. This time she laughed. He looked like he was going to be okay. Exhilaration swept her.

Wyatt laughed beside her. Her body quivered; she hadn't realized he was standing so close. Meeting his twinkling eyes with joy in her heart, she broke into a wide smile.

"We did it," she said.

"You did it." He rewarded her with a smile of his own. It had an underlying tug of intimacy, in that same long-forgotten way she remembered. Her skin flushed and she glanced away, at Melissa.

The girl, weak and exhausted, pulled herself to her elbows.

"It's a boy, honey." Emma said with laughter in her voice. She placed the warm bundle in the crux of Melissa's arm. "He's tiny, but his fingers and toes are all there. He's looking mighty strong. You did great."

Melissa's hands shook as she brought the baby's face against her own and kissed it. "You've got a lot of black hair." Laughing, Wyatt and Grandpa patted each other on the back and congratulated Melissa. The baby cooed.

Emma couldn't stop smiling. This little baby was her

nephew, her own flesh and blood. The tightness in her muscles began to slacken, starting with the loosening around her shoulders, then down through her limbs. She glanced around at the happy faces, settling on the widest, handsomest grin of all, Wyatt's.

He sent her pulse rushing. With a look of utter elation, he reached out with a firm, muscular arm and pulled her to his chest, sending tingles of excitement down her body.

Unable to keep from laughing, knowing it was just the joy of the moment, she reached up high to embrace him. She'd removed her corset earlier for sleeping, and her breasts jiggled loosely under her blouse. Her blouse slid up her back, and his fingers accidentally grazed bare flesh. She gasped. The whisper of his warm breath at her throat cascaded over her skin. His breath caught, and for a long sensual moment, his dark eyes captured hers.

Flushed, she pulled away. The embrace meant nothing. They'd been through an ordeal together, were simply relieved in the happy outcome. That's all.

Melissa called out to him and he turned. While Emma finished up and made Melissa comfortable, the men slipped out of the room to share the news with Tommy and Ruth. Emma waited until the girl and baby were fast asleep in each other's arms.

She stroked the downy face of the sleeping baby and gazed over Melissa's contented face. Emma had managed her first delivery just fine.

Now that the baby was born, everything would change. Wyatt would soften, it was happening already, and Cole would see his son. It couldn't be any better.

She looked down at her blouse. It was splattered with blood, and this time she would change into Wyatt's shirt.

As she was stepping out of his room and buttoning up the last button, the smell of fresh coffee reached her.

Heading downstairs, she felt on top of the world.

Outside in the awakening mist, a rooster crowed.

Wyatt pulled in a cool, wonderful breath of air. Walking from the stables to the side of the house, he watched the golden sun rise over the hills. It was his favorite time of day, early morning, cool dew on the grass, such serenity over the valley he felt nothing could disturb it. And this morning, of all mornings, he felt better than ever.

Because Melissa and the baby were going to be fine.

His heart pumped with excitement as he took giant invigorating steps. The children were asleep upstairs and he'd just finished hitching up the buggy for Grandpa, who'd be taking Ruth back to her farm. Emma was in the kitchen tending to the baby. He'd already taken the smooth pine cradle from the attic and placed it in the cozy nook between the stove and window. A wooden cradle, he recalled with pride, the first piece of furniture he'd ever built, carved with the name Barlow on the headboard, and first used for Melissa, then Tommy. He grinned. And now the baby.

A little baby boy, son of a gun. He pushed the problems with Cole out of his head for a minute and allowed himself to contemplate the good stuff.

Glancing to the cookhouse, he noticed a ring of smoke rising from the chimney. Hank was already up, preparing food for the hands. The ranch was about to come alive. Like most mornings, Wyatt enjoyed being one of the first to rise. It gave him a jump on the day and the chance to plan the duties for his men.

He pushed the screen door open and stepped into the warm, fragrant kitchen. Breakfast for the family had come and gone, but he'd left the fire going in the cast iron stove to keep the baby warm. By midmorning, it'd be warm enough outside to let the fire die down in the kitchen.

Emma was humming beside the wooden cradle, wearing one of his best blue shirts, sleeves rolled up and shirttail loose above her skirt. The collar at her throat parted, revealing soft shadows at the hollow of her neck, and the nubile way she moved suggested womanly curves beneath the cloth. He felt the heat rise inside his body and averted his gaze.

While Emma changed the baby's diaper cloth, the newborn kicked his tiny legs. "Is Ruth gone?"

"Yeah, she'll be home before you know it." He tossed his Stetson on the rack, gave his boots a swipe on the mat, then joined her.

Lifting the squirming little baby in the air, Emma smiled. "Would you like to hold him while I change the sheets?" Her face was pink with eagerness.

He gulped. "He's so tiny, I'm afraid I'll break him."

"You won't break him, he's tough."

"Well, all right." Wyatt held out his arms and cupped the baby gingerly, the baby's soft head in the palm of Wyatt's hand, the curled toes beneath the cotton nightshirt reaching halfway to Wyatt's elbow. "Good Lord, he's small. But he sure can move. Hurry up with the sheets!"

Emma laughed. She'd knotted her rich hair at the back of her neck, but wisps of fallen strands framed her face. "You're doing well." She stepped beside him, her body brushing his as she peered at the baby's angelic face. She radiated a vitality that drew him uncontrollably. He breathed her in, that musky, womanly scent.

He'd never have her, he thought.

She tossed the wet sheets into the soapy bucket. "He's a little fighter."

Turning to the baby, Wyatt leaned into the little cheeks that felt as soft as feathers. "You are, aren't you? You're a little fighter." He placed two fingertips against the baby's chest and felt the rise and fall of his breathing, and the pounding of his heartbeat.

Wyatt frowned. "His heart is beating fast, you sure he's doing fine?"

Her lips curved with tenderness. "He's fine. See, he's nice and pink and he's breathing calmly. His pulse is supposed to be fast, twice as fast as an adult's. Especially if he's active like he is now."

She had a way of explaining things that relaxed Wyatt. "How did Melissa do with the first feeding?"

"Good, he ate well. But he may slow down after a few days. Feeding too vigorously for long periods of time might tucker him out. It's better if he eats smaller amounts, but more frequently." She spread the clean sheets into the cradle with slender hands. "You'll have to encourage Melissa to nurse him every two or three hours the first week, until Doc Brady sees how he's doing."

The mention of Doc Brady jarred him to reality. She'd be leaving soon. "Should Melissa feed him that often even during the night?"

"Yes. But if you see Melissa needs more sleep, you can supplement the baby at nighttime—so she doesn't have to get up—with goat's milk." Her eyes sparkled at him. "Did I see goats in the yard yesterday?"

"Yeah, Grandpa's got a few. One of them is nursing her own right now; he won't mind milking her for the baby."

The baby kicked his feet again, grabbed hold of one of Wyatt's fingers and squeezed, making Wyatt laugh out loud. "Owww," he said, pretending the baby had squeezed too hard. "I think this little guy doesn't know his own strength."

Emma sighed comfortably and stroked the baby's cheeks. "He's beautiful, isn't he?"

Contentment filled him, in every pore. Sometimes, times

like these, the wonder of God and nature awed him. "Yes, he is."

Wyatt turned his face from the baby to Emma, whose own relaxed face lingered a breath away from his. His fingers ached to touch her. "You've turned into a fine doctor, Emma."

Flustered, she shook out a baby blanket. "Thank you."

His voice deepened. "If you hadn't been here, both Melissa and the baby might have died. How will I repay you?"

Smiling shyly, she slid her warm fingers between him and the baby and lifted the infant back into the cradle. "I was pleased to do it, as the baby's aunt, and as a doctor...." Her creamy cheeks tugged and she averted her eyes, but not before he saw the overwhelming pride in them.

He watched the play of emotions on her face, and the buried longing in his heart tenderly surfaced. With a will of their own, his fingers wove themselves around a silky tendril of hair that had worked its way free of her knot.

His heart turned over in response. Her breath caught, she gasped, but didn't draw away. He lowered his exploring fingers and brushed them against the soft nape of her neck, causing his loins to stir. "Such smooth, velvety skin, Emma, such beauty beneath the skin."

He felt her quiver beneath his touch. She slowly raised her smoldering eyes to his. They shimmered with a womanly invitation he wasn't even sure she knew she was sending. And then, because he was a man and she was a woman, he did what he was helpless to stop himself from doing. He slid her close, tangled his fingers in her mound of hair, and covered her lips with his.

The pleasure of her hot mouth was almost too much for him to bear. Moist and supple, opening for his. It felt right to take her. They melted into each other, the years of loneliness peeling away until it was the two of them, lost in their own heat.

A wave of animal instinct undulated through him. He tightened his hold, and her yielding body responded to his. He groaned softly. He wanted to protect her from the world.

She gave him strength.

He felt her shudder. The way her body flowed in rhythm to his touch sent a quiver all the way down his spine into the muscles of his buttocks, and down again to his hardness.

She made him weak.

Her touch was more potent than he remembered. She stole his breath away. No one, not ever, affected him the way Emma did.

He felt her hands grow rigid against his chest. She tore away, her breathing ragged. "Stop..." She staggered back. With a glance at the baby, her hands fluttered to her throat. Shaking her head back and forth, she pulled in a heavy breath and he knew it was over. "I...we...I don't want to do this."

He steadied himself. *What was he doing? What was he trying to prove?* Tunneling a hand through his black hair, he tried to regain a semblance of control. How could he possibly be kissing *her* when he wanted to strangle her brother?

"I'm sorry." He shrugged his shoulders as he watched her pull herself together. He didn't want a woman in his life. Especially not this one. It'd been over between them for years. And there were so many reasons to stay away from her. Like Cole. And even Melissa. How could he lecture his daughter on self-control when he was behaving like—like this? Did he have no sense in his empty head?

"I'm sorry," he repeated. "It won't happen again." He could feel himself growing tense and resentful. He didn't need *any* woman. Women were complications he wasn't very good with. Hadn't he proved that?

"You're right, it won't." She whirled away and headed for the door. "I'm leaving for Philadelphia tomorrow." She mumbled something about needing air and the screen door slammed behind her.

Rubbing his hands along his face, trying to erase her scent, his palms stung from the bristles. He gazed into the cradle at the innocent sleeping face.

The only reason he'd kissed Emma was because he'd got caught up in the moment. He was so elated Melissa and the baby had pulled through the delivery, he'd gotten his feelings mixed up. Nothing more. He was grateful to Emma and wanted to say thanks.

Like he'd say thanks to the stagecoach driver for a smooth trip... Well, he'd never kissed a stagecoach driver before....

Emma had become a good doctor and used her skills to save Melissa, and he was grateful. Anything wrong with that?

The baby gurgled. Wyatt pressed his fingers along the cradle's edge and rocked.

At least the question that'd been nagging him for years was suddenly answered. Last night had proved it.

He was right to have left Emma.

All these years he'd been wondering if he'd done the right thing. He had no choice but to tell her he didn't love her, or she wouldn't have gone to Philadelphia to study medicine. The year before, he'd tried to broach it with her, suggesting she go to college, move there without him, but she'd raised a storm fighting him. Made him promise he'd never mention it again. She'd told him it wasn't important, she'd make do with her life in Pine Creek.

But they didn't come from money, and he knew her aunt

and uncle's offer to help wouldn't come again. So he came up with his own plan and kept his mouth shut. But he had eyes, and he could see how passionately she felt about medicine, how good she was with people, how tenderly she cared about everyone.

How could he take a dream away from a young woman he cared so deeply about? How could he rob the world of her?

After witnessing how effective she was with Melissa last night, his heart surged knowing that because Emma had become a doctor, the world was a kinder place.

He was glad he never stood in her way, no matter how hard it'd been for him those first few years. Thinking about her all the time, comparing her to—

Taking a breath, he broke free and leaned against the wall, gathering strength. It didn't matter anymore.

Wyatt Barlow and Emma Sinclair were strangers now.

More than an hour later, Wyatt discovered Emma asleep in the rocking chair beside the cradle. He didn't disturb her. There was a soft color to her sweet proud lips and a deep rhythm to her breathing. He figured she could use the sleep, and he needed to put distance between them.

After bounding up the stairs to check on a sleeping Melissa, he tossed his Stetson on and escaped to the stables. Relieved to get back to work, grateful to get his mind off Emma, he swung a sack of oats over his shoulder and entered the stalls. The comforting scent of fresh-laid straw and horses greeted him.

He'd acted like an idiot with Emma and he wouldn't allow it to happen again. Hell, she was right, she was leaving. Things would be back to normal soon. Back to the way things were before she'd set foot on his ranch yesterday.

Was it only yesterday?

One of the mares whinnied and he gave it a passing pat as he made his way to the Arabians, checking on the horses, saying good morning to the working men.

As hard as he fought, Emma crept back into his thoughts. She'd told him she'd wait until Doc Brady arrived, then be on her way. Good, he told himself, good. The sooner the better.

He kept up a deliberate stride, but couldn't control his runaway mind. How much time did he have left with Emma? Was that what their lives amounted to—sixteen years of nothing between them, one intense night delivering a baby together, then how many more years of nothing?

A faint thread of loss twisted around his heart. He brushed it aside. That's the way it was and he would face it. Emma was practically gone already. His concern rested with Melissa and the baby.

And Cole. He'd been doing a lot of thinking about Cole. Now that the baby was born, had anything changed?

Wyatt yanked the cord on the sack of oats and measured it out to the Arabians. Shoving a hand into his pocket, he tilted his head and watched them feed.

Cole's situation hadn't changed. His capabilities hadn't changed. He couldn't magically look after Melissa today any better than he could yesterday. Only time could tell if he could shoulder responsibility, put food on the table and provide the necessities of life.

Emma was willing to help in any way she could, she made that clear. But what, in the name of heaven, could she do from two thousand miles away? Write a few encouraging letters to Cole? What could her twice-yearly visits accomplish?

It was Wyatt who had to make the decisions. He'd be here every day with Melissa. Emma's heart might be in the right place where her brother was concerned, but it was the soft heart of a woman wishing her brother was responsible. Wishing and dreaming didn't make things happen; hard work did, and that was entirely up to Cole.

It was up to the boy to prove himself. The situation was out of Wyatt's hands. And out of Emma's, too.

He kicked at the straw, thinking of what Cole had put Melissa through. Cole wasn't the one who had to listen to her screams, or pretend everything was all right when her bleeding was soaking the bed. He didn't have to pin her down by her shoulders and watch the doctor wrench out her guts. No, Cole was probably having a drink at the saloon with his friends, like usual.

Well, to hell with Cole. And to hell with his sister, too. Wyatt had a ranch to run.

He spotted his foreman in the far corner. "Morning, Jack," he hollered, weaving his way toward him.

"Howdy, boss." Jack leaned up against the boards and surveyed the rolls of fencing wire. He tipped his hat back on his blond head and set his friendly eyes on Wyatt. "I hear congratulations are in order."

Wyatt nodded and grinned.

"Melissa all right?"

Wyatt fingered the brim of his hat. "Yeah, a little shaky and tired."

"I can't believe the baby made it, so young and all."

"I can't believe it, either. Course, he's still small and has a way to go, but he's strong." *Thanks to Emma,* Wyatt thought. "How did fencing go yesterday?" *She's waiting, back in the house.*

Jack yanked work gloves over his callused hands. "Good. If the weather holds up, we'll be done by the end of the week. You hear about the cougar we trapped last night?"

"I heard. Glad our hard work putting up the fence is doing something."

Wyatt grabbed his work gloves from a keg on the wall and tugged them on. *Emma.* He hoped a little hard work would knock her out of his head. Stepping into the sunshine, he started loading up the wagon with rolls of wire. Beside him, Jack loaded the cedar posts and they fell into a stride.

She'll be gone soon. "I don't care," he muttered to himself. He increased his pace until his muscles ached and strained. It felt good to tax himself. "The two new mustangs, they eating any better?"

"Yeah, they're beginning to settle in. Not as jittery as they were two days ago."

When will I see her again? One year, two years, sixteen years?

He slammed a roll of wire onto the wagon. It hurled against another and knocked the stack down.

"Whoa," said Jack.

"Sorry."

They worked in silence. *The woman sure can kiss. Stop thinking about her. It's over, dammit, it's over.*

Congratulations from the other men started rolling in, interrupting the morning's work. Wyatt's mood lifted. He felt the tension lifting from his shoulders as the morning wore on.

Concerned about his palomino, Wyatt headed to its stall. He walked it out to the corral, noticing it still protected its weak side, but the tendon was almost healed.

While the horse circled, he glanced to the west hills, expecting some of his family to gallop over at any time. They'd be hearing the news about Melissa from the ranch hands working in the area. Wyatt was itching to tell the news himself, but he wanted to stay near Melissa in case she needed him. Grandpa, on his way home from delivering Ruth, would probably stop off at Mary's and tell her.

Squatting by the stallion, examining its lifted hoof, Wyatt heard a buggy crunch along the dirt. Must be Grandpa.

"Hello," called the familiar male voice, sending an uncomfortable jolt of surprise through Wyatt.

Doc Brady. Startled, Wyatt swung up, nearly spooking the horse, and watched the buggy roll to a stop.

He felt an ice spreading through his body. He should have been ready for the sharp chill but he wasn't.

Watching the old man hop out, Wyatt braced himself for the inevitable truth.

Emma Sinclair was about to walk out of his life, totally and completely, for the second time.

Chapter Five

"In my opinion, you had no choice, Emma," said the old doctor after checking on Melissa and the baby. "An internal rotation is a terrible thing to have to do to a woman, but sometimes you got no choice. You did a good job."

Emma smiled at the comment. It meant a lot to her, coming from the doctor she'd admired since she was a girl.

Doc Brady nodded as he walked, bushy white brows sprinkled with blond, muttonchop sideburns reaching down to his square chin.

Emma sighed in satisfaction. "I didn't do it alone. Ruth was there, and Wyatt—"

Wyatt pushed open the kitchen door for her. "Don't let her downplay it, Doc, she did a great job." He looked at her in an odd, resigned manner.

She breezed by him, very careful not to let any part of her graze him, and still her stomach fluttered. His faint smile held a wisp of sadness. When his eyes flickered, it was gone and she wondered if she'd imagined it.

He looked fresher and more awake; he'd found the time to shave the dark stubble from his jaw. It gave him a sleek, boyish appearance, as if he were heading to town for Sunday school. He caught her studying him. She glanced away, the memory of his kiss stinging her raw lips. Her chest grew hot with shame.

What on earth had possessed her to succumb to him? How could she look him straight in the eye, knowing how wantonly she'd reacted to his kiss? Was she so desperate that the first man to kiss her in over a year was railroaded with her favors?

And him, of all men, him. The one who'd out-and-out told her he didn't want her. Could he have made it any plainer?

"You always were quick on your feet," Doc Brady said. "I knew all that readin' in my office would do you good one day. Remember, Wyatt, how much readin' she used to do?"

"I remember." His eyes sparkled deep brown. She warned herself to be cautious. "Coffee, Doc?"

"Sure could use one."

"Emma?"

Coffee would perk her up; she had a long day ahead of her, announcing the news to her family. "Yes, please."

The baby fussed in his cradle and Emma stepped beside him, sliding her hand under his head and lifting him into her arms. What a soft bundle of warmth and innocence. It felt wonderful to hold him. She returned to the table with him and slid into a chair. With the baby lying on her lap, she checked his diaper cloth. He was dry.

Doc Brady seated himself beside her. "Can I examine him more thoroughly, as you hold him?"

Emma nodded and swung her knees, along with the baby, closer to Doc Brady and his awaiting stethoscope.

Tucking the earpieces into place, he slid the bell under the baby's gown. "Even with all your readin', Emma, we never did find a cure for your weak muscles, did we? And all those balms never made the scar go away, did it?"

Silently pleading the doctor wouldn't go on, she stilled the wriggling baby on her legs. They were such personal memories—her longing to cure her leg wrapped up with her longing for Wyatt, a boy she hoped would never notice her scars.

Looming above her, Wyatt was setting the tin cups of coffee onto the table. For a second, his hands halted in midair, but fortunately, he saved her the embarrassment of looking her way.

The doctor probed the baby's abdomen with skilled, gnarled fingers. "One thing's for sure. All that readin' sure gave you an appetite for medicine, didn't it? Got so you got ahead of me in my readin'. You've got a fine mind, there, young woman, a fine mind."

The floorboards creaked by the counter where Wyatt stood. "Emma's turned out to be a hell of a doctor."

She stiffly managed to nod and reply, "Thank you." As kind as the words were, her body yearned for other words. Why couldn't he say what a fine woman she'd become? Not a fine doctor. *Emma's turned out to be a hell of a woman, hasn't she, a real beauty.* Was that so ridiculous?

Would he ever consider her beautiful? Beautiful first, before thinking of how darn capable she was?

Now she was being ridiculous. How many women fought to be accepted on the merits of their intelligence, not their appearance? Yet here she was, hoping otherwise. She almost smiled at her own silliness.

But there was that kiss.

It'd been a deep, rough kiss, full of desire. She felt the back of neck flush, thinking of how quickly her own body had betrayed her, melting into his. Mercy, that's how they used to kiss as senseless teens.

She dismissed it. The kiss had happened accidentally, from the overwhelming relief for Melissa and the baby, nothing more. Emma would leave tomorrow and that would be the end of that. She'd be gone, simple and clean, as it was meant to be.

Doc Brady removed the diaper cloth, lifting the baby's legs in the air and pressing the tiny heels together, checking for hip displacement. Looked fine, Emma noticed.

"You plan on deliverin' a lot of babies in Philadelphia?"

"I'd like to."

The doctor smiled and scratched his sideburns. "Babies and children, that's where you lady doctors are needed the most."

Emma didn't argue with him this time. He had his opinion on lady doctors, she had hers. Over the years, she'd learned she couldn't change him by arguing.

He was a respectable man, she knew, advising and helping her learn whenever he'd had the chance, and she appreciated all he'd done. But she felt his limits. *No place for a woman in surgery,* he'd told her many times, *never will be. Women can't stomach surgery, can't handle the gore, can't do what's necessary. Babies and children is what women know best.*

She could almost follow the logic in his thinking, and most of his male colleagues thought the same, but she hadn't become a doctor to limit herself. There'd come a day when she would perform surgery, with or without male approval, and she'd be good at it.

All she needed was firsthand experience, and she'd get that quicker in Philadelphia than anywhere else, observing and learning from the highest skilled surgeons in America. A dream she'd held for years.

The examination ended. Emma tucked the blanket around the baby.

Doc Brady stood up and turned around to Wyatt. "I think Melissa was a couple of weeks further along than we thought. The boy looks healthy. Tiny, five and three-quarter pounds by your kitchen scales, but perfectly formed and strong. You gotta keep him warm, and keep an eye on his feeding.''

''Emma's already explained the importance of that, and it'll be my top priority.'' Sunlight streamed through the window around Wyatt's broad shoulders, making him appear huge. Stop noticing, she scolded herself.

''You got Ruth nearby, if you need any help with the baby, and your sisters.''

''Yeah, there's a lot of women around I'm sure will want to fuss all over him.''

They drank their coffee. The baby squirmed in her lap and Emma drew him close to her face, basking in the fresh smell of his skin. She wished she could be one of those women living nearby, spending more time with her nephew than just one day.

''He looks an awful lot like Melissa, doesn't he?'' asked the doctor. ''Dark hair, dark eyes.''

Emma regarded the round little cheeks and pudgy nose. ''Why, he's the spitting image of Cole.'' Delighted with her observation, she smiled. ''Cole's going to be thrilled, and I can't wait till he sees him.''

She looked up in time to see Wyatt stiffen. With a firm air of disapproval, he gathered the empty cups.

A knot rose in her throat. Wyatt wasn't still thinking of keeping Cole away...? She shook her head. Of course not. How could he keep the father of the baby away? And Cole certainly wouldn't tolerate it. She shuddered to think what Cole would do, if Wyatt made the absurd demand....

Doc Brady looked at her strangely, like he had something on his mind, something he wanted to say, but he shot a glance at Wyatt and clamped his mouth.

The baby wailed and shoved a pink fist into his mouth.

Emma laughed, forgetting the problems with the adults. The baby was hungry. "He looks like he wants to nurse, I'll take him up to Melissa."

She brought him upstairs and settled him with his mother, who was eager to spend time with him. Ten minutes later, when she was sure things were going well, Emma left them and returned to the kitchen.

Bacon sizzled on the stove. Wyatt flipped it over in the pan. "Breakfast for Doc Brady," he explained.

She stifled a yawn and glanced at the wall clock. It was close to ten.

"Tommy still sleeping?" she asked.

Wyatt nodded. "He must be tired from all the excitement last night. He'll be up soon, hungry as a lion."

While Wyatt prepared the food, Doc Brady flagged her closer, careful not to catch Wyatt's eye. Her curiosity was rising.

He whispered, "I haven't had a chance to tell you. It was Cole who found me in Levi Valley, around midnight last night."

She grew serious. "Cole came riding after you?"

"Yup. As soon as he heard you were headin' here with Tommy. All alone, he rode like hell, nearly stark crazy with worry. Found me and the missus at my sister's, in a deep sleep. We had a fine party last night at the steak house. They got a new cook there from Santa Fe. Grilled steaks and chili peppers, he sure knows how to fix up a fancy meal—"

"So Cole knows about Melissa?"

"Only that the labor pains started, and that she was bleedin'."

Tenderness stabbed her heart. "Poor Cole, he must be so worried. I've got to go to him and tell him the baby's been born, that Melissa's all right."

The doctor whispered real low. "He's waitin' outside."

Emma pulled back in momentary panic. "Here? On the ranch?"

He motioned toward the window. "Under the first tree, beyond the first hill. He aimed on comin' straight to the door, but I convinced him to be patient. I wasn't sure what kind of situation he'd be ridin' into, if you know what I mean." His eyes darted to the back of Wyatt's head. "You know how impulsive and hotheaded Cole can be."

Her stomach quaked. This was a fragile situation, and Cole being here, unexpectedly and uninvited, might not go over smoothly. "What do I do now?" she whispered.

"Ask Wyatt."

"Ask me what?" She watched Wyatt turn, hands on his hips, boldly intimidating. His breadth and width and power sent her pulses spinning.

She searched his unreadable dark eyes and told herself to calm down. Maybe it was for the best, that Wyatt's hand was played out for him like this. They could bring Cole in quickly, seize the opportunity at hand and make a smooth transition. The longer they waited, the more difficult it would become.

She inched taller, kept her voice firm. "Cole's waiting outside."

He jerked his dark brows downward. "For what?"

"Well for heaven's sake, he's worried about Melissa."

"He's the one who made *us* worry if she'd make it out alive."

She stared at his hard, cold-eyed expression. "Cole rode all night and brought the doctor and his wife back from Levi Valley. Now he's waiting outside, calmly, for you to invite him in."

He looked at her intently, then strode to the counter. "He's not welcome."

Her hands fluttered to her waist. "I know we're all tired, and you're not expecting him to be here so soon, but wouldn't it be easier to let him in now than to prolong the inevitable until later?"

Wyatt took his time answering. The icy set in his eyes didn't waver. Gritting his teeth, he glanced out the kitchen window, then back to her.

Her heart pounded with a heady mixture of hope and fear. His black eyes glinted like metal. "No," he finally said, his challenging gaze daring her to cross the line, daring her to push him into a corner.

She stared back, silent. All right, she'd back down for the moment. Arguing would do more damage than good. "Maybe you're right. Maybe it's better if we come back later, after everyone's got some rest."

A muscle flickered at his temple. Taking a deep breath, he crossed his arms and leaned against the counter, that stubborn set to his jaw.

Doc Brady gave a little cough and cleared his throat. She ignored the doctor, and her own humiliation for having to beg in front of a witness. "When would be a good time to return? When can Cole see his son?"

Wyatt shook his head solemnly. "When Cole proves he can hold a job for more than a few weeks, bring in money, and take care of Melissa and the baby."

Her palms grew moist, and she twisted them into her skirt. "But that'll take months to prove. Cole is the father, the baby's flesh and blood. Doesn't that count for anything?"

"Cole rarely thinks of anyone but himself. He'll get over it."

She shifted indignantly from foot to foot. Her temper flashed. "What in thunder happened to you? I don't know you anymore. How can you be so cruel?"

He gave her a cool, level stare and shrugged away her comments. "I'm thinking about what's best for my daughter."

"What about what's best for Cole?" She could barely control her resentment.

His face clouded. His eyes narrowed. "Did you get a good look at Melissa last night, holding on to her rag doll while she was giving birth? A doll, for cripe's sake. She's still a kid, and it's my responsibility to look after her. I bet if you look in your woodshed, you'll still find Cole's toy guns."

"He doesn't play with toys anymore. He's a young man. *A father.*"

"When he starts acting like one, he can come around." He paced the floor. "Believe it or not, I'm thinking about Cole, too. If I allow him to come in, hold the baby awhile and get attached, then what? It'll be harder on everyone if it breaks up then. What do you think that would do to Melissa? If Cole can't keep the job he has right now, I don't hold out hope for them, and I don't want him around. *Ever.*"

She gasped and stepped back. Who did he think he was, assuming right off that Cole would fail, doomed before he even started? Cole had a family behind him, one who'd help him. "And the rest of us Sinclairs? When can my mother see the baby? And my sister?"

Doc Brady, silent until now, hitched up his pants. "Wyatt, it seems only fair—"

Wyatt raised a palm and silenced the doctor. "I'm not saying never. I just want to wait until we've all got a handle on our tempers. I'd prefer if your family waited until things cool down. Until Cole cools down."

"Maybe he's right, Emma," said Doc Brady, shifting

his focus. "Maybe waitin's better, until Cole and Wyatt both cool down. No tellin' what they might do...."

Emma ignored the doctor. Her heart beat wildly. She was mad enough to spit fire at this arrogant man. "Do you think you can shoo Cole away?" she said with quivering lips. "Like an irritating fly buzzing around your head? Do you think that will *cool him down?*"

Anger flashed across his dark face. He recovered quickly, drew his lips together and stepped back to assess her. "How much do I owe you?"

"I beg your pardon?"

"What's the charge these days, for a delivery?" His tone cut through her with a curt, dismissive edge.

She stared at him in astonishment. He considered her hired help rather than family? "You want to pay me for my services?"

"I appreciate what you did for Melissa, and I'd like to square it with you."

She couldn't read his voice or face, but she was deeply insulted. He was treating her no better than a maid. She was the baby's aunt! "How dare you try to pay me. If it honestly came from your heart, I'd accept, but you only mean to dismiss me!" She swung a hand onto her hip and thrust out her jaw. "This baby is my nephew, he's part of my family as well as yours."

"You mistake my intentions." He sighed. "I don't expect you to work for free." He opened the cupboard and pulled out a billfold. "Give me the city fee, not the country. You're from the big city, you deserve big city fees. I don't intend paying you with chickens or eggs."

What nonsense was he talking about? She stood her ground, arms crossed.

He had the gall to ignore her and turned to Doc Brady. "Doc, how much would you charge?"

The lines in the older man's face deepened. "You two..." He shook his head, looking from one to the other, but she was well beyond being embarrassed. "Ten dollars, plus one for the night call. Eleven," he said in a resigned voice.

"How much do you figure she could get in the city?"

"Well, no medications were involved, but there was the version...city doctors usually charge about three times as much. Between thirty and thirty-five, I reckon."

"We'll say thirty-five." Wyatt took out the bills and placed them on the counter in front of her. With large firm hand, he slid the bills toward her, as if they were playing poker, for crying out loud, and she'd won.

What kind of a man had he become? "You'd sooner pay me off with money than pay me or my family any respect! Well, you can't buy me and you can't dismiss me! Keep your dollars!"

Her words seemed to finally get under his skin. His face darkened, he took a step toward her, but before he could retaliate, Tommy walked through the door, bleary-eyed and yawning.

"And for your bloody information, I'd charge you two thousand!" With a furious shake of her head, Emma snatched her bag and pounded out the door. As she marched to the stables, her boots thundered with every step.

She muttered a few choice words under her breath, ones she never said in public. She couldn't stomach another moment on the same ranch with the man, and someone, *someone* had to speak to Cole.

At her icy request, one of the ranch hands saddled a horse, with the promise that he'd pick it up this evening at the livery stables in town.

She gulped down chunks of air as she tore off into the crisp morning, chilled in every muscle, wondering how she'd ever explain this to her brother. Wondering what in blazes she'd ever seen in Wyatt Barlow. She rarely lost her temper, and knowing she'd lost it today made her arteries pound even harder.

Honest to God, if she were a man, she'd knock him senseless.

Her anger somewhat under control, Emma stared at the ruts in the road ahead of her, practicing what she'd say to Cole. The sun twinkled off the dew on the grass and the heat soaked into her shirt—Wyatt's shirt, that blasted man—and into her bones. She'd remembered to take her medicine bag with her, but she wished she'd asked for a shawl. The air was cool.

She spotted Cole and her breathing hitched. She slowed her horse.

His short, lean figure stood underneath a spread of pines. He was gazing into the distance slopes at a herd of wild horses. His own stallion grazed beside him, and every now and then he reached out to pat the horse's head. She noticed he was still wearing his work clothes from the livery stables. He must have dashed from work yesterday as soon as he'd heard Melissa needed Doc Brady.

He was a good boy, deep down. He had his problems, like any young man, but he was slowly learning the importance of hard work, to think before speaking, to react with his head and not always with his fists.

Looking at ease here among the hills of Wyatt's property, as if he had the right to be here, his confidence was about to be blown sky-high. By her.

He must have heard her horse approach. He swung around and waved. Removing his hat, his boyish face looked younger than his seventeen years. Unfortunately, looking a few years older would help his situation. He was growing a mustache, but you had to stand under his nose to see it.

"Emma!"

She had an overwhelming urge to hug him. "Hi, Cole." With a tender smile, she pulled in her reins and slid down her mount.

His forehead creased with lines. "How's Melissa? She all right?"

"Melissa's fine, her bleeding stopped."

The tension in his stance eased. "God almighty, I was sick with worry." He peered at her with new concern. "What's wrong, then? You look upset."

How could she say it kindly? How did Wyatt expect her to deliver such a message? She looked into Cole's youthful eyes and wearily forced a smile. "I'm just tired. It's been a long night."

"What happened to Melissa?"

"She started bleeding and went into early labor."

"You sure she's all right?"

"Yes. She had the baby, Cole. It's a boy."

His mouth dropped open. He ran a hand through his dark windblown hair. "Did the baby make it?"

Emma grinned. "Yeah, the baby made it. He's tiny and he's got a long way to go, but he looks like a little fighter. Congratulations."

He seemed stunned at first, then other feelings washed over his face. Happiness and delighted shock. He threw his hat in the air. "Yee-haa. A little boy." He grabbed her and swung her around.

His excitement was contagious and she found herself laughing along with him. It was an occasion to celebrate, now wasn't it? A little boy. A new little Sinclair. Her new little nephew.

"What's he look like?"

"He's got a pile of hair," she said, laughing. "Black, like yours. He's got a little nose, and a dimple in his chin, just like you and Pa."

He giggled. "Is Melissa happy?"

Emma nodded. "She sure is, but she's exhausted. It was a rough delivery. She had some problems that had to be worked out."

"What kind of problems?"

"The baby was stuck and we had to rotate him."

Cole shook his head. "I'm glad I'm not a woman."

Emma laughed. Most men would faint if they'd seen her last night, up to her elbows, delivering the baby.

Cole picked up his hat from the ground, dusted it against his thigh, then fingered the brim nervously. "How's Wyatt?" His boots shuffled in the dirt. "He mad?"

She snorted. "Yeah, I'd say he's mad."

"Poor Melissa. He never lets up on her." Cole turned his face to the valley and exhaled, long and deep. "And no matter how hard I try, he doesn't seem to like me."

In her opinion, and she didn't mean it unkindly, Cole didn't try hard enough. From all accounts, Cole seemed to clam up around Wyatt, never seemed to get much out of his mouth except his anger.

Cole shrugged and looked at her, another smile building. "I've got to forget about Wyatt. I've got a little boy to look after now. And his mama. You've come to get me, right?"

Emma jolted. The hard knots in her stomach twisted. She avoided his gaze and glanced to the green valley. How should she break the news?

"I've been patient, waitin' here like Doc Brady told me. It's my turn now, isn't it?" he said eagerly. "To see my son?"

Her horse was roaming a few steps away and she walked over to it and grabbed its reins, glad for something to do with her hands. "I think it's best if Melissa gets some rest. She lost a lot of blood. She passed out after the delivery."

Cole paled. "You sure she's gonna be fine?"

"I'm sure. But she needs her rest. Let's leave her be, for now."

Cole swallowed and nodded gently, his slender Adam's apple bobbing in his throat. He gazed out over the hills. The sadness in his eyes made her tremble. "If that's what's best for her...."

Suddenly, he jerked back and squinted at Emma, studying her face. "*He* said I couldn't come, didn't he?"

Her stomach dropped. She didn't answer.

Cole clenched his fingers around his hat, his face hued with tones of red. "*His majesty* said I couldn't come, didn't he?"

She felt weary, as tired as the hills, as she stared at her brother. He knew the legal ramifications as well as she did. Cole had no rights. He was unmarried. In this situation, all legal authority belonged to Wyatt.

He kicked at the dirt. "Son of a bitch!" He stomped to the edge of the hill. She followed, reaching out to him, stroking his shoulder. There wasn't much else she could do to comfort him.

"We'll see tomorrow," she said, softly. "Let's give them a day to get settled, and we'll try again."

With a blast of curses, he whirled around and dashed to his horse. "I'm not waitin' for Wyatt's permission, I'm going now. And if he tries to stop me, so help me—"

He grabbed his saddle horn, about to swing up when she tugged at his arm. "No, Cole, don't. Doing battle with him won't work."

With a look of complete despair, he turned and faced her. "What's this doin' to Melissa?" His voice was gruff. "I bet it's tearin' her apart, too, isn't it?"

Again, Emma had no answer. The hollow pit in her stomach ached as she stared at her brother. She was utterly at a loss. Wyatt was to blame for this agony. Who the hell was he to set all the rules? Who was he to deprive the baby from Cole, his own father? It was heartless and cruel.

As a father himself, why couldn't Wyatt see that?

And the shame of telling her mother and sister they couldn't see the baby…. She groaned and lowered her head to her hands.

An idea sparked in her mind.

She raised her head and a slow smile came to her lips. She grabbed Cole's hand and faced him. "Your turn will come, Cole. With my help, I'll make it come."

He flung an arm in the air. "How are you going to help? Your stage is leavin' bright and early tomorrow morning."

She felt a calm power rising within her chest, an unwavering control that rooted her to the ground. Like hell was she backing down from Wyatt. If there was going to be a fight, she'd give him a good one. "There's been a temporary change of plans," she said, crossing her arms with newfound confidence. "I'm not going anywhere. His majesty's going to have to deal with both of us."

Chapter Six

"What's wrong, darlin'?" Wyatt asked. Melissa was still in bed. It was nine o'clock, the best part of the day was already over. She sat up in her wrinkled nightclothes, glancing to the sleeping baby in the cradle. He could tell she'd been crying, her eyes were red and tiny. She hadn't bothered to comb her hair yet.

She huffed at him. "What isn't wrong?"

He felt a blast of accusation glinting from her eyes. Now what had he done? He sighed and tossed his hat to the dresser. He didn't understand it. The first day had gone well. Yesterday, she'd been quieter, but distracted by all the visitors. The crying had started last night. By this morning, he wasn't sure what in tarnation was going on. One minute she was happy and playing with the baby, the next she was ripping off Wyatt's head and wailing.

When Doc Brady had checked her early this morning, he said some women were emotional after the birth of a child, especially a few days in. Wyatt had to let it ride, Doc said.

"Your aunt Mary promised she'd swing by later, after the twins' nap," he said, hoping the news would pick her up. "Mary said she'd spend the day with you and bring the children to keep you company."

Melissa scowled and tossed her auburn head in defiance. "You reckon I should be grateful?" she snapped. "To Aunt Mary, and to you for settin' it all up?"

The muscles in his face tightened. "I reckon you should hold your tongue." His words came harsher than he intended, and she tossed her head in the other direction.

The baby stirred and she went to him, gingerly easing her weight onto one leg, then to the other. Wyatt winced at her obvious pain. She was sore, and he had to learn to be kinder.

He stepped closer, aching to help her, but she flicked his hands away. Her youthful face looked so fragile, he felt ashamed of himself. "I'm sorry, I didn't mean to be harsh. It'll take time for this to settle in, for all of us. Let me help you. Your hair needs brushing, and I'll find a dress for you to wear."

"I don't want your help," she said in a grudging voice. She stubbornly clutched the baby to her chest with one hand as she shuffled back to bed. Wyatt hung his head. She didn't want his help. Wincing with every movement, she tried to sit, but then gave up and laid down. She nestled the baby beside her.

Wyatt sank onto the bed. "We've done a lot of arguing these past seven months, and I'm sorry about that." He entwined his fingers and leaned forward, resting his forearms on his legs. "I'd like to start over. You've got a beautiful little boy here, and I'm proud of him. I'm proud of you, too."

In a mask of gloom, Melissa stared at the baby's face. A strand of hair dropped across her face, hiding her expression.

He looked down into his woven fingers. "I want you to

know that—that I love you and that I'll always love you."
With an awkward hand, he reached out and patted her leg,
wishing she'd respond.

She hesitated, then lifting her shoulders, gazed up at him.
Her watery eyes and trembling mouth imprisoned a sob. He
felt like a heel. Why did women always have to cry?

"You do, Pa?"

"Very much."

A sob escaped her as she wiped away a tear. She tried
to laugh. "That's wonderful news."

"News?" he asked, pretending shock. "I've felt this way
about you all along." He rubbed her shoulder.

Her face gave way to a bright smile. He stared back and
enjoyed it. Lord, the world was a wonderful place when
his daughter smiled.

She tried to rise on her behind again, but couldn't settle
comfortably. "Oh, to heck with it, if you give me a boost,
I'll stand up."

Her helped her to the window, holding the energetic bundle in his arms.

As she gripped the sill for support, her eyes sparkled at
him. "You want what's best for me, don't you, Pa?"

"Nothing but the best for my fine daughter."

"You want me to be happy, right?"

"Absolutely."

"Oh, Pa, I'm so glad we're talking again. It feels like
old times, us standing here together. I knew you'd come
around to see it my way."

He tingled in apprehension and leaned back uneasily.
"Come around?"

Smiling, she turned and peered down through the window, to the direction of the stables. "Yeah, come around
and allow me to see Cole again. I'll send word through one

of the ranch hands. You don't mind, do you, if I borrow one of them for a couple hours to send for Cole?''

The smile froze on his lips. He inclined his dark head. Sighing, he set the warm baby into the cradle. ''Wait a minute, we're talking about two different things here.''

A dark shadow fell across her face.

''I haven't changed my mind about Cole,'' he said softly.

Her chin quivered. ''He's the baby's father.''

Wyatt's heart stilled. Why couldn't she see it? ''He'll hurt you, even if he doesn't mean to.''

''Please, Pa.'' Her voice croaked. ''If it helps to beg, I'm beggin'. Please let me see him.''

''Oh, Melissa,'' he said, trying to be as compassionate as he could. ''I know it'll hurt for a while, darlin'…but in the long term, you'll be better off without him.'' Standing here, staring at the pain in her face, he wavered in self-doubt. He wasn't sure, really, what was best for her, or even if he should be the one trying to tell her. Maybe it was something she had to learn for herself, discover the kind of person Cole was, all by herself.

With a chill to her features he'd never seen before, Melissa turned away and stared out the window. The baby fussed and whimpered. She ignored him. Wyatt went to him, rocked the cradle, tried to soothe him, but the baby cried harder. Melissa stiffened and ignored them both.

Frustrated at not being able to calm either one of them, Wyatt increased the rocking and blurted, ''I'm thinking about sending you to your aunt in Helena. It's just a couple of days travel. Remember the last time you were there, how much you enjoyed it?''

Melissa gasped and wheeled around. ''I'm not goin' there.''

He was halted by the tone in her voice. ''All right, I

won't force you. But I meant what I said, Melissa. I love you."

Her mass of unbrushed hair quivered. Her shoulders gave way and she started sobbing. "Well I *hate* you."

"Oh, Melissa, please—"

She stepped toward him and pulled the baby from his arms. "Leave me alone."

He stared at her in defeat, unable to move. Finally, he backed out of the room, knowing he had to cancel his plans for working on the ranch today, knowing he couldn't leave her alone like this.

Is this what Emma had meant about the extent of Melissa's loneliness? He'd never seen his daughter like this before, and it bewildered him.

What should he do? What was the right thing to do? Send for Cole or give Melissa more time to get over him?

He tunneled nervous fingers through his hair. Whatever it was, he knew it wasn't going to be easy.

"Tell me again, dear, you say the baby looks like your pa? My poor William, may God rest his soul." Emma's mother asked the next morning.

Emma smiled and answered in a happy rush of words. "He looks like Pa and Cole rolled up in one."

Her mother beamed and her wrinkles faded. "It'll all work out, you'll see. Cole will marry Melissa, nice and proper." Ma's fingers raced along the colorful fabrics on the display table at the Sinclair Fabric Store. "I've been speaking with the reverend and he says he'd be happy to marry the two, anytime we're ready. When do you think Melissa will be strong enough?"

Emma's heavy lashes flew up. She was too startled by the suggestion to answer quickly. Marriage? She was praying Cole could just get in to *see* the baby. "We'll see, Ma. Let's take it a day at a time."

Ma adjusted her apron around her thick middle and patted her bun of coiled, gray braids. "Oh, of course we'll wait until she's strong enough—"

The doorbell rang again, and Emma was grateful for the interruption of customers.

Some of them offered congratulations to old Mrs. Sinclair. Ma delighted in their questions, telling them Cole and Melissa were waiting until she was stronger to set a date.

Listening to her mother's hopeful voice, Emma swam through a haze of turmoil. How would it all turn out before it was over? With determination in her step, she grabbed her shawl and left for the telegraph office. Her last remaining errand.

When she got to the caged window, she addressed her message to Dr. James Preston, the hospital director in Philadelphia, the man who'd hired her. Surely he'd understand the situation and not put her job in jeopardy because of it. She twisted her hands in her skirt as she dictated the words, "Been delayed. Emergency delivery of brother's child. Cannot commence work until end of August. Letter following. Waiting for reply."

Before she'd accepted the offer of employment at the hospital, Emma'd mentioned her brother was expecting a child, and she'd asked for time to visit in September. Dr. Preston had given his permission, and she was just rearranging the time, she rationalized.

He'd hired her because of her grades, he'd said, and because his wife had encouraged him to hire a woman doctor from the college. He didn't seem to be as enthusiastic about women doctors as his wife was, but he'd hired her. Emma knew she was treading on soft ground, rearranging her leave of absence, but from her interviews with him, she'd detected Dr. Preston was a kind and understanding gentleman.

Unlike that horrible Wyatt Barlow. He was no gentleman at all.

Emma slammed the cutting board onto the harvest table and took great pleasure in axing the cucumber into tiny pieces. Out the kitchen window, she watched her mother weed the garden. Ma's face was a mask of anger. Two more days had passed, and they weren't any closer to seeing the baby.

Ma was asking serious questions now, the fire in Cole's eyes was burning redder, and Emma'd had just about all she could swallow. When, in thunder, was that man going to invite her family to see the baby? From what Doc Brady had told her, Wyatt didn't know she'd remained in town. If this was how he intended on treating her family when she was gone, then she was doubly glad she'd stayed.

The man was an ogre. A rat.

She grabbed the crusty loaf of bread from the sideboard. Squeezing it roughly between her fingers, she sliced it up and whacked the chunks into the cloth-covered basket. She gritted her teeth and filled the water glasses on the lunch table.

Doc Brady thought she should stay away at least a few more days. She'd spent the morning in his office. Before she knew it, she was assisting him with a fractured leg and later, because there was no dentist in town, he'd extracted a rotten tooth. All the while, she'd questioned him on Melissa's condition and Wyatt's state of mind.

Melissa was troubled, he told her, and Wyatt was cranky as hell.

Well, welcome to the picnic.

Emma hadn't slept more than an hour last night. Every

time she'd closed her lids, Wyatt's smiling, nasty face sprang up.

The kitchen door swung open. Cole, his face as dark as a brewing storm, yanked a chair from the table and sat down. That was odd. He looked rather fresh for having worked all morning at the stables. Before she had time to question him, her sister Rose breezed in, the ribbons in her hair whirling as she settled her three girls at the table. She was trying to remain cheerful around them, and Emma did the same as they ate quietly.

In his own quiet cloud, Cole gathered up his dishes. They rattled as he stacked them.

"Be careful Cole," chided Ma, irritation showing in her broad face, "you'll break my china. Here, let me wash those. Isn't your lunch break over? Don't you have to go back to work?"

With a look of rebellion, Cole shoved his hands into his dungarees. "I'm going for a ride into the hills."

"What about work? Shouldn't you ask Mr. Wolf's permission to leave your duties?"

"Aw, he don't care. I'm sure he's heard by now Melissa had the baby. He knows why I'm not there."

All three women simultaneously gasped. Even Janie knew something was amiss and stared from Emma's lap.

Emma's breathing suddenly felt restricted by her waistband. She choked on her words. "Don't tell us you haven't been to work for four days!"

Cole's spine grew rigid. "It's not every day a man has a son. I'm sure Mr. Wolf's heard by now."

Ma turned white and started to shake. Rose's eyes doubled in size.

Emma felt heat stealing to her face. "What in blazes have you been doing for four days?"

"Whad'dya think I been doin'? I been thinkin' about

Melissa. I can't think of anything else but Melissa. That's what I do, up in the hills.'' Anger singed the corners of his mouth. "And while I was thinkin', yesterday I caught me a wild horse. It's a beauty.'' His eyes shone calmer. "A stallion. Long black mane, real shiny coat, real fast—''

"How could you do this to us?" Rose interrupted. "You're making fools of all of us!''

He swayed a step backward and scoffed at her comment. "Isn't anyone interested in my horse?" He glanced around in disbelief. "Melissa would be, she'd understand. She knows how much time I like to spend in the hills. She knows when I'm thinkin' about her, I go to the hills.''

"Cole, you could lose this job.'' Alarm rippled along Emma's spine. "All you're doing is giving Wyatt more ammunition on why he shouldn't allow you near Melissa.''

Cole flung a china cup onto the counter, and it spun out of control. He tried to grab it before it hit the floor, but missed. The cup smashed on the wooden planks, and he stood, dumbstruck, staring at it. "I don't want to hear that man's name again.''

Ma dissolved into quiet tears, and Emma could barely watch the painful scene.

Cole leaned closer to Ma as if he wanted to hug her, but couldn't quite manage. "I'm sorry, Ma. I didn't mean to break your cup.''

"I'm sorry," he repeated. "I'm sorry as hell for everything!'' He kicked the door open and stormed out.

Ma fled the room.

Emma shook her head and met Rose's anguished gaze.

With a sigh, Rose got up from the table and brought back a broom. Emma helped clean the broken china.

"I can't bear to see Ma like this," said Rose. "All she wants is to hold the little baby. You should have seen her yesterday at the general store. Mrs. McCullough, that old snoop, asked how the new baby was doin'."

"Oh, poor Ma."

Emma felt miserable the rest of the afternoon, wondering how she could bring the two families together. The next time she saw Cole it was in the evening. Dusk was falling and she was stepping out for a walk. He was stepping out of the livery stables. At least he'd gone and talked to Mr. Wolf. That was good. Heaven help Cole if he lost his job.

She decided not to lecture him since he seemed to be making amends on his own. Her instincts were right to keep quiet, for Cole asked if he could join her in her walk.

She felt him unwinding beside her as their footsteps padded along the boardwalk. She glanced across Main Street. "The mercantile's open, I see the light's still on. Would you like to go in and buy something for your son? I'm sure you'll be able to give it to him real soon."

Cole thought about it for a moment, then grinned real wide. He yanked on the brim of his hat. "Yeah, I'd like that. Could you help me pick somethin' out?"

Emma returned his smile and for the first time in days, felt some hope. She pulled her shawl tighter and swung her beaded bag on her wrist.

Inside the store, a yellow rattle caught Cole's eye, and a flannel nightshirt, and a large pigskin ball.

"What do you think a little baby is going to do with a big ball like this?" Emma asked, ribbing him lightly.

"Don't you worry about it. He and I'll be kickin' that ball around before you know it."

In pleasant chatter, they collected their packages and crossed the street. Too late, Emma caught sight of Jim Barlow and his gang exiting the saloon, half a block from their path. By nervous instinct, her eyes flew to their holstered guns. Cole wasn't wearing any.

"Hold your temper," she whispered to her brother in the cool night air. "Don't react the way you always do. Jim is Melissa's cousin. Think of *her,* and keep your head."

Making their way under the light of street lamps, they cast long shadows on the boardwalk. From the tail of her eye, she saw one of Jim's friends nudge him in their direction. She could smell the liquor from five paces away.

Jim turned around as they neared. "Evenin'," he said sarcastically, tipping his hat. He towered a foot above her. Lean and clean shaven in his early thirties, he flicked back his long, black, Barlow hair. If he took care of his teeth, he'd be a handsome man, Emma decided, and if he weren't such a bully.

"Evening," she replied, with a respect she didn't feel. She dug her fingers into Cole's elbow, maintaining their fast pace.

Jim narrowed his glistening eyes. She shuddered at the ice she saw there. "That wild stallion you caught a couple of days ago, Sinclair, you know belongs to me."

"How do you figure?" Cole slowed down as they passed and Emma yanked him along. The packages in his arms shifted.

"I've been watchin' it for days." Jim's thin blue lips curled up. She found his gaze terribly disturbing.

"Well, while you were watchin', I was ropin' it in."

The men laughed. Everyone except Jim. Emma elbowed Cole with a trembling arm. Did he want to get himself shot? It didn't help to be mouthy.

Cole smiled belligerently and kept walking, weaving around the group. "Any time you need a lesson, you know where to find me."

She pinched his arm, determined to make him listen. He rebuked her with his eyes and she sent him a look of alarm.

They were almost clear of Jim, another few steps. Why didn't Cole just keep his mouth shut?

"How's the baby?" asked Jim with a lewd smile.

Emma felt Cole jerk under her arm. One of the packages almost fell. A faint thread of hysteria pulsed at the back of her throat.

"Oh, I forgot," said Jim, "you haven't seen the baby." His friends snickered.

"Keep walking, Cole," begged Emma. "He's not worth it."

To her horror, Cole stopped and confronted Jim, despite the fact that Cole was a head shorter and more than ten years younger. "We all know what this is really about," Cole growled. "How long do you think everyone in town's gonna turn the other way, every time you start thinkin' about what happened thirty years ago? I'm sorry you lost your mother and I'm sorry for my father's part in it, but fighting isn't gonna solve anything."

Jim swaggered and thrust a finger into Cole's chest. "You son of a bitch, leave my mother outta this."

Emma pulled on Cole's sleeve but he kept talking. "I can't. I never even met your mother. All this happened before I was born, but I'm sick to death it's overshadowed me and my family ever since I can remember."

"Shut your filthy mouth."

"I won't. Let's get this thing cleared up once and for all, then I never want to hear about you botherin' us again. Get this straight. My father was cleared of all charges, but he still paid dearly for what he'd done by accident."

Emma quaked in her shoes looking at the anger flashing in Jim's eyes.

Emma was a healer, not a fighter, but she stepped forward. "We're all sorry about your mother. We truly are.

It's a terrible thing that happened. I wish I could bring her back.''

"Don't you know," Cole added in exasperation, "everyone in town feels sorry for you? That's why we turn a blind eye when you start getting mean. But no more. Now let us pass."

"You think you're gonna get away with what you did to Melissa?" Jim gritted his teeth. "Laying her up the way you did? No way in hell are you gonna treat a Barlow like that."

Cole's jaw trembled. "Shut up and get out of my way." He scooped Emma's arm and took a step to pass.

Jim stepped back, as rigid as a post. "If you're wonderin' what your son looks like, I seen him yesterday. I could tell you what the little bastard looks like."

In a ball of fury, Cole lifted his arm and slugged Jim in the gut. Emma shrieked. Packages hurled onto the street. Jim doubled over but recovered quickly and slugged Cole in the eye.

"Stop it!" Emma shouted. "Both of you!"

She couldn't control them. They rolled into the dusty street like a couple of vermin.

No one made a move to help her, and she was afraid they'd kill each other. In desperation, she raced into the saloon, retrieving a deputy who tore them apart.

Her face as hot as fire, Emma hauled her brother from the dirt. With a lump in her throat, she picked up the filthy new rattle. Cole picked up the tattered nightshirt.

How naive she'd been, to imagine things had changed while she'd been in Philadelphia. For sixteen years, she'd been running away from the problems between the Barlows and Sinclairs, the buried accusations, the silent rage. She'd left to go to college, yes, to study medicine, but how mighty convenient it was, to have had that excuse to leave.

Is this what her family had to put up with while she was gone?

She understood Cole's rage was building because he was being kept from Melissa, but she had a horrible fear of what might happen if this went on much longer.

There was no other way but to go to Wyatt. Tomorrow morning, she promised herself, right after breakfast. She had to mellow this hatred, and she needed Wyatt to help.

The realization twisted and whirled inside her. They needed each other.

Chapter Seven

In an exasperated voice which bordered on a threat, Wyatt tried one more time. "Melissa, please, you need some fresh air. You can't stay cooped up in here again today."

He threw back the bedroom curtains, allowing the early morning sun to slice through the gloom. She squinted in the brightness and turned her sleepy face away, ignoring him. It was her fourth day after delivery, and she was getting worse.

Deep down, that spasm of worry inside him erupted again. She had a baby to look after. "All right, then. You're coming with me to town. Now get dressed. I'll take the baby downstairs."

With a large hand, he easily scooped the baby into the padded woven basket and carried him outside, all the while shaking his head at problems with Melissa. He sure was a fine father, wasn't he? Had everything under control. Ha!

Striding into the stables, he came back with Grandpa. Best to get an ally on this ride, and maybe a hired gun or two.

Melissa joined them outside in a rumpled-looking dress. She eased into the back of the wagon, shuffling onto the blanket he'd spread on top of the straw. The baby settled beside her, in his basket, his cloth hat sitting crooked on his head. At least he wasn't hollering.

Hoping to soothe Melissa, Wyatt reached under the wagon seat and pulled out a sack of raisins. Something she could munch on during the ride. He waved it in the air like a trophy. "Look what your cousins sent you from California."

Melissa sent him a hostile glare. "Great. Soon I'll look as fat as an elephant as well as feel like one. My dresses don't fit!"

Frustrated, he threw his hands in the air. "Well, who's going to see you out here on the ranch anyway?"

Clearly vexed, Melissa's clamped her lips tight and jammed herself into the corner.

"I'll buy you a new dress," he said, struggling to make amends, "in a bigger size."

"Huh!" She thrust out her chin, gave him a withering glance, then stiffly looked away.

They stopped at Miss Molly's Dress Shop first. Melissa mellowed. She picked out a pretty green dress with a bustle and fancy lace collar. She held it up to herself in the long mirror. "What do you think, Pa?"

He shrugged, not knowing what advice to give her. He always felt awkward in a woman's dress shop, especially with all the other ladies in the store gawking at him. "You look pretty."

After an eternity of browsing through the other dresses, which he knew was really only ten minutes, Melissa settled on the original dress.

He nearly cried with joy when they escaped the dress shop and landed back on the boardwalk, where he could breathe. "Would you like to go to the mercantile? Let's see if Weaver's got any of those fancy soaps you like, the little sparkly ones from Saint Louis."

She nodded and managed a smile. The saints be praised.

"It's gettin' hot," Grandpa said, "waitin' outside in the sun. Me and the baby are comin' in this time. Into some God-lovin' shade." Lifting the basket and sleeping child, he dashed into the coolness of the store. A fresh bottle of goat's milk dangled from his trouser pocket, like a shiny gun in a holster, ready to draw if the newborn woke up griping. Grandpa had the fastest draw in the house.

Wyatt let his eyes adjust to the dimness. They were the only ones inside, save for Weaver himself behind the counter, adjusting the spectacles on his nose, reading the *Levi Valley Chronicle.* "Mornin' folks," he said, crinkling his paper shut. "What can I get for you, Wyatt?"

Wyatt stepped to the counter and leaned onto his elbow. "What's the date on the newspaper?"

"Hot off the press last Saturday."

"I'll take one."

While Weaver reached for a paper, Melissa ducked into the aisle where the tins of soap were, taking the baby with her. Grandpa moseyed over to the shiny tins of chewing tobacco. "I'm buying," Wyatt said, to the old man's glee.

Digging into his pocket for coins, Wyatt heard the bell above the screen door tinkle a little louder than usual. Someone burst in, followed by another pair of heavier boots. Someone was in a hurry. His head shot up and spun to the person barreling straight at him.

Emma?

His heart jolted. Was he seeing things? He blinked, not believing what his own eyes were telling him. What the hell was she doing here? A warm shudder ran up his body. He stared into her unwavering brown eyes and his pulse kicked in. "What the—"

"Morning, Wyatt," she said, breathless, her chest heaving as if she'd been running. Skimming her body with his bold gaze, he realized she probably *had* been running, from the family store all the way across the street and down the block, if that's from where she'd spotted their wagon. He tried to ignore how pretty she was, her hair messed up from running, her skin flushed with a rush of pink.

Blood pumped through his veins. She hadn't left town. "I thought you were leaving."

Her compelling eyes twinkled with warmth. "Had a change of plans." Her tone was friendly. The last time he'd seen her, she'd slammed the door in his face on the way out. What was going on now? Was she happy to see *him*, or the baby?

He kept his face impassive, but inside, explosive currents raced through him. Why was she being friendly, and what the hell was wrong with him? Every time she came close, he reacted like a lonely widower who hadn't been with a woman in years.

Well, it wasn't true. Just this winter, he'd courted his sister's friend. And last summer, he couldn't recall her name, but he remembered it ended with an argument about getting married...the way these things always ended for him. Arguing about the one thing he could never give.

Glancing over to the next aisle, he saw the top of a dark head beside Melissa's, bending over the baby basket.

Cole.

Wyatt sucked in a rush of air.

"Let him be," warned Emma.

When Grandpa turned around and saw Cole, he jumped off the ground. "Holy Moses!"

Then Emma's mother burst in.

Grandpa adjusted his spectacles. "What's this, an ambush?"

"Step aside, Albert," old Mrs. Sinclair commanded,

waving her hand like a sword, "I'm here to see my grandson."

She didn't have to ask twice. Grandpa's eyes grew as big as wagon wheels as he slid out of her turbulent wake. "I ain't daft," he whispered to Wyatt. "She looks meaner than a buzzard whose nest has been disturbed."

Wyatt's gut knotted as he stood watching the unruly scene, quaking to do something, not knowing what. He had half a mind to haul Melissa out of the store, right damn now. He didn't need Emma meddling in his family affairs. Was that why she'd stayed?

But hell, he reminded himself, they were in a public place. He wasn't exactly standing on his ranch, now was he, and he couldn't exactly control the situation, now could he?

He mumbled under his breath. Remain calm. No harm in sitting tight for a moment. He leaned against the counter and folded his arms across his chest.

Emma fussed over the baby, dipping her head down low, smiling and cooing, looking more feminine than he'd ever seen her. Why did she have to complicate things? Why did women always have to complicate everything?

He gulped a wad of air. Why hadn't she left town? Did her reasons for staying have anything to do with him? He cursed himself for wishing they did. And while he was in the cursing mood, he cursed himself for being a man and devouring her the way any man would devour a woman with as many curves as she had.

He ripped his gaze away and turned his eyes to Cole. Dressed in stable clothes, looking more like the baby's brother than his father, Cole lifted the baby high in the air and laughed. Judging from the gleam in Melissa's eyes, the way her whole body came to life, Wyatt didn't know whether to shake Cole's hand in congratulations, or throttle him.

Mrs. Sinclair tugged at Cole's sleeve. "Give him to me, you had him long enough."

Cole passed the baby to his mother, who pressed the little boy to her smothering bosom. More Sinclairs burst through the door—Rose and her three children, all clamoring to see and touch the baby.

Wyatt groaned, his resolve wavering,. and annoyed that they were getting to him. Was he being too harsh on the Sinclairs? On Melissa and Cole? Should he let Melissa discover for herself, the hard way, what life would be like with Cole?

When all the hugging and laughing and crying was over, Emma brushed her hands on her skirt and turned toward him. Her moist lips quivered, her gaze as soft as a caress. "Thank you," she said simply, and it stirred a part of his heart he wasn't ready to let soften.

Cole turned and faced him squarely, and Wyatt noticed the black eye. Wyatt swayed back against the counter. It dug into his rear. "You been fightin'?" *Again?*

In defiance, Cole turned his boyish face away so Wyatt couldn't see the shiner.

Wyatt glared at Melissa and she flushed. He turned back to the boy. "Who have you been fighting with?"

Emma stepped forward, her back stiffened but head held high. "It's over. He was defending himself, I was there."

"Well that's just dandy," he said to her, feeling a fresh surge of anger that Cole would humiliate her like that. "Good thing his sister's a doctor," he bellowed in Cole's direction, "in case one of them needed mopping up." Emma lowered her dark lashes.

"Don't blame Cole," Melissa snapped, "he told me Jim deserved it."

"Jim?" Wyatt clenched his jaw. "I should have known." Cole hadn't changed at all, he still couldn't control his fists. Jim probably provoked him like he always did, but it was up to Cole to control his temper. "Boy, will you ever learn?"

Cole's mouth tightened and his gray eyes glinted. Then, taking his life in his hands, he arrogantly turned his back to Wyatt and threw an arm over Melissa's shoulders. "Jim's not important," he told her, "we have to come up with a name for the baby."

Wyatt's jaw dropped. Well how the hell do you like that? Just as easy as pie, the boy turned away and ignored him.

Before his anger had a chance to bust out, Emma quickly stepped between them, holding up her hand. "Thank you for letting us see the baby, Wyatt. My mother and sister, we all appreciate it...." She tossed a nasty look at Cole, who was ignoring everyone but Melissa. Then she looked back to him, her eyes wide and pleading.

His gaze fell to the creamy expanse of her neck.

He was mad at himself for letting her tug at his heart.

Riveted to her face, he held her gaze and softly shook his head, but decided to back down.

Old Mrs. Sinclair looked embarrassed by Cole's behavior, and Grandpa tugged at his suspenders, biting down on whatever it was he was itching to say. Rose occupied the youngsters with the baby, and Wyatt felt grateful that at least the rest of them weren't jumping in and arguing.

Remain calm. He pulled in a deep breath.

Melissa exchanged a heated look with Cole, the look of lovers long separated, and Wyatt glanced away, unable to stomach it. How did they plan on surviving? They were both so young. Penniless. Unskilled. They needed protecting themselves. How on earth could they look after a newborn? Or each other? And with an attitude like Cole's, no wonder people planted their fists in the air as soon as they saw him coming.

But on the bright side, the levelheaded side of Wyatt realized that Melissa and Cole weren't married—yet—and Cole would grow up one day, wouldn't he?

Wyatt sighed. He suddenly felt ill-equipped to handle any of them. Time to leave this place. He swung around, tossed three coins to the counter, and grabbed his newspaper. "All right, Melissa, let's go."

"But Pa, we're discussing the name I came up with. Now we're all together, I'd like to tell you."

Holding his new tin of tobacco, Grandpa edged into the conversation. "Well it's about time. We've been dyin' to know what you decided. You kept tellin' us not to rush you, and we haven't."

Wyatt was almost afraid to ask. "Go ahead."

She brushed a hand nervously against her skirt and glanced down at the baby, who was now nestled in Cole's elbow. "Pa, I thought out of respect for Cole's family, you wouldn't mind...."

Wyatt grew rigid.

"I thought...we could call him William, after Cole's father."

It shook him like a clap of thunder. William? After how William Sinclair had treated Wyatt all those years?

Mrs. Sinclair's skirts rustled as she pulled a hanky from the cuff of her sleeve. "How sweet."

Grandpa whined. "What about respect for our family?"

Melissa's soft brown eyes grew serious. "I'd like to name him William Albert, after you too, Great-Grandpa."

"How about Albert William?" Grandpa tried to finagle.

Melissa ignored him. "We can call him Billy for short."

"I like it," Cole declared. And making sure Wyatt was watching, he snatched a kiss from Melissa.

Honest to God, how much more could Wyatt take?

He noticed Emma casting a trembling glance in his direction, bracing herself for the eruption. Their eyes locked. Every fiber in his body warned him against her and her family. But it seemed everything was out of his control today, including the name of the child. Did Emma understand how he felt? How belittling her father had always been? Her lashes lowered, and he thought he saw a look of shame cross her face.

A thought struck him and his eyes shot back to Cole. It wasn't possible, was it? Was he treating Cole the same way Emma's father had always treated *him?*

The thought made his skin crawl. No one deserved to be treated like that. Was he being fair to the boy?

Oh, hell. Was he?

Melissa caught his eye. "And now, one more thing, Pa."

Wyatt growled and crumpled his newspaper under his arm. When would the day end?

"Seein' that Emma's not leavin' for Philadelphia for seven or eight weeks...that's right, isn't it, Emma?"

Emma nodded. "I'm here till the end of August, I hope."

Wyatt's heart tripped at the words.

"Seein' that she's here and everything, would it be all right, Pa, if she were my doctor, instead of Doc Brady? I mean, she delivered Billy and all, and she's so nice and all, could she be the one to come to the ranch and check on me?"

Emma smiled, sweet and seductive, and he suddenly felt he'd just been blindfolded and led to the edge of a jagged cliff. How could he say no? Melissa had miraculously come to life in the last half hour, being here with these people. If he refused them, life with Melissa would be sheer misery. Unspeakable torture. What choice did he have?

He rocked back on his boots and gave a hesitant nod.

"You'll have to ask Emma if it's all right." He said the words tentatively, as if testing the idea.

Melissa jumped into Emma's arms. Emma hugged her, all the while peering over Melissa's shoulder at him with those warm, swirling brown eyes, raising his temperature another degree.

"Can you come tonight?" asked Melissa. "After supper? Maybe Cole can bring you."

Emma darted a glance to Wyatt.

He shoved a hand into his pocket. He should have known Melissa would try to throw Cole into the deal.

Should Wyatt allow it? Was it better Cole visit with Melissa right under Wyatt's nose where he could keep an eye on them, or was it better to ban Cole from her life, knowing they'd sneak around the first chance they got?

And the question remained, nagging in his brain, refusing to go away. Was he being fair to the boy?

"All right," Wyatt relented, to a chorus of excited voices. All except for Grandpa. The old man frowned and shook his head in disapproval, looking like a gypsy fortune-teller who was seeing something awful in his crystal ball.

Wyatt turned his palms to the air in frustration. He'd tried his best. If he ever had a choice between facing a field of prickly porcupines rather than this bunch of women again, he'd pick the porcupines.

Cole rubbed a hand across his chest. "I won't be able to make it till later. I gotta make up for lost time at the stables. But I could meet you there, Emma."

Somehow in all the excitement, Emma and Wyatt had managed to be standing quite close together. When she turned her starry eyes up to him and he looked down at her pretty face and full lips, his pulse hammered. "The trail's dangerous for a woman alone at night. There's always drifters passing through, sometimes even the grizzlies." Uncontrollably, his lithe body inched closer to get a good lungful of the lemony scent she was wearing.

Grandpa's head bobbed. "Grizzlies? This time of year?"

Wyatt noticed the others were studying him a little closer than usual, and he struggled through a weak grin. "Well, maybe not grizzlies, but certainly drifters." *And if they laid eyes on a pretty woman like her…*

Now why was she blushing?

With his steady gaze boring into hers, he weighed their options. He could send a ranch hand for her, or he could send the foreman. They could even wait until Cole was finished at the stables to bring her to the ranch.

But no. A sensual pull passed between them and before he'd allowed himself time to think, his protective shield slipped. "I could pick you up around six."

When she agreed, in that charming, flustered way, he didn't know whether to smile or kick himself. He definitely knew enough not to look over at the old man.

Her stomach fluttered.

Emma was acutely aware that his warm flesh was touching hers. Once again, she yanked her thigh away from Wyatt's in the buggy. She felt the stretch of muscles in her inner thighs and wondered how much longer she could hold her legs in this position on the bumpy ride.

Why had she agreed to this? Was the torture of sitting this close to him worth it? Her body shivered every time she glanced at him, all spiffed up, dark and masculine in black denim. The mere touch of his hand sent a heated shock through her skin. She was trying too hard. Getting along with the Barlows didn't mean she had to ride in a cramped buggy with him, did it?

She turned her head to the side, allowing the cool pine

air to ruffle through her hair. She wore it down tonight, and it draped softly around her shoulders.

Dusk was falling. The evening air filled her lungs, and as she'd hoped, cleared her head. But as soon as she turned again to face the road, she inhaled him again. He smelled clean and rugged, and her senses came alive.

They hit a rut in the road and the buggy bounced. His thigh pressed along the entire length of hers for a fleeting moment. He jerked it away as if he'd accidentally touched a hot stone.

I don't love you echoed through her mind. She clenched her shawl to her chest.

He inclined his dark head toward her. "Are you cold?"

"A little."

"I've got my jacket in the back if you'd like to use it." He lifted his arm to reach for it.

"No, I'm fine, really."

The clomp of the horse grew louder as they grew silent again. She braced her foot against the side of the buggy, as far away from him as she could.

How foolish she'd been that night, all those years ago. Going to Wyatt with her heart in her hands, declaring her love openly, certain he felt the same.

She groaned inwardly, trying to suppress the worst memory of all. How could she have suggested it? She'd wanted to show him, physically, what he'd meant to her. She'd told him outright she wanted to lie in the same bed with him, the man who'd come to mean the world to her.

To make love with him.

The buggy swayed and she rolled her eyes in mortification. She'd been dead wrong about how he'd felt.

Lord, at sixteen she'd almost made the worst mistake of her life. She knew nothing then about stopping babies from coming into the world, or about protecting herself from being discarded and hurt by men who only wanted to sleep with her, with no thought of marriage. Thank heaven he'd spared her.

Some men would have taken her no matter what the circumstances, not caring if they didn't love her. At least he'd been honorable, in that way.

Sliding a glance in his direction, she studied the square line of his jaw, the dark brows, the thick dark hair that fell across his forehead. She drew her arms close to her body, suddenly conscious of the fullness in her breasts.

How could she begrudge him for not having loved her? At least he'd told her. Hadn't honesty always been important to her? He couldn't help what he didn't feel, and he didn't feel anything for her. Did that mean she should ostracize him as a friend? Who, really, had been the better friend?

He turned his head and looked at her, like a polite stranger might do. Then his gaze warmed up and his eyes twinkled. "Do you enjoy living in Philadelphia?"

Her heart beat undeniably under his gaze. Her palms tensed, and she peered ahead to the distant forest. A gray mist clung to the base of the trees. "It's an interesting city." She twisted her fingers in her lap. "It's a far cry from Pine Creek, but I enjoy it."

He tugged the reins with experienced, powerful hands. "What do you like about it?"

"Well, it's big. I was shocked when I first moved there, how much there is to see and do. But I got used to it, all the people, their way of doing things."

"Are the people friendly?"

"Mostly. They're a little more guarded than here in Pine Creek."

"How do they react to women doctors?"

Her face creased into a sudden smile. "Now there's a

good question. They react about the same as they do here. Most of them have never seen a woman doctor and don't know quite what to make of us.''

''And what do *you* make of you?''

She raised her chin thoughtfully. ''What do you mean?''

He returned her curious gaze with a calm shrug of his broad shoulders. ''I mean are you happy?''

Tilting her head, she stole a slanted look at him. ''Yes, I love being a doctor.''

He seemed to like her answer. Leaning back in his seat, he tipped his head and nodded.

It dawned on her that maybe he did care about her feelings. She leaned toward him, suddenly bold. ''Are you happy, Wyatt?''

He shrugged as if taken by surprise. His eyes grew soft and he swallowed. ''I'm happy with my children, and my ranch.''

A faint sigh escaped her. He didn't really answer yes or no to the question and she found herself caring more than she thought she should.

She turned to stare at the road ahead. The horse twitched its tail. She wasn't an expert with horses, but she knew by its smooth, sleek lines that this animal came from good stock.

Her leg began to slip toward Wyatt again and she pulled it back. Thinking of lighter moments they used to share in school, she asked, ''Do you still play the harmonica?''

His full lips twitched with amusement. He smiled and her pulse skipped. He had a handsome profile when he smiled. His whole face lit up, beginning with his magnetic eyes and flashing through his bronzed skin. ''I let it go for years, but once in a while, I play for Tommy and Melissa. Do you still play the fiddle?''

"Yes, I do," she answered brightly, a bemused smile on her lips.

"What's so funny?"

"My friends in Philadelphia insist on calling it the violin. They say calling it the fiddle makes me sound like I just stepped out of the hills."

"You did just step out of the hills."

She let out a warm peal of laughter, her entire body melting with the release.

"It's good to hear you laugh, Emma."

"You always made me laugh more than anyone else I know." Her personal admission silenced them both. He grew pensive and she felt as if her breath had been cut off.

The trail entered the forest and he pulled over by the side of the road. "There's something I want to show you."

He jumped off the buggy and came round to help her down. When she placed her warm hand in his, a wave of physical awareness shuddered through her. His broad shoulders heaved as her body slid down his, much, much too close. Her blood pulsed like an awakening tide.

Their eyes caught and she trembled. He threw a strong arm to the back of her waist sliding his hand along her spine, sending ripples through her, lowering her gently and slowly until her toes touched firm ground. Captivated by his arresting face, she lost herself in his smoldering black eyes.

If he dipped his head ever so gently, their lips would graze. His breath was moist and warm as he glanced down to her parted mouth. Wet heat throbbed inside her. *No.* His touch meant nothing. It would never lead to anything.

Breaking free, she brushed her skirt and seized control of her breathing. "Something you wanted to show me?"

He cleared his throat. Turning away, he hitched his horse

to the nearest tree. His voice was a hoarse whisper. "A few steps this way."

He led her to the edge of the road, where it dropped suddenly and opened up to the valley floor below. The lushness of the valley stole her breath. Snowcapped mountains formed a background. Birds fluttered and called to each other in the growth of bush, and on a nearby slope, a clear stream trickled over boulders. Mountain flowers, with delicate hues of purple and red, covered the hill below them, and their fragrance reached her nostrils. She inhaled. "Oh, it's beautiful."

"Look," he whispered, close to her ear, making her shiver, "a hawk." He clamped a gentle hand on her shoulder and pointed in the sky to her left. She watched the magnificent bird soar above the trees, trying to ignore the wild sensations his hand was causing.

He released her and stood transfixed in the beauty of nature. She tried to resist watching him, but his rugged stance and unspoken strength mesmerized her. Her shoulder felt chilled where he'd removed his hand.

"You're a part of this land, aren't you?" she asked, breathless.

His dark eyes seared through her and her stomach fluttered again. "I could never live anywhere else."

She considered him for a moment. How lucky he was to know where he belonged.

He shifted and kicked softly at a mound of dirt. His horse grazed a few steps behind him, quietly ripping at grass. "Do you miss Montana?"

"Very much. I was born and raised in these valleys, the earth is under my skin."

"Yet you live in Philadelphia." His tone was suddenly detached.

"It's where I belong now," she said, struggling to explain. "As a doctor. I need more practical training, and my future is there." *Was it?* she wondered. As a doctor, yes, for the next few years it was. As a woman, was that the place she'd chosen for the rest of her life? When would she return to Montana? Her heart clouded with uncertainty. Would she ever return? Would she ever find the peace that Wyatt felt with this land?

Looking out to the hills, not a person or house in sight, she wondered aloud, "I don't know how Doc Brady manages, out here in this isolation all by himself. No help. No modern equipment or hospitals. I don't think I could do it."

"I think you'd be surprised at what you can accomplish, when you have to and you're alone." The rich timbre of his voice seeped with sadness. It touched a corner of her heart.

"You're speaking about the ranch now, and raising your children alone."

A wistfulness slid into his expression. He glanced to the valley.

"You've done a fine job with them."

His dark head bobbed back to her. He quirked a brow. "Even with Melissa?"

Emma swallowed at how vulnerable he sounded. "She followed her heart and made a simple mistake. It happens to many girls. More than we all care to admit, from the things I've seen in Philadelphia." *It could have happened to me,* she added in her mind. She shoved the memory away. "You used to dream about ranching ever since I can remember. How many horses do you keep?"

He smiled, an eager smile any woman could get lost in. "We've got ninety-eight at the moment. In the springtime, before we sell, we aim for numbers between three hundred and three hundred and fifty."

"I remember when you had only five."

He drew his shoulders higher at her compliment, standing tall and she felt a wave of pride. It was silly, she told herself, for her to be proud of him. They had no ties.

The horse snorted. Restless, it tugged on its lines. Wyatt studied the sky. "It's getting dark. Melissa will be wondering where her favorite doctor is. We better go."

When he smiled and swooped her up into the buggy, she shivered again. His feathery touch made her emotions swirl. This had to stop. She had to build a resistance to him.

"And by the way, I've started saving," he said with a casual nod.

"For what?"

"For the two-thousand-dollar fee I owe you."

Her gentle laugh rippled between them. "Oh, Wyatt...I've lowered my price."

"Really?" He leaned his manly body closer. "To how much?"

"Nineteen hundred," she said with a giggle. "And a dozen eggs."

"You're very reasonable."

As the buggy sped away, Emma settled into the seat beside him, enjoying their camaraderie. She was powerless to resist his easy charm.

What was wrong with being friends with Wyatt? What harm could come of that? It was certainly more enjoyable than arguing, it'd ease the tension with Jim, and more importantly, it'd help in her cause for Cole and Melissa.

She'd be wise to get on Wyatt's good side, she convinced herself. It was harmless.

Chapter Eight

Emma's breath quickened every time she watched him work. It was Wyatt's keen ability with horses, she acknowledged, and nothing more entrancing her.

She lifted her dusty boot to the lower rung of the cedar fence and hiked herself beside Melissa. Emma kept her level gaze on Wyatt in the corral. He was breaking in his newest bronco.

He didn't look at her, and she didn't bother to wave hello. She did however, raise a palm to two of Wyatt's men who were eating their lunch on the other side of the corral, and enjoying the entertainment.

The wind stirred, cutting through the afternoon heat and cooling the beads of moisture on her upper lip. Wisps of hair escaped her braid and rustled around her face. She glanced over at Billy. Two yards away, under the canopy of trees, he slept in his cradle. Satisfied the flies weren't bothering him, she turned back to Wyatt.

While they stood in the shade, Wyatt worked in full sun. Judging by the perspiration pasting his shirt to the supple lines of his back, he'd been at it for quite a while.

His damp hair fell around his face. He wore a pair of old denims, tight on his thighs, and a crisp black hat. Sunlight glinted off the silver buckle which hung at his trim waist. His boots were worn and leathery, and he dodged around the stallion with the grace of a dancer. With his body stretching and arching under muscled control, it was one of the most sensual things she'd ever seen.

She fanned herself with her hand. Lord, it was hot.

She tried not to heed the masculinity oozing from his every movement. Other women in town might notice it, whispering to each other about his fine figure, but not her.

They hadn't been alone together for the last three days, not since the first ride to the ranch. Every time there was an opportunity for them to be alone, on the porch when Cole drifted off with Melissa, or sipping coffee after supper, he found some urgent excuse to leave.

She closed her eyes momentarily then glanced down at her feet. He didn't care to be around her. Her breasts rose and fell under her labored breathing. At first she'd considered herself lucky, but now his obvious distaste for her set her mouth firmly in annoyance. He was just putting on a polite act in public. If she knew what was good for her, she'd turn around and march back into the house and ignore him, too.

The stallion reared up on two legs, giving her a fright, and she found herself planted to the spot. Wyatt waited, perfectly still, until the horse calmed down, then tried his approach again.

Melissa crossed her arms on the top of the fence and lowered her chin on her palm. "Are you sure Cole will come tomorrow?"

"That's what he said. He can't come every day, he's working."

Melissa sighed. "I know, but I miss him."

"Be patient, it takes time."

"They're getting along pretty good, don't you think? I

mean, Pa's taking to Cole, isn't he?'' Melissa stared at her father. Wyatt had managed to capture the reins and was whispering to the horse.

"Well…yeah, but don't expect miracles too soon, Melissa.'' In truth, Cole and Wyatt did seem to be getting along, but not because they were talking and working things out. Because they were avoiding each other.

Melissa crinkled her nose. Her freckles had deepened from all the healthy time she was spending outdoors. "I wish the other problem would go away. I wish Jim would let up on Cole. Pa found out what happened yesterday. He vowed he'd deal with it in his own way, but that furious look on his face scared me half to death.''

Emma frowned, racking her brain. Had she missed something? "What happened?''

"Oh, don't tell me you didn't know,'' said Melissa, clearly surprised. "Cole's gonna kill me for tellin' you.''

"Tell me what?'' Emma prodded. A sick feeling curled inside her stomach. "What's going on?''

"Cole and Jim were at it again. This time, Jim wound up with the black eye, not Cole.''

"Oh, no,'' Emma sputtered. "I saw Cole last night as he was soaking his hand in cold water. He told me his hand was red and raw from working in the stables, that he'd forgotten to wear gloves.'' Her temper rose. She dug her elbows into the rail. "I should have known. What's it going to take for them to stop fighting?''

"I don't know.'' Melissa said, biting her lip. "And I don't know what's going to happen on Saturday, if those two get together at the party.''

Emma wheeled around to face the girl. "Hold on. Your Pa hasn't said Cole can go to the party, yet.''

"But it's Billy's christening, Pa can't stop him.''

Emma silently agreed. The christening would be a big

event. All their neighbors and friends were already invited
to Wyatt's ranch. His men were building outdoor tables.
Melissa was assembling a group of musicians and Emma
ached to be a part of it.

"Let's take it a step a time. Your Pa is considering it,
and let's leave it up to him."

Wyatt was dropping his guard toward Cole, Emma tried
to tell herself. She'd noticed it in his eyes. He said he'd
make his decision by tomorrow, and she'd abide him until
then, as patiently as she could. She was trusting with her
whole heart that he'd say yes. And if he didn't—

She drew an anxious hand across her braid and turned
back to Melissa. "How are you feeling today, honey, are
you tired?"

"Just a little."

Emma cupped a warm hand over Melissa's. "Your
body's almost back to normal. I can see you're getting
stronger."

Melissa ran a hand along the fence. "Then why am I
havin' such difficulty nursin' my own baby?" She let out
a frustrated groan. "The goat's more of a mother to him
than I am."

"The supplements won't go on forever. You're a good
mother. It takes time to get used to all the changes in your
body. Your breasts will toughen, and they won't be as sore
in another week."

"I never thought it would be this hard."

"Billy's not complaining," Emma reassured her. "He's
gaining weight and sleeping well."

Melissa hugged the rail and sighed. "At least I don't
have to discuss my sore breasts with Doc Brady. I'd sooner
jump in the pond than have him lookin' at them."

Emma's laughter floated through the air. Wyatt gazed
over at them. He tilted his hat in her direction, a bedeviling

smile on his lips. She felt an involuntary prickle of her flesh. Her eyes froze on his dark, lean face. The intense moment passed, and he turned back to his wild horse.

Melissa arched her body toward Emma in a gesture of thoughtfulness. "Emma, do you still miss your Pa?"

Emma was caught off guard by the sudden question. As she slid closer, the tenderness in Melissa's eyes stilled her. "When I come across something of his in the house, or remember something he used to like to do, I miss him a great deal."

"I've been missin' my Ma somethin' awful lately."

"That's understandable, honey. You were seven years old when your Ma passed on."

Melissa fiddled with the buttons on her blouse. "I've been thinkin', if Ma were here, I could talk to her about my feelings. She'd understand what I'm going through."

"I'm sure she would. She was a nice woman." Emma's difficult emotions swirled to the surface. She swallowed past the dull ache in her throat, reminding herself that the rejection she'd felt when Wyatt had chosen to marry Lillie had nothing to do with Melissa. Lillie had been the girl's mother, and Emma would always respect her for that.

A tremor touched Melissa's mouth. "Did you ever meet my Ma?"

"No, honey, she moved here after I'd already left for college."

"Oh. Then how do you know she was nice?"

Emma felt the sharp scrutiny of Melissa's gaze and glanced away, uncomfortable with the memories. "People told me."

"Who?"

"Well, people in town."

"*Who?*"

Emma answered quickly over her choking, thudding heart. "Mrs. McCullough."

The horse still wouldn't let Wyatt mount, but the man was persistent, as persistent as his daughter with her questioning. "What'd she say exactly?"

Emma desperately wished to change the topic, but Melissa was only trying to deal with her mother's passing. But why *had* Wyatt chosen Lillie over her? How could he have married so quickly after Emma had left town?

Because he didn't care very deeply for Emma.

"Mrs. McCullough said your Ma was very pretty and good for your Pa," she answered honestly, ignoring the turmoil in her chest. "That they belonged together, and that they had a wonderful little girl. As a matter of fact, you were just born when she told me that." She dropped her lashes quickly to hide the hurt. Mrs. McCullough had crushed her that day.

The comments lifted Melissa's engaging smile. "My Ma was very pretty. Wanna see a picture of her?"

If it would make Melissa happy, Emma couldn't refuse. "Sure."

Reaching into her blouse, Melissa pulled out a silver locket necklace. When she unlatched the oval halves, it revealed a weathered photograph of Lillie. Her curly hair, once a vivid auburn in real life was grayed in the photograph. She'd died so tragically young.

Emma swallowed tightly and smiled at the girl. "She was very pretty and you look a lot like her. I'm glad you have such a pretty keepsake." She hoped it brought great comfort to Melissa. "You know, I'm not your mother, but if you ever want to talk to someone, you can always talk to me. It'll be just between us, whatever you say."

"Really? You wouldn't tell anyone else?"

"No. And you want to know something?" asked Emma

tenderly. "I bet your Ma's up there in heaven right now, smiling at the wonderful job you're doing with Billy."

Melissa's eyes watered. "You think so?"

"Absolutely."

A fluttering smile crossed Melissa's face. "I bet your Pa's lookin' down on you, too. I bet he knows you're sorry about all those arguments you never apologized for."

Tenderness bubbled in Emma's throat. She slid an arm around Melissa. "You're very sweet."

"Maybe when you think about that, you can be a little happier."

Emma tilted her head back. "What? I don't look happy?"

"You always look sad. I mean, you're smiling and everything, but your eyes are sad. Like right now. Are you sad about Cole and me and the baby?"

Emma glanced anxiously to Wyatt. He'd been spurned by the horse again and was dusting off his pants. Were her sentiments so transparent? God, did he notice them?

"Don't you think it'll work out between us?"

"I do, but I think it'll take some time. For your father to get used to Cole, and for Cole to grow up and take responsibility. You'll have to be patient."

"I couldn't live without Cole." Melissa stared up at the blue sky and sighed.

Her face somber, Emma burned with the memories of how she, too, had felt like that once. The eagerness to see Wyatt after being separated for a day, the wonder of his kiss, the sensations of his touch.

Melissa crossed her arms and her gaze followed her father's movements. "I couldn't live without passion, I couldn't live like you."

Emma's heart lurched madly at the unintended criticism. At just that moment, Wyatt, in the corral, yanked off his sweaty shirt. Emma cleared her throat, pretending not to be affected. Her eyes roved his streamlined chest, all the way from his wide, square shoulders down to his flat, muscled waist. His skin was golden brown, the color of golden wheat, and if she were a proper lady, she'd turn away.

Was her life without passion?

With every heated breath she took, she knew she was capable of great love and passion.

"You're not at all what some folks say about you," Melissa continued, unaware of the devastating effect her words were causing. "You don't act like an old spinster, but still, I couldn't live like you."

Emma felt the blood drain from her face. People called her an old spinster? She slumped against the rail.

No, her heart whispered back. Her eyes flashed. "There are other types of passion besides love."

"Like what?"

She felt her strength returning. "Passion for work. Passion for people. Those are vital, too. When you get to be a little older, you'll understand their importance."

"But haven't you ever been in love?" Melissa asked.

Emma's gaze pulled toward Wyatt. "Once." His hard, golden biceps glistened in the sunlight, and she'd never been more primitively aware of him. Her pulse jolted and her breathing pounded. Why did he have to be so male, so alive, so alert to everything around him?

"And what happened?"

The hollow core inside her ached deeper. She shifted her gaze away from Wyatt. "He didn't love me."

Melissa sucked in a sharp breath and shook her head with pity. "That's awful. But if he had loved you, wouldn't your love have been more important to you than anything else? Wouldn't you have fought for him, like I'm fighting for Cole?"

Immobile, Emma tried to hold her raw emotions in check. Blinking away the sting from her eyes, she knew she *had* fought for Wyatt. She'd fought against her father, against her family, against every member of his family, and in the end, only one thing had mattered.

Wyatt hadn't fought for her.

Thunder rolled in the distant hills.

Wyatt pushed the kitchen door open, allowing Emma to exit first. She sailed by him with barely a glance, the citrus scent of her rushing over him.

She'd been quiet all day, and he struggled to understand her. When she'd arrived this afternoon, she was talkative and friendly, even spending time with him, Melissa and Tommy in the library. By this evening, her conversation had petered into stony silence. What in tarnation had he done to offend her? He was staying out of her way at every opportunity. Hell, he hadn't even had the chance to make her mad.

He peered up at the sky as they made their way to the stables. "Looks like rain. We better take the covered buggy."

"*You're* taking me home?" She spun around to look at him. Her glossy hair tumbled around her shoulders, shadowed with hints of gold and brown and red. Her eyes flashed.

What was so damn awful about that? He admitted, he'd tried to get out of taking her home, but everyone else seemed to have an excuse tonight.

"Yeah," he said, pulling his body taller, "I am." His gaze traveled over her face and searched her eyes. "Might be a big storm brewing. You *could* spend the night instead."

An instant redness stabbed her cheeks. Her mouth

twisted like she'd swallowed something stale. "*No*, thank you."

Well, she sure knew how to deflate a man. He unbuttoned his suede vest and popped the top button of his new shirt. Why the hell had he donned a new shirt? "I guess you're stuck with me, then."

They reached the stables and he hitched a mare to the larger buggy. When he held out a hand to boost her up, either she didn't see it or she pretended not to. She yanked herself up and arranged her skirts. "I don't intend on staying the night," she repeated, much to his annoyance. "I'm not afraid of a little rain."

He shrugged his shoulders. "Might be more than a little."

She raised her voice. "I'm not afraid of a *lot* of rain."

He jumped in beside her. "Might be more than a lot."

She narrowed her eyes. "All right then, I'm not afraid of a damn storm."

As he stared at his pretty companion for a moment, her burning eyes challenging his, he suddenly realized how ridiculous they were being. He threw back his head and roared with laughter.

She puckered her lips and glared at him with hostility. Then her mouth softened, her cheekbones rose, her eyes sparkled, and she started laughing herself.

He leaned over playfully and their shoulders grazed. He felt an instant pleasure rising in his skin. "Are you afraid of a little lightning?" he teased, sending her into another round of laughter as the buggy creaked forward.

She brushed at her cheek, her cold resentment apparently gone. He hated arguing with her. Settling into her seat, she placed her medicine bag beside her. She carried that dang thing wherever she went, as if it were a sack of gold.

He stretched his long legs in front of him. They had more

room in this buggy than the smaller one. Thank goodness he didn't have to sit shoulder to shoulder and thigh to thigh with her. It was torture the last time around.

The sky grew dark, and a warm rain began to fall. Emma stretched her palm over the side, letting the mist wash against her skin. While she enjoyed the rain, he appraised her with a roving eye.

Underneath her creamy lace blouse, her chest rose and fell with a delicious shudder. Mighty tempting. All curves and jiggles. He forced his head back to the horse, flicked the reins between his fingers, struggling to ignore the arousal in his groin. "Yah," he blurted suddenly, prodding the horse.

She looked at him in dismay as the animal picked up its speed. They settled into a comfortable silence. "The rain smells different in Montana," she said. "It smells fresh, like the mountains."

He nodded. "You've been awfully quiet today, Emma. Something wrong?"

She pulled her hand to her lap. Her brown eyes grew serious. He shouldn't have mentioned it. He didn't want to break the spell.

"It's been a long day, I guess."

"It's a long way to travel to see a patient, every day."

She toyed with her fingers. "I don't need to come here as often as I do. Melissa's coming along fine, but I like spending time with her and Billy."

"She likes you a lot." He watched the wind tug at her hair. The glow of her smile warmed him across the seat. "Melissa's been a lot...*calmer* since you started visiting."

"I can't take all the credit. It's Cole's company, too, she's responding to."

Wyatt scowled and bit down on his lip. "Right. We can't

forget Cole. He needs a little credit, too. After all, he's had a large role to play.''

She twisted in the seat. "Don't be mad at Cole. It doesn't help things. Jim's already mad enough for all the Barlows combined.''

Wyatt's fingers tightened around the reins. "Jim. Now there's another fine citizen.''

"I've decided to go see him," she said, shifting taller and leaning forward. "Tomorrow. I plan on setting him straight on a thing or two.''

"What?" He craned his neck. "Listen, I want you to keep out of Jim's way. I've already sent him a message, loud and clear. He's to stay away from Cole.''

"I just thought if I went to him—''

"No."

She drew away and took a deep breath.

Emma's meddling would only aggravate Jim. Besides, meeting with him this morning, Wyatt had made it crystal clear. Stay the hell away from Cole Sinclair. Jim had fumed, but he'd listened.

"Emma, let's not argue on this one." He shook his head, trying to persuade her of the importance of what he was saying. "I saw Jim flogging his horse once—" his voice was firm and final "—and let's just say, he's got a problem controlling his temper." And it was the last time Wyatt had allowed Jim to work on his ranch.

Her eyes fluttered at his comment, but she didn't offer an objection. That was good enough for him.

Raindrops pelted the leather top of the buggy. He flicked the reins and the horse responded, pulling them faster. The warm rain trickled down the buggy. The air smelled of her scents and he felt drugged. Hell, he wanted to pull her close and press her against his body. All she had to do was look at him and it caused his head to spin. No one aroused him like Emma did. No one ever had. Not even Lillie.

Guilt washed through him. He hadn't been very fair to Lillie, marrying her on the rebound like he had, but at the time, he hadn't realized it. What was he supposed to do, live like a saint for the rest of his life because Emma had left town? She'd left for sixteen years!

The misery of it all weighed upon his shoulders. He had to break the stifling silence. "Are you anxious to get back to Philadelphia?"

She cleared her throat. A line of concentration deepened her brows. "I miss my work there. I'm hoping—that is, I'm still waiting for a reply on the telegram I sent."

"Do you miss your friends?"

She nodded and eased a tentative smile. "I've known a lot of them for years."

He tried to sound casual, as if he didn't care. "Anyone in particular?"

She flashed him a curious glance and raised her chin a notch. "Anyone in particular you're asking about?"

He regarded her with amusement. She knew damn well he was asking about a man. "Did you leave any particular man behind?"

"I left several."

She flushed but remained silent at the quirk of his brows. Her answer didn't surprise him. She was beautiful and intelligent. There wasn't any man who could resist her, unless he was dead or blind.

Might as well come right out and ask. "I heard you were engaged, two years back. What happened?"

Her eyes grew large and her hand shot up to her throat. She chose her words carefully. "It didn't work out, and I simply called it off."

"Simply, huh. Why?"

Greenish eyes fired off in his direction. "Why is that any of your business?"

"Just curious." Lord, she had a temper. He decided to keep his mouth shut.

He was getting hot again. And sticky. A trickle of sweat rolled down his spine. The rain fell quicker now, slanting under the roof, falling on his skin. He undid another shirt button and tossed off his vest. Thunder rolled past them and beyond the forest. It'd be dark soon. Lightning flashed, illuminating the horse and buggy. He and Emma flinched in response, and she instinctively inched closer.

July already, he thought. Only six weeks left with her. His heart reversed directions.

She grew silent and they both stared ahead, rocking in unison when the wheels hit a bump in the road, listening to the drops of rain drumming on the leather. He was still thinking about her engagement, and the question tumbled out before he could yank it back. "Did he ever take you swimming in your birthday suit?"

"*Wyatt!*"

"Did he?" He held his breath, hoping for a no. The two of them had always dreamed about doing it together. Did she remember how long they'd lie under the trees by the creek, kissing for hours, discussing exactly what they'd do to each other in the water? His heart beat with the drum of the rain.

He thought he heard a giggle escape her.

"Why are you laughing?"

"The thought of Lord Jonathon Winchester in his birthday suit."

The name stunned him into silence. He was definitely out of his league with a lord. The guy had probably impressed the hell out of Emma and her society friends.

He shrugged his shoulders, more than a little annoyed.

What did he expect? She'd gone on to Philadelphia without him. She'd grown into a sophisticated city woman who was seeing the world, while most days, he was watching the rear end of a horse. Like he was now.

"Lord Jonathon Winchester," he repeated calmly. But then again, she'd chucked the man. Sure as hell, he probably needed chucking. "Did you get a Winchester rifle out of him at least, before you threw him out?"

"He's not from the rifle family, I'm afraid, otherwise I would have gotten two. One for you."

"Nice of you to think of me at a time like that."

Laughter found her again, and its sound rolled through him like a sweet morning mist. Her compelling eyes turned to his and his heart thudded.

"How do you address a Lord?" he asked. "Did you call him Sir?"

"No," said, pulling back in mock indignation. "He's a normal person. I call him Jonathon."

She *calls* him Jonathon? Hell, she was still seeing him? "I thought you said you got rid of him."

"Not as a friend."

"And he can take it, just being your friend?" Well, hell, *he* was takin' it, wasn't he?

"Jonathon is very civilized," she said with a maddening rush to the man's defense.

Jonathon sounded like an idiot.

Wyatt stared ahead at the horse's rear, feeling like one himself.

After a moment, Emma raised a hand and slid her hair over her shoulder in a provocative gesture, intensifying something within him. His buried curiosity found a voice again. "Well, Emma, have you?"

"Have I what?"

He swallowed and grew serious, more serious than he

wanted to show. His palms grew moist. "Have you ever fulfilled that wish? Have you ever gone swimming like that...with anyone?"

Lightning flashed. Her brown eyes grew round and liquid and her breathing hitched, sending his stomach into somersaults. "No, I never have. Have—have you ever...?"

"No," he whispered.

An intimate silence followed his admission. She hadn't done it with anyone else. And neither had he. The world felt right.

A clap of thunder shook the hills, rolling straight through his spine. He suddenly realized how heavily the rain was coming down. The bottom of Emma's skirt was drenched, and the bottom of his pants. Lightning cracked the sky. He leaned forward, his body tensing. "We better stop somewhere."

Concern rumpled her face. "Where?"

"We'll go into the bush a ways, and stop under the trees."

"It makes me nervous being under a tree during a lightning storm."

He quashed his own fears and tried to calm hers. "We'll be fine."

The mare remained calm under Wyatt's firm hand. They rolled into the bush and he pulled under a roof of branches. Raindrops pelted the leaves above them, driving his heart faster.

He jumped down and hitched the horse to a tree, then came around for Emma. She held out her hand, and a blast of raw desire surged through him. God, did she know what she looked like?

Damp tendrils of hair framed her face, softening the curves of her cheeks and accentuating the beauty of her warm eyes. He wanted to reach out and wrap the wet strands around his fingers. He wanted to slide the moist hair from her face and lift her full lips to his.

Gazing lower, the sight of her thin, wet blouse clinging to her corset made his heart gallop until he heard it pounding in his ears. Her firm, round breasts thrust forward through the mesh of cloth. The red circles of her nipples jutted through, beckoning for him to reach out and taste them.

His belly tightened.

He had to do something, fast. To put some distance between them before he yanked her down in the mud and said to hell with it. Before he ravished her like the wild beast she was turning him into.

But what could he do? She held out her hand in complete trust, and he, like a gentleman, swallowed hard and took it.

Her touch felt like fire, searing through his skin right through to his heart. Their moist fingers clasped, he tugged her down, his mind shamelessly filling with lust.

Her eyes grew wide and her breathing panicked. It only served to push her chest further toward him. Those succulent rosy buds. She'd taste like fresh rain if he took her now.

Their heated gazes collided. He tightened his grip on her hand and slid a powerful arm around her waist. She grabbed his shoulder to stabilize herself. For a heart pounding moment, her wet breasts pressed against him and he felt their tips jutting against his chest.

The urge to taste her sweet lips made him hard. And the way her body fit snugly against his, he knew she could feel his hardness. Her gasp of shock when he shifted his stance only fueled his fire. It was more than any man could take. Finally, unable to hold back, he plunged his fingers into her silky hair.

She gasped at his touch. "No, Wyatt—"

"Yes," he murmured, quivering at the sound of her rich voice. His lips found her slender neck, and he kissed its heavenly warmth. Again and again.

Lightning flashed. She arched and rocked against him and he yearned to discover what she'd feel like, naked on top of him, bucking and riding.

"Stop," she moaned.

"You don't want me to…"

Gazing into the dark depths of her eyes, he trailed his thumb down the curve her jaw and slowly to the base of her throat. He intended to trail farther to the swell of her breasts, but she reached up and nabbed his fingers.

He smiled dangerously, filling with pure desire. Was she taunting him? He felt her tremble and she swallowed hard. Gently, tenderly, he brought her fingers to his lips and kissed them one by one. Her chest rose and fell. Guiding her hand to his side, he placed it on his quivering thigh. Thunder rolled and he quaked.

He was out of control, and he knew it. Couldn't stop himself if he tried. Somewhere, in the back of his mind, he knew he should try. But gazing down into her soft beckoning eyes, he was lost. She moistened her pink lips and he couldn't resist. He lowered his mouth onto hers, finally tasting her sweetness. Her lips parted, and his tongue slipped inside her hot mouth.

She moaned and surrendered, hiking her hand around his neck. Running her fingers through his hair, sending shivers down his spine with every gentle caress.

Why did she control him, body, mind and soul? Their bodies strained to touch, closer and closer. He pressed into her and she responded, making him wild with desire. What would it be like to sleep with her? To ravish her in bed?

Oh, God, it would be heaven.

Her breasts jiggled against his chest and he slid his moist hand up over the firm rounds. She pulled away but he tugged her back and slid his bare hand under her blouse, daringly over the top and under her corset. She moaned and spilled her bare breasts to his hand.

Her hard nipples felt like jewels in his palm. His knees turned to water. He tugged a nipple and she groaned.

"Emma," he whispered, "you're so beautiful."

Her breathing rasped. "I...we better stop...."

"No, not now."

She tore her mouth free. Her glistening eyes deepened. "We can't do this."

Chilled, he staggered back as if they'd been cut in two by a cruel twist of a knife. "We're adults now, we can do whatever we want."

With a tremor to her voice, the pinkness in her face fading, she reeled away. "No. Nothing has changed. It'll always be the same between us."

The rain poured down on the leaves.

"No," he shook his head in despair, "it doesn't have to be that way." But in his wounded heart, he knew the truth.

She would always leave, and he would always stay.

She stepped back into the shadows and he could no longer see her face. "It'll always be the same." Her voice had lost its warmth and he shivered. "We don't belong together."

Chapter Nine

When Wyatt quietly tugged the reins and drew the buggy up to the house, Emma slid to the ground without a word. Hurt and longing choked her voice.

With a strength that surprised her, she gripped the handle of her medicine bag, swung it over her shoulder and let it smack to her side. No matter how many times she shared his kiss, nothing would ever, *ever* come of it. He didn't want to make a commitment to her, he never wanted to marry her.

A suffocating loneliness squeezed her heart. The rain beat faster on her head. Her teeth chattered and her body trembled.

Was another storm coming? And what if it was? She didn't care how wet he got on his return. She wasn't about to invite him in, to trap herself in the same quarters and have to endure his tormenting gaze. With barely a glance to his dark solemn face, she dashed inside the house.

Entering the hallway, she heard familiar voices coming from the dimmed parlor. Mother, Rose and Ben.

Weary, she glanced down at her drenched figure. Her ruffled appearance would raise too many probing questions, ones she wasn't prepared to answer. Dropping her wet bag by the door, she hiked her sopping skirt and petticoat, and tiptoed up the stairs.

Rose's girls had given up their bedroom while Emma was staying in town, and tonight, she was utterly grateful for the privacy. She stepped inside the airy room that Rose had done in yellow ginghams.

Emma slid out of her wet blouse, disturbed at the tenderness in her breasts. Had Wyatt aroused her that much? Her response to his touch had always been so physical. Unlike any other man she'd ever been with. Even Jonathon. She'd never quivered at Jonathon's kisses.

She sighed. Her nipples were still firm from Wyatt's hot touch. What would have happened, if she'd allowed Wyatt to go further tonight?

She wouldn't think about it. Pulling in a deep, soothing breath, she stepped out of her petticoat and corset and added them to the wet pile. Thank God her senses had come back to her in time.

If she could, she'd douse herself in a hot bath to scour away his touch, but a bath would alert her family she was home. She rubbed a towel briskly against her skin. The sharp movement reflected in the corner mirror, and caught and held her eye. Dropping the towel to her side, she took a step closer and scrutinized her naked body.

What was it about her that'd made it so easy for Wyatt, all those years ago, to turn his back and walk away from her? Why hadn't he wanted to make her his wife?

With the kerosene lamp flickering on the dresser, she stared at her reflection. She tried to judge herself impartially. Animation left her face and a heaviness weighed upon her heart. Her gaze slid over her smooth, straight shoulders, over the white swell of her upturned breasts, across her slim hips and down the triangle of silky curls. She wasn't so bad, was she? Other men found her attractive. She could spot desire when a man gazed into her eyes. Usually the next place he looked was down at her skirt, trying to see if he could discover the cause of her limp.

Her eyes traveled over her firm, long legs, finally settling on the disfigured calf. Was that the cause? She narrowed her eyes and peered at it, like a stranger might do, assessing it as honestly as she could. After twenty years, her calf still retained a slight purplish hue, faded brown near the scars, the calf muscles thin and weak. None of the ointments had softened the harsh reality.

She refused to wallow in self-pity, and turned in the mirror, assessing from another angle. No angle made it look better. It never had. She hadn't always been able to look at it, especially during her teen years, but she'd given up hoping it'd turn normal. Now, she counted herself lucky to have survived a rattler bite and that she had a leg at all.

Propping her foot on the bedspread, she ran her fingers over the two bumpy X marks where Wyatt had made the incisions. Were the cuts that ugly?

Were they so ugly they could drive a man away? They hadn't driven Jonathon away. But truthfully, he'd never seen her scars. He'd only told her they didn't matter. Maybe once he'd seen them, he'd have given her a swift goodbye, too.

She knew very well that a woman's appearance was important to a man. Men prided themselves on how their women looked, no matter if they said different.

It was important to *her,* too, to be attracted to her husband. Physical intimacy was an important bond of marriage.

She tossed the damp towel on the heap. Oh, she knew Wyatt had been drawn to her tonight. Her flesh prickled and her skin heated, remembering how his body had pressed against hers. His masculine arousal. He'd even called her beautiful. She lowered her lashes. But she'd been clothed, hadn't she? How would he respond to see her naked? To see this leg?

Turning away from her reflection, she raked a white nightshift over her head. She clenched her jaw to mute the sob in her throat. It would never happen. She'd never give Wyatt the opportunity to see her naked. She had too much dignity to face the possibility of rejection from him a second time around. She would rather die a virgin than have him explain again how little he cared for her.

Her mouth trembled. She slowly lowered her head to her hands. Wouldn't she?

Yes, she told herself with determination. She had no intention of falling under his spell. She picked up her hairbrush and yanked it through her mass of tangled strands.

She didn't need a man to fulfill her life. Medicine gave her more than she'd ever imagined, helping others in need.

As she tossed her hairbrush back onto the silver tray, she eyed an envelope propped against the candlestick. What was that? Why hadn't she noticed it sooner?

A telegram, stamped with today's date. She picked it up and ripped it open. A sudden flurry of nerves assaulted her. It had to be from the hospital.

"Received your letter. Holding your position open until August first. Measles outbreak. Hospital needs you. Hope brother wife and child are well. Cordially James Preston."

Measles? A wave of apprehension pulsed through her. That was dangerous news. Measles was a deadly disease. Maybe she should pack tonight and leave immediately.

Sinking onto the bed, she clutched the paper between her fingers. No. Dr. Preston would have said if he needed her immediately. He wasn't a man who minced his words.

August the first. Three weeks. Half the time she thought she had. Her stomach clenched tight. She reread the telegram. Dr. Preston obviously thought her brother was married to Melissa. She felt a guilty qualm as she glanced up. She hadn't bothered to explain the full details; as a matter of fact, she hadn't confided to anyone in Philadelphia. Would any of them understand?

She breathed a heavy sigh. Did she belong in Philadelphia?

She glanced again at the paper she held in her hand. Three weeks left. Would that give her family enough time to heal their wounds with the Barlows?

What made him think he mattered to Emma? Wyatt wondered as he pushed himself back in the saddle, marveling at his own arrogance. What made him think she gave a damn anymore?

He hadn't even seen her for two days.

Knowing how much the christening invitation meant to her, he'd wanted to invite her himself, but she'd made herself scarce. Cole had said an emergency came up, and she was assisting Doc Brady with in an appendectomy. But what had kept her from the ranch the following day?

Blinking, he glanced ahead at the shrubs. He knew what held her back. She cared about coming to the christening, but she didn't care about seeing him again. Not after that blazing kiss they'd shared.

With a curse on his lips, he slid back his Stetson and rubbed his brow. She'd sure been upset with him. He still couldn't believe how carried away he'd been by his burning desire to have her.

What would happen if he cleared the air and told her everything? Was it such a crazy thought? Would it make a difference if she knew how he'd really felt about her on the night they'd parted sixteen years ago?

I did love you, Emma, I loved you so much I did what I thought was best for you. I left, and you became a doctor.

Would she understand? Would she accept it in the tender way he'd offered it, as a young man of nineteen?

His lips drew together in concentration. A lot of years had passed. She was a grown woman, and he was smart enough to realize it'd been easier to impress her then instead of the cultured woman she was now. In his wildest dreams, if they started seeing each other again, how long would it take before she sent him packing?

What in the hell would he accomplish by explaining why he'd left her? Did he think he mattered that much to her anymore than she even gave a hoot?

Would she magically forgive him? Would she decide to stay here, in Pine Creek? *With him?*

He struggled with his pride. The shattering truth was, he was afraid that if she lined him up alongside all the other men in Philadelphia and compared point against point, he'd come up short.

And if she turned him away, in that one god-awful moment, he knew it would be the wretched end of him.

He gave a short, desperate laugh. She was a doctor, for cripe's sake, accustomed to going to the orchestra, the ballet and fine restaurants. France, even. What could he possibly offer her? What had he ever offered Lillie?

The burden of his own weakness tugged at his heart. He couldn't make Emma any happier than he could his first wife.

Morning light filtered through the pale-yellow curtains as Emma tugged her new dress over her head and let the silk glide over her hips. With a nervous fluttering of anticipation, she stepped back, allowing Rose to cinch the crisscross of thin red straps at the front of the bodice. Rose tugged hard. The tugging bounced the rows of rags in Emma's hair that her sister had applied for curling.

With dressmaker's pins perched between her lips, Rose squatted on the floor, her skirt spilling around her feet, and reached for the hem. The final step before completion. Emma turned to face the mirror and gasped, shocked at her reflection. The dress was much too revealing.

"It's too tight around the bodice," Emma whispered in a fevered hush. "It's too low off the shoulders. And much too red!"

With a look of consternation and a wave of her hand, Rose flagged away her sister's concerns. "You look as pretty as one of those catalog girls." Rose stepped back with eager eyes to appreciate her creation.

Emma stared into the mirror and when she saw the bright-eyed, sensual woman staring back, she felt her knees wobble. Her face flushed at how much her reflection revealed.

The cherry red brought out the sun-kissed color in her cheeks, color she hadn't seen for years while living in Philadelphia. Her exposed shoulders looked soft and shapely, while her waist seemed so very tiny, cinched by the straps of the bodice and accentuated by her full breasts and hips. "Oh, Rose, I'm not sure—"

"You're used to wearing those stuffy blouses you collect from the city. Honest to Harry, you'd think you were eighty years old already."

"I'm a doctor and I should look like one," she said firmly.

"Then maybe you better put on your britches and buy suspenders."

With a hand on Emma's waist, Rose twirled her sister around in the mirror, checking to see that the hem was pinned straight. "Maybe one of the Walker men will notice. Devon, in particular, is always asking about you."

Emma rolled her eyes at her sister in the mirror. Rose, married with three children, happier than a butterfly in a field of flowers. She thought everyone should be married. Lowering her eyes and fighting the anguish that assailed her, Emma knew not everyone was meant to be married. And even though she'd love to have babies of her own one day, how could she have babies without a man?

Brushing at the folds along the front of her dress, Emma knew if she thought about it too long, she'd get all weepy again, and decided it was better to laugh than cry. Mustering a casual tone, she gave her sister a nod. "Devon makes it real obvious what's on his mind, every time we meet. The way he rakes me up and down and grins like we're both sharing the same secret, honestly! He'd be just as happy with a sack of hot coal in his bed."

Rose giggled wholeheartedly and Emma slipped out of the dress, careful not to jab herself with any pins.

Her sister grew real quiet as she threaded her needle. "Maybe Wyatt will notice."

It was all Emma could do to keep from bursting into tears. It was too painful to discuss, even with her sister. Emma wasn't sure anymore, what she felt herself.

She hadn't seen Wyatt for days. She'd seen Melissa yesterday at the ranch, but Wyatt had been working in the fields, clearing brush. Emma hadn't seen him since that kiss. Her pulse tingled with the memory. "There's nothing going on between me and Wyatt," she voiced with a hollow ring.

"I saw *something* between you in the mercantile that day. I don't think it's over...."

Yanking her old dress over her head, Emma turned away from her sister. Emptiness gnawed at her, but she ignored

it. "Let's just enjoy ourselves today at Billy's christening."
She slid the red dress from Rose's fingers. Glancing to the
clock on her dresser, she added, "There's barely two hours
left till we have to leave, I'm sure the girls need your help
to get ready."

Thankfully, Rose gave in and Emma finished the hem-
ming. Emma had already made the girls' breakfast, Ben
was locking up the store, and Cole was downstairs shaving
and dressing. Ma was ready an hour ago, humming and
singing in her new dress. She'd prepared enough platters
to feed a platoon, Emma thought with a smile. Apple dump-
lings, pecan pie and finicky cucumber sandwiches she'd
gotten from the fancy cookbook Emma had brought her
from Philadelphia.

"The royalty eat cucumber sandwiches like these in England," Ma explained while they loaded up the buggy.

Emma jabbed Cole with a hard elbow to keep him from
laughing. He was in fine spirits, she noticed, smiling and
cheerful all morning, and it warmed her heart to see her
family in such a happy mood. Maybe everything *would* turn
out right before her time was up.

Her mind flashed to Wyatt. Would he notice her new
dress? How would he react when she told him she had less
than three weeks before leaving for Pennsylvania? Her
stomach began to flutter as their buggies turned into his
valley—Cole, Ma and Emma in one, Rose, Ben and the
girls in another.

A crowd was already milling in the front yard as they
approached. There were dozens of people there, many more
than she'd anticipated. She felt a tingle of nerves, descend-
ing from the wagon, hoping that their neighbors, and the
Barlows, would respect her family on this happy day. That
they'd leave Melissa and Cole in peace, even though they
weren't married yet but had a child to celebrate.

Cole was still whistling as he helped unload Ma's platters, then quickly disappeared in search of Melissa.

Standing alongside her mother and sister, Emma surveyed the grounds. Wyatt had done it up real nice.

He'd raised a canvas tarp over a square of grass for the musicians, to keep them shady and cool. Rows of wooden tables made of fresh-cut planks were lined up under the trees, and another canvas tarp was raised over the food tables. Wyatt's pride showed in every detail.

Even though Emma's family had every right to participate in Billy's christening, she was grateful to Wyatt for the invitation. She respected him for the strength and compassion it must have taken, to allow the Sinclair family to mingle with the Barlows after all the years of hatred.

Glancing to the house, she noticed red ribbons tied around the elms and cottonwoods by the porch. She'd already noticed the jars of wildflowers adorning the tables. Melissa's doing, Emma felt sure, smiling to herself.

Ma and Rose let out a shout when they spotted the guest of honor, little Billy, nestled in a knitted outfit, coming out the front door in Melissa's arms, accompanied by Cole. Melissa looked serene and pretty in a crisp green dress, her waist already slimmer from her delivery three weeks ago. As Ma and Rose walked off to join them, Emma picked up her skirts to follow. What stopped her was a muscular, black clad figure striding out from the stables, not ten feet away.

Wyatt.

Her whole being rocked with the bold sight of him. Rough and rugged, a wall of masculinity dressed in a dark suit, his sharp black hair slicked at the sides. He was gazing down at a plank of wood and a hammer he held in one hand, lost in concentration, no doubt about to make a last-minute adjustment to one of the tables or benches. He was humming a soft tune, a lullaby she recognized from her childhood, about rocking horses and moonlight.

A heated smile tipped the corners of her mouth. He was so tough and intimidating on the outside, yet so gentle and sweet on the inside. And he fought hard so no one would discover it.

When he glanced up and spotted her, he stopped dead in his tracks. The hammer and wood slipped out of his hand and thudded to the hard ground.

She couldn't breathe for the tenderness in his gaze.

With black piercing eyes, he ravaged every curve of her body. His muscular frame tightened beneath his dark suit, and he swallowed firm and hard. Mercy, he was every inch a man.

She felt as if, for a moment, the world stopped spinning and stood still around them. They were reduced to their rawest forms in nature, simply man and woman, held breathless and captivated by each other.

She gasped for breath, the muscles along her stomach quivering for release. Growing hot, she felt a shiver quake from her bosom all the way down into her legs until it raced back up and settled into her heart.

That's when the realization struck her, like a thunderbolt sent from Zeus.

She was still in love with this man.

She loved Wyatt with every exploding cell in her body. Oh, Lord, she'd never stopped loving him.

Chapter Ten

"Emma," Wyatt said, her name rolling off his tongue expertly, smoothly, "you look like heaven."

Before she could respond, before she had a second to compose herself, another woman's voice called out to Wyatt.

Lilabeth McDougall pulled him in one direction, and Devon Walker slipped an arm under Emma's, pulling her in another.

"Nice to see ya again," said Devon. Grinning wide beneath his fluffy brown mustache, he butted his thin frame close to hers. Stifling a groan, she stepped back, her heart still pounding from her awakening about Wyatt.

She barely got a moment to think about Wyatt, for Devon inched closer and closer, talking about the weather. Standing so close she could smell sausages on his breath. As he slid tighter, she swore he was trying to peek down her dress. She stepped back on uneven ground and almost bumped into Tommy and his cousins at the food table.

Trapped and flustered, she glanced over at Wyatt, two yards away. Lilabeth held his attention, wriggling her behind and pressing her chest against his arm. Emma hadn't seen Lilabeth in over five years, not since the woman had thrown her third husband out of the house.

Heavens, the woman could talk. What was she talking about, animated and batting her lashes like she had something stuck in her eye? Wyatt didn't seem to mind how close she was standing, or how tightly she pressed against him. He didn't make a move to walk away. Emma averted her gaze, unnerved by the magnitude of her own desire.

"Yes, I can't wait for the music to start either," Emma replied to Devon.

"You'll save me a dance, won't ya?"

Startled, Emma focused her concentration. She didn't dance. "W-we'll see," she stuttered. "If there's time…"

Devon got lost in conversation about himself, and when Emma glanced over at Wyatt again, his dark eyes were gazing back. Her heart whirled to the sky. Pointedly, he looked to Devon then back to her, arching a black brow in amused curiosity, as if asking *Who's the fella?* Heating to the sparkle in his eyes, Emma bit back a smile, looked at Lilabeth and arched *her* brow—*Who's the girl?*

Wyatt shrugged a cavalier shoulder and tossed her an innocent look, like he had no idea where Lilabeth had come from. Then the corners of his mouth tugged up and his eyes shone brighter. *How'd we get trapped?* he seemed to be asking, and Emma stifled her sudden desire to laugh.

With a private nod to Emma, Wyatt yanked Lilabeth closer and steered her toward Emma and Devon. Smiling, Emma knew what he was up to. She took a step toward them, too, and sure enough, lecherous Devon followed beside her until the four of them bumped into one another. After Wyatt made the introductions, Emma mentioned Devon had just bought himself a ranch on the north side of town.

"You don't say," purred Lilabeth. "A fine, strapping

man like you, I'm not surprised.'' She leered at Devon, a
dozen years her junior, as if she could swallow him whole.

Devon grinned back like he wouldn't mind being swallowed.

And Emma and Wyatt both breathed a humorous sigh of
relief. Suddenly feeling self-conscious around Wyatt, as if
he might see in her eyes what she'd just realized herself,
she felt like bolting. Out of politeness, she remained where
she was, but only for the moment, she promised herself.
During the small talk that ensued, his shoulder brushed
along hers every now and then, reminding her with a shiver
that he was near.

Wyatt was responding to something Lilabeth was asking
about the baby when Emma heard familiar voices beside
her.

Grandpa, dressed in a checkered suit and bow tie, made
his way eagerly along the food table, platter in hand, with
Miss Molly, owner of the town's dress shop. Judging by
the dreamy look in Grandpa's eyes, he was sweet on her.

In spite of herself, all the romance in the air around her
filled Emma with a warm sense of jubilation, and she
couldn't help but watch Grandpa try to woo Molly.

A widow for over twenty years, Molly was always
dressed in grand style. Her lacy coral blouse ballooned over
her very ample bosom, and the large bow at the back of
her skirt accentuated wide hips. Molly had once been ac
cused of doing away with her own husband, shooting him
with one of her own pistols, but Emma didn't believe it.
She believed Molly's version that it'd been a robber.
Molly's peaceful features seemed too kind to be shooting
people.

Their voices carried, and Emma couldn't help but over-
hear their exchange. Wyatt looked their way, and with a
glint of humor, gently nudged Emma's shoulder with his.

Her stomach fluttered as she realized he found their conversation amusing, too.

"I just learned that kings and dukes in England eat cucumber sandwiches like these," Molly said to Grandpa.

"No wonder they're so skinny," he replied. "Got any meat?" Grandpa must have washed his hair this morning, Emma noticed. It looked different, puffier and bigger around the ears. The top of his shiny head was beading with perspiration, a likely combination of the heat and his wool suit.

"Hold your horses, Albert. The ceremony comes first, then the sit-down meal. Take a few snacks to tide you over."

"A man's sure gotta fight for what he can get around here. I ain't got much time left in my life, and I'm hungry." He bit into a cucumber sandwich and turned a charming old eye to Molly. "I gotta confession to make, sweet doll."

Molly sent Grandpa a look of exaggerated terror. "I'm not sure I want to hear your confession."

Grandpa scratched his thatch of hair, his brows drawn together and eyes opened up as if he were unlocking his soul. "Well...the thing is...I'm sorta, well...I'm sorta partial to you, Molly."

Molly bit into a biscuit and tried to conceal the girlish smile creeping over her face. She looked like she was sixteen again.

Grandpa's eyes narrowed with sudden concern. "But... you ain't packin' any pistols in those stockings, are ya?"

"Don't believe everything you hear," Molly grumbled. "I'm packin' a lot of things in these stockings, but pistols ain't one of them."

He stared at her for a second, then rocked back on his shiny boots and roared with laughter.

Emma found herself smiling alongside Wyatt.

"Don't go breakin' my heart," Grandpa said, growing serious again, stepping close to Molly. "It's an old heart, and it can't take much."

"For heaven's sake, Albert, I've only agreed to sit beside you and have lunch together."

Balancing his plate in one hand, Grandpa eyed her with lust. "We both know what we're talkin' about here. Sittin' at the same table's gonna lead to a dance. One dance will lead to another. That'll lead to me takin' you home. Then before I can count to three, you'll be offerin' me a slice of that dreamy apple pie you make so well. And you know where that leads. We'll be wakin' up in the same bed and you'll be pullin' out the fryin' pan and cookin' me breakfast."

"Grandpa!" Emma gasped.

Molly's mouth dropped open, and she blushed so intensely her ears turned red. "I'll be pullin' out the fryin' pan all right, and whackin' you right over the—"

Grandpa splayed a wrinkled palm in the air. "Don't go gettin' ornery on me. You may be the prettiest little thing here, but Molly— Did I ever tell you how much I like your name, *Molly?*"

Still ruffled, her breathing erratic, she replied, "Only a dozen times…"

"Well, it's pretty. And alls I'm sayin' is, don't go breakin' my heart."

Grandpa's voice trailed off as they wound their way through the crowd. Emma watched him slide his roving hand from the top of Molly's shoulder down to her waist, and with only a slight hesitation, down to her rump. Blushing profusely, Molly tweaked his hand with a quick pinch, then a brisk slap.

"Gee willikers, your hand's quicker on me than when you're swattin' flies."

Emma laughed softly to herself as she watched them go, her heart filling with affection. Thinking Wyatt was too absorbed in his conversation with Lilabeth and Devon to have noticed Grandpa's last exchange, she glanced up at him.

His twinkling eyes met with hers and he winked. A sensuous light flashed between them. Her body flushed and for one luxurious moment, she allowed herself to simply stand beside him and bask in his warmth.

In the crowd, someone called for Melissa and Cole. Reverend Kilpatrick, a jovial, graying man, as thick and tall as the cottonwood trunk he was standing beside, was ready to start the ceremony. The crowd hushed and the families proudly found their places, Wyatt standing off to Melissa's side, and Emma, Ma, Rose and Ben standing off to Cole's.

The baby, draped in a white robe, slept in his godmother's arms during the entire half-hour ceremony. Melissa's cousin Susanna, and her husband Travis, were a good choice for godparents, thought Emma. They, too, were young, newly married, and had a lot in common with Melissa and Cole.

Emma watched with pride as Cole stood beside his son. When the baptism was over, she glanced over at Ma, who was weeping into her hanky, then over at Wyatt, who was grinning broadly.

Now all Emma had to do was get Cole and Wyatt talking.

A feast followed. Emma shared a table with her family. The Barlows weren't rude, but they weren't talkative, either. Melissa, in her good nature, made a point of bringing Billy over and eating with them. After the meal, a ball rolled under the table and Rose's girls jumped up and kicked it back to the Barlow children who'd tossed it. As they began to play together, Emma sighed wistfully, wishing life were as easy to patch up between the adults.

The music started, and Emma spotted Jim three tables away. The hair at the back of her neck bristled. He'd finally showed up. Looking over at their table, he was talking loud and laughing hard, almost as if he'd been drinking. Her fingers tensed in her lap.

Cole didn't appear to notice. Or he chose to ignore it. He got up abruptly and left with Melissa and Billy.

Emma decided Jim wasn't worth worrying about. She turned around in her seat, rearranging her red dress, and leaned back to enjoy the musicians. Their merry tune pulsed through her, as they played accordion, harmonica, fiddle and guitar.

Glancing over the crowd, she recognized many of the faces and nodded—Mrs. McCullough sitting with the reverend and his wife, the young boy with his arm in the new splint she'd helped Doc Brady apply, and her childhood friend, Sue Ellen Russell, eight months with child and still as pretty as she was in the fourth grade.

Emma caught the eye of Wyatt's sister, Mary, sitting on the porch. Mary looked tired, older than her years. A few days earlier, when Emma had bumped into her at the ranch, they'd shared coffee, but Mary had cut her hair since then. It was cropped short to frame her delicate face, and suited her. Emma smiled and waved, indicating she liked the hair. Mary waved back.

And in that one gesture of friendliness, Emma could see it reflected in Mary's tender, hopeful eyes. Mary knew. She knew how Emma felt about Wyatt.

Feeling heat in her cheeks, Emma spun away. What was Emma doing here, sitting in her fresh new dress and fancy hairdo? It hadn't been a secret, how lovestruck Emma had been as a girl. But sitting here as a lovestruck woman, still unable to get her man, made Emma shrink with humiliation.

If Mary pitied her, Emma couldn't bear it.

The dancing started and Devon barreled toward her. Wyatt, joining Mary, glanced in Emma's direction with a look of intent in his eyes. Feeling smothered, Emma jumped to her feet, made an excuse and ducked into the crowd, weaving her way around the porch to the back of the house.

Blissfully alone.

She ran along the flowing creek, through the firs and cedars and birch, finding solace beside an old oak rooted by the murky water. She recognized the oak from her childhood. Sagging against the rough bark, she closed her eyes. Music filtered through the leaves around her, a lonely ballad, not close enough for her to hear the words, but the sadness of the music wove through her heart and squeezed.

She'd never have him.

Swallowing past the lump in her throat, she told herself soon, she'd be gone from here forever and wouldn't have to endure living close to him.

The creek gurgled, and Emma watched sunlight skim over the water as the ballad finished. And when it did, she knew, without turning around, he was standing behind her.

She heard him catch his breath, heard him slow his breathing, and felt the heat of his eyes burn against her bare shoulders. She shouldn't allow him to stare, to stoke the fire, to let her imagination run with thoughts of his caress.

She didn't breathe.

"Emma," he said, so softly she wondered if he was just her imagination. "We used to read a lot of books under this tree, didn't we?"

So he recalled it, too. She looked down at her hands and

squeezed her eyes shut, trying to banish the tears. "Yes," she whispered.

"And we used to be good friends, once, didn't we?"

Friendship wasn't enough. She didn't speak.

"Remember how we used to be able to talk, to say anything to each other?"

She pressed a hand to her bosom and took a deep breath. He was quiet for a moment. A waltz began in the background. "Dance with me."

Panic shot through her. Her breath snagged and her fingers wound tighter together. "No."

She heard the ground crunch behind her, and his firm, square hand grabbed her upper arm and swung her around to face him. It was hot where he held her.

His eyes shone deep and black, swirls of marble caught in sunlight, and her knees almost buckled.

"One dance."

It would torture her to dance with him. To touch what she couldn't have. And as ridiculous as it was....she couldn't bear to tell him she still hadn't learned to dance. She wanted to laugh aloud, it was so ludicrous. Her girlfriends had tried to teach her, more than once, but in the end she'd always felt awkward and self-conscious. "No, please...I...let me go." She tried to pull away.

He wouldn't let her. His arm tightened over hers. Skimming over her skirt, his eyes narrowed. "You've never let it stop you, have you—I mean, you're not shy about your leg? Surely some man, a lover somewhere, helped you through—"

"Let me *go*." She pulled free.

They stood face-to-face. Her chest rose and fell with a tumble of emotions. His eyes lowered over her body and swept back to her eyes. "God, the way you look, how can I let you go?"

In one smooth motion, he slid his arm around her and lowered his hot mouth to hers.

His kiss was firm and demanding, then as gentle and tender as a whisper. Trembling, she felt trapped, afraid, excited. Then her bones began to melt, and her resistance mellowed. Why did he make her feel this way? Both helpless and exhilarated?

With a shameless moan of surrender, her hand reached up to his shoulder and buried itself in the silky hair at the base of his neck. He groaned and pulled her closer, if that was possible.

His lips sent waves of pleasure through her spine, through her bosom, through her moist, womanly center. The tips of her breasts ached to be suckled. She tried to fight the urgency of his touch. When he kissed her throat, behind her ear, and began searching down lower, to the swell of her breast, she felt an involuntary shudder of loneliness and confusion melded into one.

What did he want from her? His touch bewildered her. Sometimes he seemed to want her as much as any man wanted a woman, other times his eyes were as cold as stone.

Aching inside, she knew what she wanted. If she couldn't have all of him, body, spirit and soul, for always, she wanted no part of him.

She pulled away, and with a groan, he let her. Her shoulders chilled from where he'd dropped his hands.

A lock of hair fell across his forehead. His gaze deepened. His voice was rough. "There's something I want to explain."

"There's something I need to tell you, too." Voices carried in the breeze, close by. They turned their heads to the sound. Melissa and Cole, strolling hand in hand along the creek.

She'd better tell him, quickly. "I'm going back to Philadelphia sooner than I thought. The hospital needs me."

His face paled. "When?"

"Three weeks."

He staggered back and swung away from her.

She eyed him carefully. "What was it you wanted to explain to me?"

His shoulders rounded and he groped for words. "Only that...I'm grateful for all you've done for the baby and Melissa."

"The baby's taking his nap, and Aunt Mary's keepin' her eye on him. He's plum tuckered out." As Melissa talked on about the morning's events, Wyatt shoved a hand through his slicked hair and tried to catch his breath.

He was trying to make sense of what Emma had just told him. She was standing beside her brother, fully concentrating on the young couple's conversation, as if nothing had just happened between them, not a fine city hair out of place.

He felt like ripping his out. She'd shocked the hell out of him and he was still speechless. Why, she wasn't intending on staying one day longer than necessary. As soon as her job was finished smoothing things out between their families, she was leaving Montana.

Dammit all to hell.

He tugged off his jacket and flung it over his shoulder. Well that was just fine with him. Go right ahead. He'd even buy her the stagecoach ticket if she'd agree to take it.

A one-way trip, don't bother coming back.

Hell.

"Ain't that right, Pa?" Melissa's shiny face peered up at him. Her loose auburn hair glistened in a stream of light.

"Sorry, what was that?"

"I said, you and Cole have a lot in common. You both love horses."

Wyatt snorted. "Yeah."

Cole shifted uncomfortably in his snug blue suit as they walked along the water's edge.

Wyatt knew the discussion was a ploy to get him and Cole speaking. A woman's ploy, and it angered him. Melissa and Emma had probably discussed it yesterday. How they'd get the men together, throw in a couple of words about horses, and soon the men would be laughing and hugging each other like long-lost friends. Was that how it was supposed to work?

Well, to hell with Cole.

Weeds crackled under their feet. Wyatt shoved a hand into his pocket. Calm down, he told himself, pulling air into his lungs. Don't take it out on the boy.

Melissa deserved better from Wyatt. She'd been trying hard to be on her best behavior, and looking at her, all dolled up in her green dress, the one they'd bought her at Miss Molly's, he felt a surge of pride.

He didn't bother looking at Emma. He already knew how good she looked in her dress. Good enough to make him want to rip it right off her.

She was leaving him. He silently cursed Philadelphia and rubbed his jaw.

He glanced over at the boy, trying to shift himself to a better mood. What did Melissa and Emma see in Cole?

Beneath the shaggy hair, beneath the thin mustache that was almost invisible when the sun shone on it, Wyatt saw a tough young boy eager to be a man. But what was Wyatt overlooking? What did Melissa see? What did Emma see? There must be something good in Cole.

"That's a fine pair of wild horses you own," Wyatt said to Cole. "I saw them in the livery stables last week."

Cole's head sprung up. Surprise registered in his clear gray eyes. "Yup."

"He caught them himself." The freckles on the bridge of Melissa's nose squished together as she smiled. "Go on, tell him how, Cole. My pa's real interested in horses."

"Yes, tell us," said Emma, brightly. Wyatt sucked in his breath and tried not to look at her heaving cleavage.

Cole shrugged. "Nothin' much to tell. The horses were roamin' the hills. I took my time watchin' 'em, set my eyes on the ones I wanted, and roped 'em."

Melissa tugged her shoulders higher and smiled.

"Next time, though, Cole," said Wyatt, "don't wait until they're roaming Jim's property before you catch them. He claims one of the horses is his."

Cole's eyes widened and his body jerked back. "He knows the law, the sheriff told us both. Wild horses don't belong to you just because they run on your land. Besides, Jim doesn't own that property."

"I know who owns the land where that stream flows. I do. But Jim's been living in the nearby shack for the last year, making his living off that property. He claims he's stopped his drinking. I don't know if I believe him, but he swears he's going to work hard this time. Don't rile him up for nothing. He's got a short fuse, and his friends are a lot meaner than yours."

Cole mumbled under his breath.

They neared the back of the house where the grass was cut short. "Your horses for sale?" asked Wyatt.

"Nope."

"You sure? I could always use good stock for breeding. I got a stallion—a Kentucky whip—being delivered tomorrow. Now there's a fine breed of horse."

"How much do you figure my horses are worth?"

"Oh, if you got time to sit on them, break them in, I reckon you could get fifty apiece."

"How much did you pay for your Arabians?"

"They're in another league. I paid five hundred apiece."

"Then I think you might have been taken. One of my mustangs is worth just as much as one your Arabians."

Wyatt studied him. The boy sure was cocky. "You've got a lot to learn about horses, then."

Cole's face creased and he stopped walking. "You think because I'm young, I don't know squat about anything?" He suddenly jerked and clutched at his chest. "Owww..." Melissa must have pinched him. He deserved it.

"No sense getting mad over horses," Wyatt told him. "The calmest dealer always gets the best price. You might have an eye for good horses, but the price of horseflesh is based on a lot of things."

Cole raised his voice in defiance. "Every cowboy and drover I ever spoke to prefers a wild mustang over an Arabian."

"Yeah, that's true," Wyatt said in a frustrated tone. "There's a lot of distrust where a new breed's concerned."

"And every Indian I've seen from the Rockies to the Missouri can outmaneuver any other breed of horse, sittin' on top of a mustang."

"Yeah, I'll give you that, too. Mustangs are what the Indians are accustomed to. But an Arabian horse, my Arabians, no one can beat them."

Cole scoffed and looked him in the eye. "I bet I can beat 'em."

Wyatt clenched his teeth. Did the boy have to argue about everything?

Shaking her head at her brother, Emma slid her arm under his. "Now Cole, we're trying to have a friendly discussion." She nudged him along and they cornered the front porch. The lively music and the buzz of the crowd got louder.

Darting glances at each other, Cole and Melissa came to a stop, and Cole drew in a shaky breath. "Please…sir, could we talk to you?"

The words *please* and *sir* had never escaped Cole's lips in addressing Wyatt before. He glanced to Emma to see if she knew what this was about, but she looked as puzzled as he did.

With a wary eye, Wyatt peered from one to the other. "All right."

"Melissa and I," Cole began. "We've been talkin'…."

Jittery, Melissa gazed at the grass.

Cole's color deepened. "We've been talkin'…and I'm askin' for your permission to marry her, sir."

Alarmed at the suggestion, Wyatt stepped back. Marry? The two were no more ready for marriage than two newly hatched chicks. "Marriage is a serious commitment."

Cole nodded, real adultlike. "It's one I want to take."

"Me, too, Pa."

In astonishment, Wyatt glanced at Emma. Her mouth gaped open, but she recovered quickly and glanced back at him, gauging his reaction. How was he supposed to react? Cole probably hadn't even thought it all out. He peered at the boy intently, telling himself to control his temper. "How would you support Melissa and Billy?"

Cole's eyes narrowed. "I got a job."

"Does it pay well?"

"Enough for now."

"Does it pay even when you don't show up for work?"

Cole's lips thinned. He glared down at his boots and kicked at a clump of grass. Emma and Melissa glanced away in embarrassment.

What in tarnation did the boy think? That Wyatt would blindly agree to this marriage, without question?

Melissa stepped forward and nervously fingered the front pleats of her dress. "Pa, please, try to remember when you were our age." She swallowed. "We got so much feeling for each other, it's spillin' out and we can't stop it. I know old folks like you can't remember...."

Old? *Old?* He was only thirty-five, and never healthier in the bedroom department. He raked his eyes over Emma. Color rose to her cheeks. "I remember," he said in a heated voice. "But there's more to marriage than a marriage bed. You still need to eat, Billy needs clothes, and you need a place to live." He raised his brows. "Where would you live, Cole?"

Cole glanced over at his mother, sitting at the table. "At first, we'd probably live with Ma."

Probably? Wyatt whipped his jacket over a nearby chair and tried to simmer the pounding of his pulse. "Have you asked her? Have you thought it all out?"

Emma jumped in with pleading eyes. "Our family would help in every way we could. I could send money from Philadelphia."

"That's not the point. The point is that these two have to figure things out for themselves." Wyatt stepped back and placed a hand on his hip. "When were you thinking of marrying?"

"Right away."

Oh, blazes. He shook his head, biting back a sarcastic remark, and tried to be diplomatic. "Wait two years. You can save up some money, Cole, put it toward a house. Melissa, two years will give you time to mature and look after Billy."

Melissa's lower lips trembled.

An artery throbbed at Cole's temple. His nostrils flared. "We'd like to marry sooner."

Emma slid an arm around Melissa's waist. "Wyatt, please, won't you take more time to think it over?"

He didn't need more time. It was out of the question. And furthermore, he didn't appreciate Emma's meddling. None of her womanly charms were going to work this time. He was immune. Besides, she was leaving soon, and that set him off even more. "You're not ready," he shouted at Cole. "The problem is you can't support her."

Cole's eyes blazed. "Don't tell me what my problems are, you're not my pa. You've got a few problems of your own."

"Cole," Emma warned.

Wyatt rubbed his mouth and seethed.

The boy gritted his teeth and glared at Wyatt. "Are you sayin' *no?*"

"You've got a hell of a lot of nerve, confronting me like this, standing on my property."

"I said, are you sayin' no?"

Wyatt voice dropped to a dangerous level. "Don't make me say it here."

Melissa shrank back and sobbed, and Wyatt, turning to her, didn't immediately notice the raised fist sailing through the air.

It cracked against his jaw and decked him.

Chapter Eleven

Wyatt's jaw throbbed.

Emma shrieked and dropped to her knees beside him. "Wyatt!"

The crowd parted and the music faded.

Wyatt shook his head and rubbed his pounding chin, then slowly rose on an elbow. Outrage choked his words.

Emma bent over him, her eyes widened in horror, scanning his face. "Are you all right?"

The boy got in a lucky punch at a man with his head half-turned in another direction. And lucky for Cole, Melissa was holding him back now. The only reason Wyatt didn't jump up and box the boy's ears was the look of shame in Melissa's eyes.

Rising in thunderous silence, Wyatt ignored Emma's outstretched hand. He wiped a dribble of blood off his split lip and faced the little son of a bitch.

Cole stood defiant, rubbing his knuckles, his eyes smoldering. "Quit treatin' me like I don't exist."

The boy desperately needed to learn a lesson, and Wyatt desperately wanted to teach it to him. But glancing around the circle of trembling faces, Wyatt decided now was not the time. His muscles quivered, primed and ready to hit something, but he held his fists in check.

Fighting wouldn't prove a damn thing.

Emma raced to Cole and shook him by the arms. "You've lost your senses," she implored. "How could you start a fight, here, of all places, on this important day?"

Cole just kept glaring at Wyatt. Before anyone caught wind of the figure sneaking up behind Cole, Jim Barlow wheeled the boy around. Amidst the horrified shrieks, Jim slammed a hard fist into Cole's stomach. "I'm not sittin' still to watch this, you bastard!"

Cole doubled over and bile rose to Wyatt's throat watching it. Not here. Not at the christening.

Melissa screamed. Wyatt shot forward to separate the two, but just at that moment, Cole belted Jim in the side of the head and the two rolled to the ground.

It didn't take long before Cole sprang back up and they continued their punching by one of the tables.

The crowd gasped, Emma's pale lips trembled, and Mrs. Sinclair and Melissa sobbed in each other's arms. Rose and Ben pressed their hands over their daughters' eyes to shield them from the view.

That was it. Wyatt had reached his limit. He stomped over to the two, intending to grab them by the hair and haul them into the cold creek.

The reverend appeared, and he was closer.

Shame leaped to Wyatt's face as he watched the reverend, in his flowing black cassock, try to break up the skirmish.

The gentle old man tapped Jim's shoulder. "Now boys, stop this." A loose arm struck him in the face and sent his eyeglasses flying through the air.

Wyatt's heart drained of blood.

Emma and her mother gasped.

Cole and Jim realized the clergyman had been hit and with a mighty heave, Cole shoved Jim off his chest.

"Sorry, reverend," Cole pleaded with an outstretched hand, "we didn't mean to hit you. Please, I'm—I'm sorry...."

Jim straightened and looked sheepishly to his boots.

The reverend clamped a thick hand over his nose. Gingerly, he lifted his hand off his face and peered into his palm. Apparently, no blood. Humiliation slithered up Wyatt's spine. Someone handed the clergyman his wire spectacles, and he stared at the bent frames.

"You're behaving like barbarians on this fine, wonderful day of celebration." His voice croaked. "You shame me to the bone." He turned and left, shoulders drooping, shaking his pitiful gray head and twisting his glasses back into shape.

Wyatt starting shaking. The crowd shuffled and began to part, most of them unable to meet Wyatt's ashen gaze. Ben led his family away, Rose's fallen voice exclaiming, "We'll never be able to show our faces."

Emma and Cole stood frozen to the ground, their eyes glistening with fear as they met with his. Melissa looked horrified when she caught his rage. "Please Pa, no."

Wyatt leaped toward Cole, inches from his face. "Thank you for proving you're not worthy of marrying my daughter."

Cole's eyes glinted and he gritted his teeth. "You're makin' a mistake. You're ruining your daughter's life."

"*I'm* ruining my daughter's life? Get out of my sight and don't you ever, *ever,* come near my daughter again."

Jim lunged in Cole's direction. "Yeah, Sinclair! You stay the hell away from Melissa or I'll beat you to a bloody pulp!"

"Shut up!" Cole heaved forward, clenching his fists, ready to pounce.

"Stop it!" Wyatt's gut churned at the sight of them both. He stepped away and turned to Melissa. She was caught in the middle of this, and by the pained expression on her face, her heart was breaking. Cole's doing.

"Please, Pa, no," she sobbed. A stream of tears slid down her cheeks.

Wyatt reached out and she buried her face into his shoulder. "Shhh…don't cry. Everything will work out, you'll see. You're going to Helena. Your aunt Elizabeth said you can stay six months, a year, however long you need."

Melissa pulled away from him. "*No.* I don't want to go. Helena's more than a hundred miles away. Please, Emma," she begged, turning around, "stop him."

Emma stepped forward, opening her arms to Melissa, but her eyes beckoned to him. "Please Wyatt, don't make any rash decisions—"

"Rash decisions? *This* is not a rash decision. Everything else raging through my head is, but this isn't."

The green in her eyes flashed. She opened her mouth to add something more, then clamped it shut and shook her head.

Running a hand along her skirt, something stopped her and she glanced down. Wyatt noticed the waistline of her dress was ripped a good six inches. Another jolt of anger raced through him.

She glanced over to where Cole was standing, but he'd vanished. With a final blast of blame in her eyes, she glanced at Wyatt, then slipped into the crowd and disappeared. Sobbing, Melissa hiked up her dress and tore off to the house.

Jim stepped forward. His eyes narrowed and his breath came in short furious gasps. "Don't worry, Wyatt." He rubbed his bleeding fist. "I'll pay the bastard back for what he's done."

Staring at the dangerous glint in Jim's eyes, a wave of raw fear gushed through Wyatt. "Like hell you will. Stay away from him. This is between him and me."

Jim's head reared back in dismay. Indignation infused his face. His lips curled in a frightening display of unchecked hatred. "Why, he punched you right in the head. Nine months ago, he took advantage of Melissa." He narrowed his churning eyes on Wyatt, and his mouth trembled with rage. "And his father killed my mother. No Sinclair's ever gonna treat a Barlow like that again."

Wyatt's gut rumbled at the ugly, black tone of contempt spewing from Jim's mouth. He stepped in front of Jim and stared him down. "I *said* leave him the hell alone."

Jim stalked off, shouting curses, more enraged than Wyatt had ever seen him. Wyatt hauled himself up, watching the furious shoulders disappear into the stables. With any more prodding, what would Jim do?

Wyatt shuddered and looked around. The crowd had thinned. Half the folks had left already, Emma and her family among the first to go.

Sighing, his bones weary, Wyatt looked on. He didn't say much the rest of the day. He helped clear the tables, dismantle the wood, and near suppertime, he saddled up a horse and went for a ride. Maybe the cool mountain breeze would restore him, give a tiny thread of pleasure to hang on to.

No matter what angle he approached it from, he knew the best thing was to send Melissa away. She needed time and space to look at things from a distance, to grow into an adult. And Cole Sinclair, well, he'd proven what kind of a hot-tempered, irresponsible person he was. Maybe two years would change him, maybe it wouldn't. Wyatt couldn't care less. Cole had put himself out of the running.

Wyatt spent the next afternoon in the stables. His Kentucky whip arrived, and for a few hours at least, he was able to bury his problems. Melissa wasn't speaking to him, and he didn't have the heart to go up to her room to tell her to pack her things. He'd give her a day of rest, and talk with her tomorrow about leaving for Helena by the end of the week.

In the evening, he was riding in from the pastures with his men when he spotted Emma on a horse, riding toward the ranch.

Now what? he wondered, shoving back his Stetson from his brow. What was her damn hurry? He thought she'd already said goodbye to Melissa in the note she sent last night. And why was she riding alone? How many times had he told her it wasn't safe?

Spotting him on his mount, she galloped toward him. With an angry tug on his reins, he met her halfway, at the fence, two strings of wire between them.

He pulled in his horse. "After what your brother did yesterday, I'm surprised you can show your face."

She was out of breath, overheated from the ride. And she could barely control her horse. "Where's Melissa?"

Wyatt reached over the fence and grabbed her reins. He patted the horse. "Whoa, boy, settle down." The horse calmed.

Glancing at her medicine bag flung over the horse's neck, Wyatt frowned. Irritation seeped into his voice. He'd had enough of the whole lot of them. "Melissa is no longer your concern. It'd be easier on her if you stopped showing up here. Doc Brady will tend to her now."

Emma winced and swallowed. The sight of her crumpling figure tugged at his conscience, but it didn't stop him from continuing. The words needed to be said if his daughter was ever going to be left in peace. "Melissa's torn in half because of all of this," he nearly shouted. "It's Cole's fault, not yours, but your presence is a reminder." He glared at her with hardened features. "Turn your horse around," he said in reckless anger. *"For God's sake, go away."*

She choked with silent tears, but he steeled himself against her. Blinking and fighting for breath, she fought for composure. He pulled on his reins, about to leave. "I'll have Jack ride back with you."

She flung her arms over the fence in desperation. "Wyatt, listen to me."

He suddenly noticed her trembling hands. Her pale, drawn face.

A fresh fear took hold of him. "What is it?"

Her eyes begged to be heard. "Cole's gone. He's disappeared." Her voice hitched, rough with emotion. "Do you know if— Did he take Melissa? Oh, God. Did he take the baby?"

Emma listened to his curses as he leaped the whole way up the stairs. She wasn't as fast because of the pain shooting through her leg, but she wasn't far behind him.

With fear quelling inside her, she watched as Wyatt reached Melissa's bedroom door. It was closed and locked. He rattled it, hollered Melissa's name, then lifted his boot and kicked it in.

The door splintered.

The room was empty.

The bed was made, but the pillow gone. Melissa's armoire lay open, with half her clothes missing. Billy's cradle was rocking softly from the blast of the door. The padded yellow quilt that usually lined the bottom, and his flannel blankets, were gone.

The room echoed like an empty shell, and emptiness pulsed through Emma.

A note lay on the bed. Wyatt's boots thudded across the rug. He reached for the note and read it silently.

With a heavy sigh he pulled his drawn lips together and he let the note slide to the bed. He walked to the window and simply stared out at the valley. Immobile.

Emma picked up the note.

Dear Pa,

Please forgive me for leaving and please try to understand. I can't live like a prisoner in my own life. I'm not like you, content to live my life alone. I want to be with Cole.

I'm sorry I can't tell you where we're headed. If I did, as surely as snow melts in springtime, you'd chase us down and separate us. So, may God forgive me, you'll never hear from me again.

Trust me, Pa, this one last time. Trust me that I'll take care of myself and Billy. Please let Emma know I'll look after Cole. Let Grandpa and Tommy know they'll always be a part of my heart.

And you, Pa, I will love you until the day I die.

Your respectful daughter, Melissa.

"Oh, Melissa, *no*..." Emma was silent for a long, long time.

After what seemed an eternity, Wyatt surged to life. He crossed the room, a new purpose in his stride.

Emma shrank back at the deadly look in his eye. "What are you doing?" she asked, following his looming figure down the hallway.

He didn't answer. His mouth stubbornly set in a firm line, he strode into his bedroom and started yanking out the drawers.

"What are you doing?" Emma repeated, twisting her fingers together. Her stomach fluttered when he still didn't answer. "In the name of heaven, tell me what you're doing!"

Leaning over his bed, he slid a muscular arm underneath it, and with ease, tugged out a leather bag. He blew the dust off, unbuckled the strap and tossed it onto his bed.

Her eyes widened with sudden apprehension. "You're going after them."

He spun toward her. "What do you expect me to do?"

"I don't know, I need time to think."

"There is no time." He ripped through his chest of drawers and flung his clothes onto the unmade bed. "I'm gonna kill him, I swear I'm gonna kill him."

Emma's heart grew cold at the words. "You shouldn't have goaded him yesterday," she snapped. "He wouldn't have left if you'd kept your cool."

When he lowered his threatening dark gaze to hers, her pulse hammered and she stumbled back a step.

"Tell me everything you know," he growled. "When did Cole go missing?"

She was actually trembling under his level stare. "No one's seen him since ten o'clock last night. This morning, we all assumed he got up early, saddled his horse at the livery stable and went for a ride to the hills." She pressed a hand over her stomach, to stop the rise and fall. "When he didn't show up for supper, I headed to Mr. Wolf's house. He seemed surprised to see me. He thought I was in Levi Valley with my friends from Philadelphia who'd come for the christening."

Wyatt tilted his head and frowned.

"I don't have any friends visiting from the city." She sighed, realizing she and Wyatt were on the same side. They both wanted Cole and Melissa to return safely. And if they worked together, they'd figure something out. "I didn't understand at first," she rattled on. "But apparently, Cole told Mr. Wolf at the livery stables I wanted to rent a buggy, the largest covered buggy he has, to show my visitors around. Said Cole oiled up the wheels, polished up the rims and gave him a big deposit, even though Mr. Wolf said it wasn't necessary."

Wyatt lurched forward and sped up his packing. "Did he take his horses?"

She laced her fingers together nervously. "He took one, the one that's broken in. But he sold the other horse to Mr. Wolf. That's when I knew Cole doesn't intend to come back."

Wyatt shot her a disturbing look. She shrank at the dangerous glimmer pulsing in his eyes.

His voice got real cold. "Do you have any idea where they might be headed? Any relatives in another state, where they might go?"

She brushed away a loose strand of hair from her brow. "Just Pennsylvania." Wyatt crossed the floor and dug into an open drawer. She furrowed her brows, deep in thought. "But Cole wouldn't go to Philadelphia. He hates the city."

"Has he talked about any other place he might like to visit?"

"No."

Wyatt snorted. "Of course not. That would be too easy."

"How about Melissa? She ever talked about traveling?" Inching closer, she gripped the bedpost and watched as Wyatt jammed socks into his bag.

"No. She won't go near our kinfolk. She knows I'd chase her down."

"Wait." Her hand froze along the smooth wood as she remembered. "Cole's developed quite an interest in wild horses. He has a friend from Oregon, a fellow he met in passing at the livery stables last week. Cole went on and on about him, even brought him by for supper three days ago. The man says there's a lot of wild horses in Oregon, that someone like Cole could make a fine living."

"You think Cole's headed there?"

"I don't know. But he has a thing for horses, and he seems to be good at catching them."

"Then he could make a good living anywhere up and down the mountains."

"Oregon?" asked Emma. Her eyes narrowed, trying to comprehend it. It seemed their best bet, but where, exactly, in Oregon would they search?

Wyatt shrugged, the lines around his eyes deepening. "We can narrow it down to two choices. If he's heading across the mountains, he could swing south for a couple of weeks, then down across to Oregon. Or he might head north a few days, across Eagle's Pass through the mountains. Then he could settle in any town he pleases on the other side of the Rockies."

She watched him quickly wrap his razor blade in a cloth, his broad shoulders dipping over the bed. "The ride south is a little safer for horse and buggy," he said with a scowl. "Eagle's Pass is a dangerous trail to cross, through heavy woods and mountain crags, but it's closer. It'd only take them three or four days to get there." His voice grew harsh and she tried to keep herself steady.

"Those woods are full of desperate people," he continued, "itching to steal anything you got." He shook his head. "Rusty Jordan got mauled by wolves last year coming back through Eagle's Pass. He lost a leg."

Her body stiffened at his bluntness.

He slammed a pair of pants into his bag. "You think your brother would try something so dangerous, with a baby?"

She hesitated to answer, staring at him, tongue-tied. She didn't know what Cole was capable of anymore, and it frightened her beyond words.

"Sure," said Wyatt, gritting his teeth. "'Course he would." He cursed under his breath. "Well, he's got to leave the Territory, that's for sure. The law's going to be looking all over for him in Montana—"

"The law?" Her throat seized.

"Yeah, the law," he growled, causing her to shiver. "I've been too soft. He's not getting away with kidnapping as well as taking advantage of a minor."

Reaching into his night table, he slid out his Colt and coolly jammed it into the waist of his pants.

Shock flew through her. She swayed back and stammered, "W-what's that for?"

"Protection."

"Protection from a seventeen-year-old boy?"

"Protection *for* a seventeen-year-old boy. Does Cole know how to use a gun? Do you think he took one?"

Her head spun. Her trembling fingers fluttered to her temples. "Oh, please, don't ask me that...I can't bare to think about the danger...."

"I'm asking. This is no game."

Ice ran down her spine. "I suppose he did. Yes, yes, I'm sure. He's a good hunter. He spent most of last summer with his cousins, hunting and trapping in the woods west of here."

"That's good. Maybe he's good enough with a gun that my daughter won't get robbed, or attacked."

She was barely able to control her gasp.

Watching Wyatt buckling up his bag, a sudden thought

occurred to her. She had a plan. With a quick breath of determination, she stepped forward. "I'm coming with you."

His head shot up. "Like hell you are."

"Yes, I am."

"Be reasonable. You'll only slow me down."

"I'm going." She steeled herself, glaring back into his swirling eyes, refusing to back down. If Wyatt and Cole came face-to-face, there was no telling what could happen. "If I don't go, you're liable to kill each other. And little Billy, God, if he picks up the measles, or smallpox…I've got to be there."

Wyatt straightened and ran a hand through his wavy hair. He studied her closely, then turned his back and briskly continued packing. "Fine. You go home and pack. I'll meet you at your door in about an hour. I'll pack the food bag. Jack's waiting outside by the stables, he'll help you. Think you can be ready and packed in an hour?"

"Yes," she said. Gratitude welled up inside her. She nodded and flew out the room and down the stairs. When she reached the bottom, she stopped dead in her tracks.

Clenching her jaw, she raced back up. Her soles hammered on every wooden tread, the soreness in her leg forgotten.

Wyatt glanced up from his bag, speechless.

With her hands propped on her hips, she confronted him. "You bloody coward, why can't you just say it to my face?"

He sighed, looking very weary. "I tried."

"You have no intention of meeting me in town. As soon as I leave this house, you're ducking out the other way."

"You'll only slow me down."

"I can ride fast."

"Not as fast and long as I can."

"Cole and Melissa are traveling in a buggy with a small baby. They'll be going slower at a safer pace. I can catch up quick, riding single."

"I have a feeling that Cole's idea of a safe pace is a lot different from mine." He skimmed her body up and down with an intimate gaze. Her warm shudder of response irritated her. He continued, "Aren't you concerned about what the folks in town will think? You and me, taking off alone without a proper chaperon?"

She flushed from head to toe. With a quick wave of her hand, she brushed off the question. "I don't care what they think. Besides, after what happened at the christening, I can't hold up my head anyway." Her mouth set with new determination. "Let me go with you. If something should happen to Billy, if he caught a fever or some deadly illness, would you ever be able to forgive yourself, turning down a doctor?"

His black eyes sharpened, and he eyed her carefully. "That's an underhanded question."

"It's a valid question. And you're wasting time thinking about it. Let's go." She raced to the drawers and flung a pair of his pants and socks onto the bed.

"What are you doing?" he asked.

"I'm packing clothes *I'm* going to wear."

He tried to grab the clothes but she ripped them out of his hands and threw them back onto the bed. "I'm *going*."

"You can't take these."

"Well, I am. Melissa's clothes are too small. Yours will have to do."

"Not these," he said, tossing them aside. "The pants have holes and the socks are ripped."

"Oh."

"Bachelor's clothes," he explained. He tossed her some others. "Take these, they're newer." Pulling out another bag from beneath the bed, he helped her pack. "I know I'm going to regret this." He shook his head.

She glanced down at her long skirt and constricting blouse. "I'll change into pants, it'll be easier to ride." Bundling up the clothes, she added, "I'll change in the other room."

"I'll wait for you downstairs."

She took one long, hard look at him and swore. "Bloody hell, you'll take off on me."

Before he had a chance to blink, she took the pants and clawed them up her legs, then shed her skirt and flung it onto the bed.

He stood there, amazed. His eyes lit up, watching her contorted efforts. A smile found its way through his mask of anger and broke on his lips.

A flash of humor crossed her face. "I'm glad you still have it in you to smile."

He tilted his head in a gallant gesture and her pulse skittered, to her annoyance.

She strode to the armoire and slid out a belt. It wrapped one and a half times around her waist. She'd leave her blouse dangling the way it was, her corset would have to come off later. "There, that's better. Do you have a jacket?"

"Downstairs in the kitchen. We'll get it and your medical bag on the way out. But here, you need one more thing."

He pulled out a shiny derringer from his night table. "Put this in your bag."

Suddenly sobered, she drew back. "I don't think so."

"Take it." He held it out.

She made no move to get it. "I hate guns."

"I'm not asking you to love it."

"I could never shoot anyone. Ever."

"We're riding into dangerous territory. Even doctors have a right to defend themselves, don't they?"

She hesitated for a moment, staring down at the shiny little pistol. It was almost pretty. Then she shook her head. "No, I could never pull the trigger."

He let out a moan of frustration. "Then take the pocketknife at least. I'll keep your pistol in my pack for now and show you how to use it later."

He tossed her the knife and, not wanting to argue further, she slid it into her pant pocket.

On the way to the stables, they met up with Grandpa, who was obviously distressed. He squinted in the fading orange light, his blunt gray hair poking out under his rumpled hat. "Jack just told me. What's this about Cole disappearin'?"

Wyatt explained everything as Emma listened in anguish.

Grandpa slumped back. "That's why her hair was combed."

"What?" asked Wyatt.

"I heard the baby cryin' around two this mornin', and I came down to the kitchen. Melissa had just finished feedin' him. She was still in nightclothes and shooed me back to bed. When I went back to my room, I thought somethin' looked strange. I didn't put my finger on it till later. Her hair was combed. Who would comb their hair at two in the mornin' to feed a baby?" He looked from Emma to Wyatt.

"Did you see her after that?"

"No, I let her sleep. I figured she'd been up durin' the night, she was tired. And later, I—I went into town, visiting with Miss Molly...."

"They must have left shortly after two." Wyatt's eyes met with hers and she swallowed the desperation in her throat.

He peered at the blazing red sunset. "It's seven. They

got seventeen hours' lead on us.'' His commanding voice picked up urgency. "Grandpa, I need you to go into town with Jack. Tell Sheriff McCabe what's happened. Tell him we're headed to Eagle's Pass—"

"Why not Oregon?" Emma said.

"Because Cole's probably counting that we'll do just that, go south, on account of his friend. And Cole also strikes me as the impatient type," Wyatt added sarcastically. "Eagle's Pass is a shorter ride to freedom."

As much as she hated to agree with him, it made sense.

Wyatt swung back to Grandpa. "Tell Sheriff McCabe to charge Cole with everything he can think of—"

"Now just a minute—" Emma interjected.

"Well, it's about time you threw the law books at him," said Grandpa. His mouth twisted at Emma. "Don't give me the evil eye, woman. You know your brother's nothin' but trouble."

Emma struggled to restrain her tongue. Some sixth sense told her it was a good thing she was going with Wyatt, otherwise Cole would be lynched in the blink of an eye. It was up to her to avert the deadly confrontation.

Wyatt's jaw tightened. "Send Jack to Emma's mother to let her know Emma's coming with me. Then tell Sheriff McCabe to press charges, and to telegraph the law in every town he can think of. Tell him I'll pay. And listen, Grandpa, this is very important. Jim will come by, if not tonight when he hears the news, then in the morning. Listen carefully. Tell Jim we *are* headed south, to Idaho Falls, then on to Oregon. Don't tell him the truth. It'll buy us some time."

Grandpa squinted. "You figure he'll go after Cole?"

"Damn right he will."

"Oh, lordie, lordie."

Emma wasn't convinced. Her mind floundered with the

heavy thought. She hadn't even considered Jim. "How do you know? How can you be so sure?"

"Because I know Jim." Wyatt's face hardened. His voice held an edge Emma had never heard before, and it sent chills down her back. "Because I grew up with him and know what he's capable of. Because I saw the menacing look in his eye yesterday when Cole punched him in the face."

His gaze riveted on her face. "And because I can feel it, crackling in the air around me."

Chapter Twelve

Cool wind whipped through Emma's hair and over the brim of her hat. The hard saddle pressed up against her as she clamped her legs around her mare's straining muscles. Her own clenched thighs and buttocks screamed for release. She and Wyatt had been riding for three hours, but she sure as thunder wasn't going to be the first to suggest they stop for camp. She'd show him how tough she was. She wouldn't be slowing *anyone* down.

The dim blue light of a three-quarter moon lit their path. Fortunately, a cloudless sky allowed the brilliant stars to shine, otherwise the dirt track beneath them wouldn't be as clear, and they wouldn't be galloping as fast.

Wyatt charged ahead of her on his sleek, black gelding, every now and then glancing back. Emma supposed he was checking to see if she was still there. Half of her wondered what he'd do if he happened to glance back to find her gone. He'd probably keep on riding and say to blazes with her.

Well, to blazes with *him;* that wasn't going to happen. She leaned into her horse and urged it faster.

Come hell or high water, she'd be at Wyatt's side when he found Cole and Melissa. To protect her poor brother from Wyatt's wrath. Her lips twisted in anger at both men. Secretly, she intended to blast Cole with a few words of her own. How could he lead everyone through this danger? Especially a newborn child?

Her mouth set in a grim line. Billy hadn't reached full term yet. He was gaining an ounce of weight every day, up to eight pounds now. His feedings were going well and for the last four days, he hadn't needed goat's milk. But what if Melissa's milk dried up because of the strain of the ride? How would they supplement the baby? Had they thought of it?

It was one of many ugly scenes playing through Emma's mind, and one she dared not mention to Wyatt.

She tugged at the soft cloth of her jacket, *his* jacket, and wrapped it tighter. Although the summer days in Montana were hot, the evenings and nights were cool.

They kept riding until the path grew darker. Brush and trees closed in on them, and the wide-open stretch of the road they began on shifted into narrow ribbons.

Wyatt slowed his horse to a trot and she fell in behind him. A fork appeared in the road and, without hesitation, Wyatt veered to the left. Emma settled back into her saddle. Wyatt obviously knew this land, and his confidence was reassuring.

Up ahead, between a cluster of pines, moonlight skimmed across a glistening lake. Her mare whinnied.

Wyatt slowed his gelding and pulled over beside her. "We'll make camp here. We've pushed the horses hard. They need water and rest."

He dismounted with expert agility. Her legs shook like marmalade as she descended. When her boots hit the ground, her body wavered and kept on going.

Wyatt shot out a powerful arm and steadied her. "Whoa...take it easy."

She flicked his tight grip off her arm. It'd be easier if he didn't touch her. "I'm fine." But she wasn't. The dirt road heaved up in front of her eyes and nausea welled up her throat. She tried to gulp down a bitter mouthful, but it crept back up.

In the smoky moonlight, Wyatt stared at her. She couldn't see his eyes, but something about his intense gaze caused her thoughts to scatter. She gazed over his silhouette, the strong outline of his hat, his gently rounded cheek and the straight line of his jaw.

"Take it easy," he said. "I imagine you haven't ridden this hard for years."

Her back straightened. She stammered. "I'm a little out of practice, but...I'm fine."

He released her and she, like a spinning top out of control, stumbled forward into the forest. "I need to use the bushes." Sour bile bit at her tongue. She reached the first tree, ducked behind it, bent her head down and vomited.

Heaving in relief, she sagged against the gnarled trunk and filled her lungs with cool forest air. Bloody hell, she'd get through this, without Wyatt noticing her difficulties.

When she finally stepped out of the woods, he'd already hitched the horses to the trees by the lake, and was collecting kindling. Their saddlebags lay propped against a fallen log.

She wove her way to the clear water, kneeled on a boulder, and rinsed her face and mouth. That was better. She felt more herself.

Returning to the small clearing, she watched Wyatt, crouched low to the ground, stacking the wood in a triangle to build a fire. The combination of his broad shoulders and unbuttoned, open vest made him look large and forbidding. His hat was slung low, over his eyes, and if she didn't know better, she'd swear a part of him was in his glory, building a fire and making camp.

He didn't bother to look up at her and she felt a little snubbed. "There's some jerky in my bag if you're hungry," he said.

The thought of jerky made her nauseous again, but she braced herself, realizing she needed to eat to keep her strength. "I'll wait for you, whenever you're ready."

"Suit yourself." Reaching into the pocket of his vest, he pulled out a tin of matches. "You all right?"

"Never better," she piped up with an exaggerated smile. Watching him ignite the crackling wood, she slid onto a log directly across from him in the circle of fire. Her shoulders jerked up with a revelation. Lord, he hadn't seen her getting sick behind the tree, had he? "Why do you ask?"

The warm glow of firelight danced across his face. "I could hear you vomiting clear across the lake."

Her face tingled. "Oh." She thought she'd been quiet.

He added thicker logs to the fire. She could see his eyes now, between the blazing flames that separated them, and they gazed straight at her. "Sorry you came?"

"Not at all."

A smile curved across his full lips. "You're tougher than you look."

She quivered at the way he said it, then squirmed her rear end on the hard log, irritated his opinion meant so much to her. "Damn right I am."

The warmth of his grin echoed in his features and for an uncontrollable second, she had an urge to whip a stick at him.

Instead, she wriggled closer to the fire. It calmed her. She basked in the warmth that seared her cheeks, her arms and through the supple denim of her pants into her thighs.

Rising, he reached into his saddlebag and pulled out two

sticks of jerky. He tossed her one and she took a bite, then chased it down with a swig of water from her leather pouch.

He returned to his log. After a few moments of watching the fire, he said, "You're awfully quiet."

"Mmm-hmm." The muscles in her legs felt loose and warm. Without thinking, she absently massaged her left calf. It felt wonderful, releasing the tension in her body. When she noticed him watching her, his eyes moving slowly over her body, she stopped rubbing.

He bit off a piece of jerky like a man who hadn't eaten for days. "How long do you think Cole and Melissa have been planning this?"

Emma frowned, irked by his question. She peered into his eyes. It was a mistake to look at him. Her pulse strummed at the intensity of his gaze and sighing, she turned away, preferring to stare into the fire. She had more control over her feelings. "I don't think they've been planning it for long. Only since yesterday, when you refused them permission to marry."

His body stiffened and his mouth dropped open. "Are you blaming me for their disappearance?"

Her muscles tensed. *Yes!* "It doesn't make any difference. They're gone." The fire crackled. "I never saw Cole once today. How did he contact Melissa? Did he come by?"

"No chance. Someone would have told me. The last time I saw Melissa was last night, when the messenger delivered your goodbye note."

"What note?"

He stared at her. "You didn't send one?"

"No."

He shook his head. "Well, there's our answer. Cole sent her a note. Hell, right underneath my nose. If Cole weren't so damn cocky—"

She cut him off with curt words. "Whatever else you believe about Cole, you do know he'd die protecting Melissa and the baby, don't you?"

"That's what concerns me. He's putting them in a situation where he may *have* to die protecting them."

She crossed her arms. "He'd never do that, knowingly."

His stare drilled into her until she was forced to look away. "He's not taking them to a carnival. He's taking them into the Rocky Mountains. Untamed wilderness. Drifters, Indians. None of whom are partial to strangers."

Why did he have to keep reminding her of that? She was well aware of it.

Wyatt jumped to his feet. He poked the fire with a stick. "One of the last things Cole said to me at the christening was that he can beat my horses. Remember? Now he's trying to prove it to me."

Emma shook her head in exasperation. "Oh, for crying out loud..." She stared into the fire. Why did Cole and Wyatt have to argue about every single thing? Honestly, they were two of a kind, if they could only see it.

The wind shifted and he batted a whisper of smoke that drifted his way. He peered down at her, a line of suspicion deepening around his eyes. "Are you telling me everything you know about Cole's disappearance? You're not hiding anything, are you?"

She shrugged to hide her guilt. It gnawed at her. She did know one more thing, but should she tell him?

His eyes narrowed. His voice quieted as if he were talking to a child. "Let's make a truce. If we want to find Melissa and Cole, we have to be honest with each other."

Her lips thinned with irritation. "I'm not sure I can trust you. When you find him, what do you plan on doing to him?"

Wyatt sighed and stared into the fire. "I don't know myself."

She gulped. "You said you were going to charge him with everything you can. What does that mean? Rape? Kidnapping?"

"He's guilty, isn't he?"

Her heart squeezed. "Not of those things." Emma shook her head gently. "As difficult as this may be for you to hear, Melissa had a hand in all of this. She's a willing participant, and their only fault is they love each other. Is that such a crime?" She trembled, looking into his eyes.

He swallowed. The hard edge to his expression softened. His eyes glistened and he stared at her as if he wanted to add something, but then he slid off his hat and ran his fingers through his hair. "You didn't answer my question. What more do you know?"

The intimate moment was gone, replaced by an emptiness in her heart. "If—*when*—we find them, what do you plan on doing?"

"I plan on taking Melissa and the baby home, screaming and kicking if I have to."

"And Cole?"

The fire spit and crackled in the silence. "A good bout in jail might do him some good. Not to mention how good it would make me feel."

She jerked back at his harsh comment. How can he be so cruel? Her braid bounced off her shoulders. "Then I'm not telling you what else I know."

He flung his hands into the air. "Look, I'm not sure what I'm going to do to Cole. But if I hadn't told the sheriff to press charges, he wouldn't be helping us search for them right now." She glanced up in surprise, and he inclined his dark head and stared at the fire. "The sheriff's got other things to do than help us find two runaway teens. But if one of them broke the law, with serious crimes like kidnapping, that's another thing altogether.''

Her breathing snagged. That was why he'd sent the sheriff that menacing order to press charges? To ask for help, not to punish Cole? Well, yes, of course, what a wonderful idea. And when the sheriff caught the two young people, Wyatt could drop the charges. She looked across the fire at him with newfound respect and amused wonder.

He scowled at her reaction and shrugged her off. ''Now stop smiling. I didn't do it for Cole. I did it for Melissa.''

He sighed, then his expression softened. His eyes shimmered. ''Come clean. What else do you know?''

''All right, a truce.'' She motioned to her medicine bag, sitting among the saddlebags. ''I have a secret flap in my medicine bag, where I keep emergency money when I travel. Cole saw me slip some money into it last week, after I came from the bank. A hundred dollars is missing.''

''He stole money from you?'' Wyatt pushed his hat off his brow and shook his head. ''His standard of virtue never ceases to amaze me.''

She jumped to Cole's defense. ''If my brother needs money, I'm happy to give it to him.'' She hadn't disclosed the information to Wyatt in order for him to judge her brother. ''He left a note, saying he'd pay me back.''

Wyatt gazed at her in disbelief and stretched his legs out in front of him. ''Did he say where you could write to him?''

''No,'' she said, his silly question hitting a chord of amusement. Her voice filled with undiluted laughter. ''The note didn't say where I could reach him.''

He grimaced in a smile. ''So they have a bit of money on them, added to the sale of Cole's horse and any money he might have saved while working for Mr. Wolf. Enough to last six months, maybe?''

Wyatt clapped his hands on his thighs, rose and dusted off his pants. "I'll go get the bedrolls."

Her nerves jangled, and her face flushed at the mention of bed. She watched him get the blankets and come back to the fire. Where, exactly, did he intend on unrolling them? Together, or apart? Catching her off guard, he tossed a bundle toward her, letting her choose for herself.

"I'm sleeping over here," he said, spreading his roll out by the fire. While she was still deciding, he lay down, tugged his hat over his eyes, and crossed one arm over the other. "You can sleep over here, beside me, if you're afraid of the animals, or over there where you are. Your choice. Best to stay close to the fire, though. Animals are afraid of fire."

Animals? She gulped. What kind of animals, she wondered, peering through the thick bushes. She couldn't see a thing through the dark trunks in the forest.

"Coyotes, wolves, skunks," he answered, as if reading her mind. "We don't have to worry about the grizzlies until we reach higher ground. Even snakes."

Her pulse leaped at the mention of snakes. Squinting into the darkness, she gasped at the two shiny circles staring back at her. They flickered and disappeared. Her imagination? Mustering courage, she slid forward, taking a closer look. Was there a creature out there?

A twig snapped and she jumped. That's all the motivation she needed. Scooting over to Wyatt's side of the fire, she unrolled her bedroll in line with his, their heads almost butted up against each other's.

She longed to rub the smirk off his face. "I hate snakes," she muttered. She darted underneath the top blanket, clutching the rough wool in her hands. Turning on the hard ground, she removed her jacket, *his jacket,* and punched it into the shape of a pillow.

They didn't talk. Soon, the heat from the fire warmed her front, and when she rolled over to allow the fire to heat her backside, she drifted into a soothing sleep.

She didn't know what time it was when she awoke. It was the middle of the night, judging from the black stillness. She was facing the fire again, it was blazing high and Wyatt was standing beside it, leg propped on a log, poking at the flames with a stick. What was he thinking about, so lost in thought?

She watched him for a while, his strong, dark features illuminated by the warm glow of light, his broad triangular back silhouetted as he twisted. She grew warm with longing. Her whole being filled with an ache to touch him.

Under different circumstances, what would it be like to be here as his wife or lover? Traveling to another town with him, maybe to pick up a new horse, or to see a new sight? A shudder passed through her and her heart began to pulse. They'd share the same bedroll then. They'd make love by the fire.

She blinked and watched his worn leather boots shuffle in the dirt. Reality tugged at her, and her heart twisted and crumpled. These weren't different circumstances. She'd never be his lover or his wife, no matter how much she loved him.

A knot rose to her throat. Silently, she closed her eyes and let grogginess overtake her. Sinking her face into his jacket, she inhaled deeply. His intoxicating scent enveloped her and soothed her frayed soul. At least she'd have him for a few days, while they were on the run.

And at this moment, it was perfect. To safely close her eyes, to turn her back to the fire and know she'd be taken care of by Wyatt.

She believed in his strength. If anyone could find Melissa and Cole and the baby quickly, it'd be him. If anyone could take care of her and make her feel protected out here in the wilderness, it was Wyatt. He'd tend to the critical fire, and he'd watch for nasty predators.

She mellowed and let her body float on a dreamy cloud. For the first time in years, since before she'd entered medicine, it felt magnificent to let her guard down and bask in the fact that she was the one being protected, and not the one doing the protecting. Someone was looking after her.

She tucked the blanket under her chin, smiling softly to herself, and fell into a deep intoxicating sleep. Dreaming wistfully, sensually, of the man standing three feet away.

Wyatt had a crick in his arm. Lying on his bedroll, he slowly rose on an elbow and shook it out. It was still dark between the trees, but shafts of light were filtering through the branches. The air was fresh and damp. Judging from the coolness, the fire had to be out. He rolled over to take a look and almost rolled on top of Emma.

His breath trapped in his lungs. She was sleeping peacefully, and for a minute, he didn't move.

His eyes traveled over the soft curves of her face and over her long dark lashes to the gentle upturn of her full, pink lips. In her sleep, she clutched the blanket over her shoulder and held it tightly under her chin, but it was impossible to hide the gentle round of her breasts and the alluring curve of her hips.

His body tightened. Tenderly, he reached out with a slow hand and stroked her supple cheek. Her eyes fluttered but she didn't wake.

She looked like an angel when she slept. Too bad when she woke up, all she seemed to evoke from him was the devil. She was as stubborn as she was tough, and even though that made it more difficult for him, he was glad she was here.

He drew his hand back with hesitation, torn in conflicting emotions. He was glad she was here?

His heart stilled in contemplation. He did find pleasure in her company, and appreciated her point of view. As much as they argued, he knew she had nothing but the best of intentions for Melissa and the baby.

Emma was strong. She could shoulder a lot of problems. And he didn't feel so all alone when he shared his problems with her.

Ah, well, she was not for him, though, was she? In a lithe and silent motion, he rose to his feet. She was leaving the Territory in less than three weeks. In his kinder, quieter moments, he knew he wished her nothing but happiness in the life she chose in Philadelphia. With any man she chose.

Grabbing the coffeepot, he walked to the lake and filled it with water. Cole, on the other hand, was another matter. Wyatt would square it with him first chance he got. Where were Cole and Melissa this morning? Had they made it safely through the night? What had happened with Jim? Had Grandpa been able to stop him? Wyatt's skin bristled thinking about the possible dangers. And the little baby, how was he?

When Wyatt returned to the fire, he sliced up the smoked bacon he'd packed and tossed it into the frying pan. It was sizzling and heating up the air when Emma awoke.

"Is that bacon I smell?" Emma rose on her elbows. "If you pull some eggs out of your saddlebag," she said in a groggy voice, "and throw them in as well, I'll be mighty impressed."

He returned her warm smile. "Sorry, no eggs."

She sat up. Her face was rumpled and her hair fell in a tangle. When her blanket slid down her body, her baggy shirt gaped open and revealed a bare shoulder. His breath caught. His gaze traveled further down the cloth, and he realized her corset was gone.

He threw his gaze back to his cooking.

"Good morning," she said, rising slowly, stretching her arms above her head. He was grateful when she shoved her arms through her jacket sleeves and covered up her body.

"Good morning." He noticed she didn't look as green as she had last night. Seeing her dressed in his clothes, he felt a strange sensation flash through his gut, a crazy kind of pride. He shrugged it away.

They finished breakfast quickly, and he wondered if it was his imagination, or was she racing with him? Emma was fast. She was packed and ready to go as he was shoveling the last scoop of dirt onto the fire.

She dashed to the lake, unhitched their horses and brought them back. She stared at him in silence when he slid out his holster and tied it to his leg.

"There's no sense hiding my gun," he explained. "We might as well show we know how to defend ourselves, to anyone who might be looking."

She only nodded.

He slung his rifle back over his horse, and while he had her attention, he removed the loaded derringer from his pack and showed her how to pull the trigger. She watched but wouldn't agree to take it. He shook his head at her reluctance. Walking over to her horse, he slid it inside one of her packs, where she'd know where to find it. He hoped to hell she'd never need it, but just in case, it was there.

She mounted her mare. With a backward glance, just the right amount of impatience in her voice and a hint of a smile, she asked, "Are you ready yet?"

"I knew it! You were racing with me."

"And I won, too."

He found it impossible not to laugh.

The morning passed in serenity. The whitecapped mountains grew steadily closer, and the foothills got steeper. Even the vegetation was changing. It was thicker, more firs and pines, and the birds and animals calling to each other grew louder, if you stood long and still enough to listen.

Wyatt stopped several times to peer into the dry earth, desperately hoping to catch sight of their tracks. It hadn't rained for weeks in this area, and it was difficult to follow tracks. There were two sets that might be Cole and Melissa's. By a process of elimination, he vowed he'd find them.

Right after lunch, they met up with a furniture maker and his wife, making a delivery to Great Falls. The couple huddled together in a covered wagon, three small children sleeping in the back, with two newly made rockers and a shiny wooden chest.

Wyatt snapped to attention when they said they'd passed a youthful couple and their baby, fitting Cole's and Melissa's descriptions, yesterday at noon.

Emma tugged anxiously at her reins. "How did the baby look? Did he look well?"

The man nodded and ran a hand along his unshaven cheek. "Mighty fine. My wife here had a closer look."

Wyatt tensed, waiting for her reply. She fiddled with her bonnet. The children mumbled behind her and she motioned for them to hush. Turning and smiling at Emma, she revealed half a row of yellowed teeth. "He was sleepin' as cozy as a little bird in a nest, all wrapped up in his basket."

Wyatt's heart warmed at the news. "Did they say which way they were headed?"

The man motioned to the mountains behind him. "Said they were going to visit kin near Eagle's Pass, who hadn't seen the baby yet. Said not to worry, they weren't going far." The man squinted at Wyatt. "Are you kin?"

"I'm her father."

The man peered at Wyatt with polite curiosity. He tipped his hat as he rolled out. "Well, hope whatever disagreement you may have had with your daughter works out and that you and your wife have a fine day."

With a twinge of embarrassment, Wyatt nodded goodbye. He glanced at Emma. He couldn't read her expression behind those round, shimmering eyes, but it was a natural conclusion, that someone should think they were married. She glanced at him and their eyes locked, awakening a flame inside him. Neither of them bothered to correct the furniture maker.

Wyatt watched them pull away. Halfway down the rutted road, the wagon shuddered to a stop and the furniture maker peered around the corner. "Be careful on that narrow stretch of road between here and the village of Bloomington. Some low-down thief's been attackin' and robbin' people. Marshal's been notified from Great Falls."

Grateful for the warning, Wyatt tipped his hat. He'd be extra careful.

They rode hard for the rest of the day, stopping long enough to rest the horses. Dusk was starting to fall when rain hit. A warm trickle, not strong enough to keep them from riding, just wet enough to dampen their enthusiasm. They'd soon be at the base of Mount Eagle, Wyatt figured, then Bloomington. He'd be happy with their day's travel if they could make it to the inn there. They'd have a hot meal.

Emma didn't raise an ounce of complaint. As they galloped side by side, he slid his gaze over her, taking in the damp jacket and the rain-splashed hat that dipped low over her face. His flesh shivered at her feminine curves. He admired her for her perseverance. Not many women would ride this hard, for this long. Especially a city woman. She must be sore all over. At least she was off her feet, and he didn't have the extra guilt of making her sore leg worse.

The path dipped ahead and she leaned forward, her brows furrowed. "Wyatt, what's that on the road? A fallen branch?"

His body rose on the horse to look. His pulse sped up at the view. A huge branch was draped across their path, but there was no lightning or wind to have caused the fall. There was a clearing to the side of the road. He couldn't tell for sure, but it looked like someone may have dragged the branch across the road. *To make them stop.*

His pulse started pounding. "Don't stop, Emma! Speed up, jump over it, it's a trap!" He leaned into his horse and gathered momentum, safely making the leap to the other side.

Gasping, he looked back. Too late. Emma hadn't gathered enough speed, and her horse reared to a stop.

Good girl, though, she held on tight while her horse simmered down. He pulled his own horse to a stop and circled back. His nerves bouncing inside his chest, he darted glances to the woods. He drew his gun. The forest was too quiet.

Rain flickered off the brim of his hat. His horse snorted.

Emma's eyes widened with fright as she looked around her. "Sorry, Wyatt," she whispered in the eerie silence. "I couldn't do it in time."

"Don't worry. No harm done. It's probably just my imagination." With a final glance and nothing visible, Wyatt slid off his horse. He had to turn his back to Emma for a moment. With his gun clutched in one hand, he pulled the branch off to the side of the road with little effort. "There you go," he said, his muscles relaxing as he stepped back to face Emma.

His heart stopped beating at the sight of her.

A rusty rifle was pointed at her head.

The man was old and grimy, about sixty, unshaven gray whiskers matting his face. "I ain't playin' any games, missus," he addressed Emma. "Get off your horse and tell your husband to drop his gun, real slow."

Chapter Thirteen

Emma shuddered and didn't dare breathe. She felt an icy dread spreading through her stomach. Trembling, with the cold metal barrel pressed against her temple, she watched the look of horror pass through Wyatt's eyes. As the stranger coolly held the gun to her head, she dismounted.

With a curse, Wyatt lowered his gun and tossed it to the ground.

If only she'd listened and taken the derringer, if only she'd been able to leap over the branch—

The barrel jabbed against her face. "Where's yer money?"

With shaky knees, Emma battled whiskey fumes. Without moving her head, she turned her eyes to the ugly man holding the gun. Dressed in dirty rags, his cheekbones hollow, one of his front teeth wobbled as he spoke. It dangled over his bottom lip as rain dripped over the brim of his hat.

Wyatt looked at him as if he were a vulture who needed his neck snapped, and the way Wyatt's fists were clenching open and closed at his sides, it looked as if he were contemplating doing just that.

"Where's yer money?" the man repeated louder. He

prodded Emma with the rifle between her shoulder blades and scooped down to pick up Wyatt's gun.

Wyatt gritted his teeth, standing tall in the rain. She wished she could run into his protective arms. "Leave her alone. I carry the money. It's in my saddlebag. The right side, second pocket down."

"I ain't fallin' for yer tricks. Yer wife can git it. You stay put."

Swallowing her fear, Emma shuffled to the black gelding with a gun jabbing her back. Breathing deeply, she pulled out a billfold and passed it to the old man.

She'd give him whatever he wanted.

He stepped back and she swung around slowly to face him. Wyatt stepped forward to grab her and she instinctively melted toward him, but the man jerked his rifle higher, stopping Wyatt in his tracks.

"Stay where you are, mister." He slid his moist dark gaze toward Emma, and she noticed his eyes were bloodshot. Lack of sleep? Whiskey? "Where's yer jewelry?"

"I don't have any."

"What's that chain danglin' from yer pocket?"

Her pocketwatch. The one her family had given her for graduation. She gulped and clawed it out, tossing it toward him. She'd gladly give him anything as long as he left.

He rubbed his greasy palm on his dirty pants. "And yer weddin' ring?"

Her heart turned over. She glanced at Wyatt and his brown eyes glistened with compassion. "I don't have one," she said in a firm voice.

The man looked at her ringless fingers and sneered. "Sure. Why bother gittin' married?"

Her shoulders jerked back in outrage. With a blast of contempt, Wyatt lurched forward and the man cocked his gun at him, stopping Wyatt cold.

Her throat closed up. "No, please," she begged. Gazing at Wyatt, her eyes pleaded for him to back down. A muscle twitched at his throat. He stepped back.

"A little touchy aren't ya, about yer woman? How touchy are ya about yer horses?" He whistled in delight at the horses. "I was hopin' the next people who passed by would have a fine horse, but I didn't expect them to be this fine. Horses like this could fetch me a good dollar."

Her thoughts raced through a muddle of logic. Their lives for their horses. That wasn't so bad. He could take whatever he wanted, as long as he disappeared. With a sickening quake rolling through her insides, she motioned to her mare. "Take my horse and be done with it." He could take one, and she and Wyatt could still share the other.

Wyatt's mouth contorted. His face darkened and his whole body leaned forward. *"No."*

Oh, God, he wasn't going to fight this man, was he?

The greedy, bloodshot eyes narrowed and Emma took deep breaths until she was strong enough to look at Wyatt again.

Wyatt's lips twitched. An artery throbbed at the base of his throat. "Horse thieving's a major crime. You'll be hanged if they catch you."

"I ain't plannin' on gettin' caught."

"But if you do, you'll be hanged."

The gray head jerked back. "You tryin' to get me riled up?" He raised the barrel of his rifle, which was rusty and twisted. The man didn't take care of himself, or his weapons.

Wyatt shifted straighter, and spoke with confidence. "I've got something you can have that's more valuable than these two horses put together."

The man squinted. "Yeah? Like what?"

What was it? Emma wondered, hoping, by some miracle, he could send the man on his way.

"Something no one's got within hundreds of miles of here. Something even a gang of criminals would pay a hefty dollar for—I'd say at least three hundred dollars, maybe more. And it's not horse thieving, and you wouldn't be hung."

Emma squirmed nervously in the dirt as the soft rain misted against her cheek. Was Wyatt bluffing?

The man pointed the rifle straight at Wyatt's head and she froze and held her breath. "I ain't got time fer games. What is it?"

Wyatt swallowed and nodded at Emma's horse. "A medicine bag."

She gasped in horror. *"Wyatt!"*

Wyatt slid his calm gaze toward her. He inclined his head and clamped his lips, as if to say *Be quiet.* Damn him, he was serious!

The gun lowered. "A medicine bag?" The man grinned and leered at her. "Is that yer medicine bag, missus?"

Outraged, her mouth gaping, she glared at Wyatt, and then at the seedy face staring at her. "You can't have it!"

"You a doctor? I ain't never met a woman doctor before."

"You can't have it!" she insisted.

In the dusk, the man grinned again, and light bounced off his shiny forehead. He shook his head with pleasure. "Must be worth a lot."

Emma kicked the dirt with her boot, trying to control the heated throbbing in her veins. "Take one of our horses, they're worth a lot—"

"Not as much as a medicine bag," Wyatt interjected, infuriating her beyond words. "And stealing medicine to help sick folks, criminals or not, I don't reckon a judge would look down on you for that.''

Her muscles wound like tight springs. How could he even suggest it? Her whole life was in that bag! Melissa and Cole and Billy might need those medicines. And how could she be a doctor without a medicine bag? Didn't he understand? Her gut clenched and she shouted, ''Nooo!''

With a humorless smile on his face, the man gazed from Wyatt to Emma, to the horses and back. Maybe he'd take everything, medicine bag and horses! What would Wyatt do then? He was getting them deeper into trouble!

Wyatt must have been thinking the same thing. ''On second thought, maybe you should take my horses. They're branded and their tracks are visible. The marshal from Great Falls is on his way, and he could track you down in no time. But if you only had a doctor's bag, I reckon you could disappear in a puff of smoke, just like magic.''

''Just like magic,'' the man mumbled.

Emma seethed with mounting rage. She wouldn't be a victim. She wished they'd brought the Arabians and every horse Wyatt owned so the thief could take them. ''My personal instruments are in there,'' she blurted madly, ''some of them forged in England.''

''You can buy more,'' said Wyatt in a tempering voice.

''Not like these! It took me years to find the ones that suit me best. And what about my medicines? I've built a collection.''

The man rubbed his scruffy chin. ''Medicines are worth a lot, 'specially in these parts.''

''So are sutures and bandages and modern tonics,'' said Wyatt.

''Listen,'' Emma implored Wyatt, clenching her teeth, ''we *need* those medicines. For your daughter. For our trip.''

Wyatt shook his head stubbornly.

The man pointed his rifle at the bag. "Got any opium in there?"

The question stopped her cold. Alarm rose to her throat. She'd seen opium users in Philadelphia, and she couldn't remember a sorrier sight. "Opium is strong medicine," she said in a blunt tone. "It'll kill you. *Please,* don't take it."

The man grinned. "Untie the bag and toss it here."

Wyatt did as he was told, relief washing over his face, and Emma knew, as long as she lived, she'd never forgive him for giving away her doctor's bag. She shrank as she watched her shiny leather bag, her source of pride and accomplishment, disappear into the shaky hands of a thief.

As he grabbed the bag, he stopped and peered down the road, his head tilted as if he were listening for something.

"I hear them, too," said Wyatt. "Horses coming. Maybe the marshal."

Thank God, help. Her breathing hitched with a flurry of hope. Before she could say more, the man shoved them down to the side of the road. While Emma trembled from head to toe, he knotted their fists together behind their backs and tied a handkerchief around their mouths.

In a cloud of whiskey breath, the man sneered. He crouched down low beside Wyatt. "Now, you see, if I shoot my gun, I'm liable to attract some attention. Lucky for you, I'm feeling generous. Oh, and thanks for the rifle, mister," he said, caressing the shiny gun he'd taken off Wyatt's horse, "I never had me a gun this fine."

Disappearing into the black woods, he left them stranded. He didn't even have the decency to hitch their horses to a tree.

She tried to spit the rag out of her mouth with no success. With her rigid back pressed up against Wyatt's, her curves molding to the contours of his muscles, she sat in a puddle of mud, so very conscious of where his warm flesh was touching hers. She was going to kill him.

The sun was almost down behind the treetops. Cool mud oozed around Wyatt's thighs. Thank God they were safe. He didn't know which burned deeper inside of him. Fury or relief.

The dirty rag in his mouth stunk like whiskey and cigars. The rope dug into his wrists. He tugged at his hands and Emma's, and managed to loosen the slack. He'd kept his hands rigid while the old man had bound them. The geezer had been in a hurry and didn't do as tight a job as he should have.

Wyatt peered through the dark woods for any trace of him, but saw nothing. His blood churned with rage. If he didn't have Emma to protect, he sure as hell would chase the vermin down and deliver him personally to the marshal.

Up ahead around the bend, he could hear their horses, chomping on grass. The horses weren't going anywhere.

Emma's warm backside wriggled and slid along his. He could learn to like the feeling. He heard her spit out her cloth. *"How dare you give away my bag!"*

Did he have to contend with her anger now? Why couldn't her rag have stayed in for a little longer? A final tug with his tongue and he shoved his own cloth out of his mouth. "I had to do it, he would have taken our horses."

Her body heaved up and down. "We could have ridden on one horse." Her shoulders jerked forward, dragging his own with them.

He had to fight her to regain his balance. "Sit still and I'll untie us! Do you honestly think he'd take one horse? He'd hang for one horse just as high for two. So why not take two?" He clawed at the ropes.

Her voice was hoarse. "Billy and Melissa might need those medicines. How could you do that to them?"

"We wouldn't have a prayer without horses. Move closer. There's a pocket knife in my front vest pocket. If you could manage to slide around me, I think the ropes are loose enough, you could try to reach inside my pocket with your mouth and grab the knife. We could cut the ropes."

Obeying his order, she squirmed to his side. "I can't get that close." She yanked hard and nearly pulled his shoulder out of his socket.

"Owww!" Wyatt tugged at the muddy knot and it loosened another inch. He curled his body closer so she could twist around him to reach his pocket.

"You should have negotiated better. He would have left us one horse."

"You're wrong."

"Don't tell me I'm wrong," she hurled. "Not after giving away a *six-hundred dollar* medicine bag!"

"I knew it was worth a lot." He felt her fists ball up next to his and was glad her hands were tied.

"Don't talk to me!"

"All right, just move closer."

Madder than hell, she slid up against him real tight, and with an amazing feat of agility, turned her head slowly and slid the knife out of his pocket with her heated mouth and tongue. If his heart wasn't pounding so hard in his ears, he might have been able to enjoy the charming experience.

When he finally cut them loose, she sprang up from the damp earth, her pants caked with mud.

He rose and tried to dust off his seat, but the cool dampness had soaked right through. "Can you hear them now?"

"The horses? Yeah, I hear them." She swiped the messy strand of hair off her brow and unknowingly streaked a line of mud across her forehead.

"We don't know if the riders are friendly. Let's keep out of their way."

He whistled for his horses. They came. He pulled them into the woods. In the heavy dusk, they'd be invisible to passersby. Taking the derringer from Emma's pack, he held it to the road and waited. He tried to lower a protective arm around Emma, but she shirked it off.

Two riders galloped past, young men in their twenties, concentrating on the road ahead. As they turned through a fading streak of light, Wyatt noted they looked bred from the same stock, as if they were brothers, fair skin and blond hair. By their heavy saddlebags and stubble of beard, they'd been riding for days. He let them pass without a word.

Ignoring Emma's curses, he helped her mount her horse. Her legs were soaked. From the map he'd studied earlier, he knew they were only miles away from the inn, and they'd be able to clean up there.

They rode off, and within an hour, he proved to be right. The dark road widened and a welcoming sight stretched before them. A central log cabin, clustered with several smaller ones, rose out of the mountainside. Smoke poured out of its chimney, and three horses were hitched to the post outside. The corral outside the barn contained the two horses that had recently passed them on the road.

Finally. A warm meal. A soft bed. A place to change their damp clothes into dry ones. He sighed, his body and thoughts filling with pleasure.

He turned to Emma but the icy look in her eye caused him to clamp tight. Best to keep his mouth shut while she was in her ornery mood.

When they pressed the bell at the polished front desk, a plump woman, rosy cheeks and coils of braided white hair stacked on her head, greeted them. An oil lamp in the corner flickered, creating a shadow over her broad nose.

"Evening ma'am," said Wyatt, removing his damp hat and being careful to avoid stepping on the rug with his dirty boots. He could see her watching to make sure he didn't.

"Evenin' mister, missus." Her hair jiggled on top of her head as she smiled. "Welcome to our inn. My name's Belle, and this here is my husband Harry." Her husband swung around the corner, shoving a last bit of pie into his mouth. He had black fuzz for hair. Belle gazed curiously over Emma's dirt-streaked face and disheveled attire.

In a self-conscious gesture, Emma flicked the hair from her cheeks.

Wyatt thought Emma looked good in a layer of dirt. She was looking more and more like a Westerner and less and less like an Easterner by the minute. Her belt was cinched tight around her narrow waist and her heaving bosom under her soft shirt poked out enticingly beneath the wet jacket.

Wyatt dipped his head towards Belle. "You'll have to excuse our appearance. We ran into trouble five miles back. We were robbed."

Belle clutched her throat and sniffed. "Oh, no."

Her thin-boned husband stepped to the desk and worry furrowed his brows. "Was he an older fella, dirty and gray, one tooth hangin' over his lip?"

"That's him," Emma said. The soft lamplight played over her pretty, smudged nose.

The couple seemed distraught. "He's been botherin' people for weeks, and we can't seem to catch him," Harry informed them. "Marshal should be here any day, but until then, you make sure you stay real close to your wife, here."

Belle played with the cameo brooch at her neckline. "Our sons, Clay and John, just rode in from Billings. I feel much safer, now they're back."

Wyatt leaned on the counter. He had to duck his tall frame under the overhead log beam. He loomed over the other heads. "Are they the two blond fellas, their horses in the corral?"

"Yeah, have you met?"

"We saw them pass on the road."

"Well, did the thief harm you in any way? You hurt ma'am? You look shaken."

Emma drew her arms close and smiled at Belle. "I'm fine. He didn't hurt us, thank heavens."

Wyatt gazed at the older couple. "We're looking for my daughter, Melissa. A young couple with a baby?" He described them as Emma glanced around.

Harry stroked his chin with his finger. "They were here at noon."

Belle smiled, displaying dimples. "Nice young couple. The baby didn't take to the goat's milk, though."

Wyatt grew uneasy. "Goat's milk?"

She pointed through the square window pane behind her. "We got us a few mountain goats in the yard, but the baby didn't take to the milk."

Melissa needed to supplement the baby? Why? His nerves tensed and he took a deep breath to steady them.

Emma leaned in with sudden concern. "Did the baby look sick?"

Belle waved it off. "Oh, no. I got seven children of my own. Sometime they get fussy, that's all. Melissa shouldn't have been upset by it. Sometimes a baby is hungry, sometimes he ain't. He'll eat when he gets hungry, I tried to explain it to her. And by the time they finished lunch, just like I said, he was hungrier than a little runt, feedin' at his ma. Melissa was still cryin' though."

Wyatt's back went up, thinking about what Cole was putting her through. He tried to probe for information delicately. "We're trying to surprise them by meeting up with them at Eagle's Pass. They tell you they were headed that way?''

Belle nodded, and Wyatt shifted anxiously from foot to foot. Seems Cole and Melissa were leaving a lot of clues about where they were headed. Was Cole that confident he wasn't being followed, or was he leaving a false trail? What the hell was the boy up to?

"Well, I'd say you're about six hours behind them," said Belle. "But surely you'll rest here for the night? You look like you could use it. Especially the missus. She looks plum wore out."

Wyatt turned to Emma, and he felt guilty for how tired she looked. He'd been dragging her along as if she were one of his ranch hands. "If we rest tonight and rise before the sun," he said, "we might catch up with them by tomorrow night. The horses could use the rest. So could we, after today."

Emma nodded in agreement, fire still flashing in her eyes when she looked at him. How long was she going to keep this up? The woman had such a temper....

Harry stepped behind his wife and sat down at the desk, rummaging through a stack of papers. "I'll jot down a few notes for the marshal."

Belle poised her quill pen over the guest registrar. "Mr. and Mrs...?"

Wyatt straightened to attention. He figured he should at least try to save Emma the embarrassment. "Mr. and Mrs. Wyatt Barlow—"

"Sinclair—" said Emma, her eyes wide and indignant. She tapped her fingers by the open page, motioning for Belle to keep writing. "Mr. and Mrs. Sinclair."

Belle raised her eyebrows. "It's none of my concern. We get all types through here."

Emma flushed crimson and Wyatt felt a tickle of amusement. When his twinkling grin met with her ruffled gaze, she snarled at him. Lord, what happened to her sense of humor?

She thrust out her chin. "Please write us down as Dr. Sinclair, and her…her assistant, Mr. Barlow."

Belle slid a questioning look toward him. Wyatt had been called many things by many women, but never an assistant. He winked at the older woman. "She's still going by her maiden name," he whispered, "she's a very proud woman."

"We need *two* rooms," declared Emma.

The pen wrote their names in very carefully, while Wyatt slid closer to Emma. His broad shoulders dipped low against hers. "Do I need to remind you, *dearest,* my bill-fold was stolen? I have a stash of money in my boot, but it's not much. We don't have money for two rooms, *darling.*"

"Then I guess you'll have to sleep with the horses, *honeypie.*"

His eyes narrowed and a thought dawned on him. "Unless…unless you hid some money, too?"

"Only an idiot would travel without emergency money."

He broke into a wide-open smile. Well, thank goodness. With a lecherous gaze, he scanned her tight figure, wondering where she hid it.

She glowered at him. "It's tucked nice and neat in my medicine bag. *All two hundred dollars.*"

He withered at her look and spun back to the desk, a shrunken man. "The cheapest room you've got, please."

The woman pretended she wasn't listening to them argue, but Wyatt noticed she was biting back a smile. Well, who the hell cared what she thought anymore?

She glanced up from her book and turned warmly to Emma, ignoring Wyatt altogether. "I can tell you two have been arguin'. Travelin' always does that to us, too, honey. Why, every time we take a trip into Great Falls, by the end of it we're ready to pull each other's hair out.'' She called over her shoulder to her husband, who didn't look up from writing. "Aren't we, sweetheart?"

"Yes, sugar."

"Throw in a couple of young-uns with their fighting and never-ending stops at the side of the road, and we'd pay good money to have someone tie a noose around our necks. Am I right or am I right, sweetheart?"

"You're right, sugar."

Her face darkened and she shook her head at Wyatt. He jumped back, startled at the accusatory glint in her eyes. "You men. You don't help any. And you're all the same, every last one of you that comes through here. Always pushin' those horses to make the best time you can. What's your damn hurry?"

Feeling suddenly weak and powerless, Wyatt shrugged his shoulders.

"What you need is a hot bath and a quiet room," she said to Emma, pressing a key to her hand. "Here's one. Nothin' fancy, but it's quiet, right at the end of the hall. Mister, if you want to do something to help your wife, rub her shoulders. Massage her aching backside. Once in a while," the woman rolled her eyes to the ceiling and drawled, "tell her how pretty she is. God almighty, would it kill ya?"

Emma raised her brows and gave him a smug smile.

Wyatt hoisted the saddlebags off the floor. When women stuck together, they sure stuck together, and speaking up now with both of them glaring at him would be like throwing a stick of dynamite into a keg of gunpowder. Silently, he followed Emma down the hall.

There was only one bed in the room when they got there,

barely bigger than a single. They both couldn't fit into it, unless they slept on top of each other. *Hmm, now there's an interesting idea.*

He looked up at Emma's stiff back. Judging by the way she tossed her bags onto the bed to claim it as her very own, his thought wilted.

He tossed his bedroll onto the sofa by the wall, claiming it as *his* very own. On second glance, it looked too short for his bulky body, and he eyed the thin carpet on the floor. In the end, he knew dang well he'd wind up on the floor, might as well start there to begin with.

Dropping the rest of the bags, Wyatt stepped to the stone fireplace. Dry logs were stacked along the hearth. A fire would dry their clothes.

He noticed Emma eyeing him nervously. The streak of dirt across her forehead was half smeared off, but she still looked as dirty as a savage, and he enjoyed that. Her hair was sticking out all over her head and her lusty curves were even more accentuated by the tight pants clinging to her rump, and the absence of a corset.

A knock at the door startled them. Wyatt opened it, turning his back to Emma, blocking her view. Harry was holding out a tray. On it sat a slim, blue perfume bottle and an unopened bottle of red wine. Two clear glasses flanked the wine.

Wyatt picked up the finely crafted blue glass. It was filled with liquid. "It's massage oil," Harry whispered. "Belle's sister sends it from New Orleans, and the women here go crazy over it. And a complimentary bottle of red wine. Belle insists. Says it's just what your wife needs. Belle's honored there's a doctor staying at the inn."

Wyatt shook his head, doubtful that anything could soften Emma in the mood she was in. It would take more than a few baubles to simmer her down. As if anything this simple could work on a complicated woman like Emma. But on the other hand, it couldn't hurt. "Thanks."

Harry nodded, the black fuzz on his head shaking, and gave Wyatt a sympathetic look that seemed to say, *Good luck.* "There's an adjoining room next to yours," he whispered, pointing to his right, "that connects to a bath, if your wife's interested. There should be pots by the fire to heat water. Call me if you need more."

Wyatt thanked him again and closed the door.

Emma looked up from unpacking her wet bags. Her dirt-streaked face mellowed into a gentle smile and she cooed. His pulse danced watching the warm glow come to her skin.

"Oh, how lovely. Did Belle send these?" She slid her wet jacket around the chair and stepped forward to pick up the blue glass. She lifted the decanter to her mud-caked nose and inhaled.

Wyatt nodded, marveling at the transformation. Perfume and wine? That's all it took? He wished she was half as interested in getting close to him as she was to the perfume.

He gulped and saw his opening. Maybe Belle was right. All he had to do was tell her how pretty she looked, and things would be fine. He hated arguing with Emma, not when her smile alone could melt a glacier.

"Emma, you look beautiful tonight."

He ducked as the pillow hit the door. It slid to the hard wooden floor, and he realized with a thunk that he didn't understand women at all.

Chapter Fourteen

Emma bit down hard on her lower lip, trying to bridle her temper. Clamping the wine bottle between her knees, she rocked back and forth on the bed as she struggled to dislodge the cork. There was no bloody way she would accept Wyatt's offer to help uncork the wine. Who in tarnation did he think he was?

Giving away her medicine bag without a second thought, making all the bloody decisions without her! She didn't need his wretched help for *anything*. From the corner of her eye, she saw him looking on in helpless amusement from the sofa, as she fought with the blasted cork.

Two pots of water swung over the fire, gently simmering, and wet, rinsed clothes were strewn nearby as Emma yanked and wrestled. She didn't plan on drinking much. She hadn't had a glass of wine since leaving Philadelphia, and after the tough day she'd had, she could sure use one.

Wyatt had already secured the horses in the barn, she'd changed into her dry blouse and skirt, and he'd pulled on a fresh pair of pants. All they had left to do was wait for the water to boil to finish filling the tub. And get the bleeding, good-for-nothing cork out of the damn bottle.

Muttering to herself, almost ready to fling the whole

thing into the roaring fire, she hammered the cork into the bottle neck with the pocketknife Wyatt had given her at the ranch. Her chest bounced with the final jolt, and her behind dug into the mattress.

Holding up the knife toward him in eager triumph, she gave him a generous smile. She felt her cheeks warm as his smoky black eyes slid up her body, from her rump to her face, as if he were appraising a side of beef.

He stretched his long legs in front of him and folded his arms behind his head. Secretly, she hoped the loose wire springs sticking out of the sofa were digging into his backside.

"I knew this knife would come in handy," she said sarcastically. "You were wise to make me bring it." She twisted on the bed, reached for her glass and filled it. She raised the bottle toward him. "I'm sure Belle wouldn't mind if I offered you some." On the contrary, Belle was probably thinking a bottle of wine would heal everything between them. Huh!

He waved a palm in the air, about to decline. Then she saw him gazing at his thin bedroll resting on the hard plank floor. His mouth twisted on a sour note. "Just one glass."

She poured him one and sat back to savor the taste. "Tastes good." She rolled the sweet wine on her tongue and making sure he wasn't looking, picked the cork granules off her tongue. So help him, if he lodged one complaint about the cork bits floating in the wine...

He didn't.

She sighed and squirmed on the bed, making herself comfortable. After a few sips, feeling better, she asked, "Do you think they'll catch the man who robbed us?"

She cleared her throat, pretending not to be affected by the handsome man sharing the same room with her. Dark stubble shadowed Wyatt's jaw, giving him a striking aura of danger and undeniable appeal. Her pulse beat erratically just looking at him leaning back on the sofa.

He swirled the burgundy wine in his glass, gazing at it as it rested in one large palm. A lock of black hair fell over his brow, that same unruly strand that always seemed to go its own way, and she had an urge to set it back straight. "Maybe. If he gets into that opium, they won't have a problem tracking him down."

Emma winced. "I feel sorry for him."

"Don't. He's got what's coming to him."

As he drank, she watched his Adam's apple ripple. She gazed at the way the firelight danced along the muscles of his throat, all the way down the opening of his shirt to the patch of glistening dark hair. He turned a tender eye toward her and her senses leaped to life. "I'm sorry about your medicine bag."

She tried to deny the quivering in her veins and took another sip before she answered.

It wasn't his fault they were robbed, she told herself. Deep down, she knew her anger at Wyatt stemmed from her real fear. Of a medical emergency—that someone might need her skills as a doctor, and without her bag, she wouldn't be able to help. She couldn't think of anything worse, watching someone suffer, knowing she could do more, but not having her equipment. "I'm not much of a doctor without my bag."

He inclined his head and stared at her long and hard. "Is that why you're so upset? *You're* the doctor, not your fancy bag. I saw what you did for Melissa, I was there. I've never seen a doctor work as hard, with as much courage as you showed."

His words gave her some comfort, but he didn't understand. "There's only so much my bare hands can do. My books were in that bag. With Melissa, I was able to read the notes on emergency labor, how exactly to extract the baby. The pharmaceutical notes, too—I could look up doses and fixes.''

''You're worth much more than your bag,'' he insisted, ''more than all your notes.''

''I don't mean to complain, especially out here where folks don't seem to have much of anything in the way of doctors or medical supplies, but...I rely on those books. It's not all in my head yet. I don't have the skills Doc Brady has.''

''You can buy another book.''

She sank lower into the bed. ''They're hard to come by. I'll have to wait until I reach Philadelphia. In the meantime, what if we come across an emergency, someone needs me, and I have no medicine, no instruments, no books?''

''I hope like hell that doesn't happen. But if it does, you'll do like the rest of the people do out here. You'll do the best you can with what you've got.''

She nodded in slow agreement. ''I admire their courage, living out here in the middle of nowhere. They don't even have vaccines for smallpox. How do they do it?''

''They're strong, rugged people. Just like you.'' His eyes appraised her and something invisible pulled between them. ''Emma, have you...have you ever considered staying in Pine Creek?''

She inhaled sharply at the suggestion. How did he mean?

''People need you out here as a doctor.''

Flustered, she shook herself. Her heart was hammering foolishly. For a minute, she thought... Oh, of course he meant as a doctor. She was crazy to let her mind jump to any other conclusion.

''I'm not ready yet to practice alone.'' She sifted her words carefully as she swirled her wine. ''One day, yes. But Doc Brady doesn't think surgery's a place for a woman, and even though he means well, he'd never give me the training in surgery I need out here. The only way I can get it is the hospital in Philadelphia.''

His eyes probed hers and she tingled under his gaze. She could almost imagine running her fingers over his chest, feeling the movement of his heavy breathing. Her pulse quickened at the speculation of what his touch would feel like.

His jaw quivered. He broke the spell and jumped to his feet, checking on the water. ''Almost boiling.''

She finished the last mouthful of wine and poured herself another glass. A rush of tiredness washed over her. Her body felt warm as she gazed into the crackling fire.

Tugging at her loose braid, she unraveled her hair and let it fall over her shoulders. She felt his nearness overwhelming. Rising to her feet, she walked over to the tray on the table, pulled out the massage oil and lifted the top, letting its fragrance waft through the air.

Wyatt groaned and his lips twisted. ''You're not really gonna use that stuff, are you?'' Tossing a blanket onto the rug by the fire, he stretched down on it, long and lean, and propped an elbow under his head, peering up at her.

She sank down onto the bed, her sock feet crossed under her skirt, and set the tray beside her. ''Why not? It smells pretty.''

''It smells like—''

''Like what?''

He shrugged and buried a smile. ''Never mind.''

Now she really wanted to hear it. ''Tell me.'' Her hair bounced around her and the effects of the wine tingled in her legs. ''What does it smell like?''

His grinned suggestively. ''It smells like a cheap whore.''

She laughed, slow and easy. "How do you know what a cheap...*woman* smells like?"

This time he laughed, roving his eyes over her face, then over her wild hair, then over her body nestled on the bed. "You're lit."

She sat up indignantly. "I'm not lit."

His laugh was low and rich and made her knees tremble. "Yup, you're lit. How many have you had?"

She glanced at the half-empty wine bottle. "Just a couple of glasses. Lowering her lashes over him, she felt a rush of heat through her limbs. "Have you ever visited one of those places?"

"A whorehouse?" The way the corners of his lips tugged up when he said it made the thought seem appealing, exciting, even erotic. He must be right, the wine must be affecting her.

Her heart took a perilous leap and her whole body flushed. "Mmm-hmm. Have you?"

He arched a dangerous black brow. "As a matter of fact, yes, just last week."

With a genuine exclamation of shock, she sagged into the bed.

He added smoothly, "But purely for business reasons."

She pursed her lips in sudden disappointment and splayed a palm in the air. "I don't want to hear any more." Her head felt heavy.

"Not *that* kind of business. Beula and Patsy needed horses. I sold them two of my finest."

"Oh." She paused to let that sink in. That was different.

His dark eyes rounded in amusement. "Don't make me out to be a saint, Emma. I'm not. Believe me, if I didn't have two young children to raise, I'd be frequenting that place every night."

She sat up. "Now why did you go and say that?"

"Because it's true."

The image of him roving through the whorehouse, searching for the right woman to bed, gave her a delightful shiver. "What kind of a woman would you choose?"

His eyebrows jutted up and his mouth opened in amused dismay.

She added boldly, "What kind of a woman appeals to you, if you were paying for her? If you had to choose one?"

"I'd take the one who talked the least."

The bed swayed. "I'm serious."

He laughed. "I am, too."

"I'll tell you, if you tell me."

When his eyes narrowed on her, his look was so galvanizing a fluttering arose at the back of her neck. He cocked his head. "You'll tell me what?"

"I'll tell you what kind of a man I'd pick out, if I was paying for him."

Slowly, he looked her up and down, every inch of her, and the way he drank her in was as if he were undressing her. A hot ache burned in her throat. "No man in his right mind would take money to bed you."

Lord, it was hot in the room!

She fanned herself. There was no stopping her now, she was going to ask exactly what was on her mind. "What appeals to you, as a man? Do you prefer...*enjoy*...ah, like...big breasts or little breasts? Big fanny or little fanny?"

He rolled his whole body lazily toward her, giving her his undivided attention. "Yup, I do."

Breathless, she was almost afraid to go on. "You do what?"

"I like 'em all. Big and little."

She moaned. "You're not very particular."

"I particularly like all women."

She eyed him under lowered lashes.

"Don't look at me like that," he warned with a tremor to his deep voice. "I'm being truthful. I love women's bodies."

She shuddered at the heat in his eyes. Gulping, she reconsidered where the conversation was heading. It was heading to a place too dangerous to go. "What about her mind?" she asked, trying to divert the conversation. "Is her mind important to you?"

"If I was taking a woman to bed, I wouldn't be thinking about her mind, much less be reading Shakespeare to her."

She giggled, the tension in her muscles gloriously released.

"What about you?" he asked, watching her closely. "What type of a man would you enjoy in your bed?"

"I'd like a man who reads Shakespeare," she said, as seriously as she could in her hazy condition.

He laughed, long and hard. His laughter filled the room and caressed her, soothing her tired body, tingling over her warm skin.

"You *would* enjoy that," he hooted. "God help the man who doesn't bring along a volume of good English verses."

His laughter now brought her to the brink of irritation. She didn't think it was that funny. "I'd like him to do other things, besides just read."

His eyes twinkled in that private way and she blushed down to her toes. "Please," he said, "my...ahhh... curiosity...is up. Describe the type of man who appeals to you."

It seemed so logical. She wanted someone strong and bold, a red-blooded man who'd fight for her to the ends of the earth, yet someone gentle and tender, too. "Someone hard and soft." Her words were slurred, her mind drowsy.

His face sure looked confused. "I'd really like to understand this. Hard *and* soft?" He rubbed his jaw and leaned closer. "Do you mean physically, or mentally?"

"You can finish the picture...." her voice trailed off as she fell back onto the bed. "You're the one who told me you like big fannies and little fannies...."

"All this talk of breasts and fannies, I've got images of naked women floating in my head, one in particular—"

The room was on a tilt. Was she dreaming, or was he still talking? She closed her lids.

"What about the bath?" he whispered, his breath hot at her ear.

Her limbs were as heavy as stone. She couldn't move.

Strong hands scooped her up and slid her under the sheets. She was dreaming...he kissed her forehead...his soft, warm lips brushed her face and it made her heart glow.

"If I had to choose, I'd pick you Emma. I'd pay 'em twice what they asked, and I'd pick only you."

Was she dreaming? She wasn't sure, she didn't want the dream to end. He wasn't talking to her as a doctor, he was addressing her as a woman. Smiling, she felt her heart bubbling with joy, bursting with the bottomless satisfaction of knowing that if she were a whore, he'd pick her.

"Why didn't you wake me?" Emma thrust her folded skirt into her saddlebag. The sun wasn't up yet, and they were packing by the light of the oil lamp.

"I tried, but you were in a drunken stupor." Wyatt wasn't trying to get her worked up on purpose, but he couldn't help it. When she got fired up, her eyes sparkled, her face flushed, and her whole body jiggled like nobody's business.

And after leaving him in the lurch like she did last night,

all heated up with no place to go, she deserved some ribbing.

Emma's mouth gaped open, she was speechless. He could only stare back. He'd never seen her speechless before.

"I was *not* drunk. I was tired."

"I know you were." His voice lowered and he shoved his rolled shirt into the bag. "That's why I let you sleep. You looked worn-out, and I didn't have the heart to disturb you."

He watched the anger in her face fade. She held out a clump of hair, tugging her fingers through it. "My hair's caked with mud, and I feel grimy."

She didn't look grimy to him. She'd washed up at the basin, and only her hair looked untamed. "You can wash tonight when we make camp. Admit it. You had a good sleep, and you feel better."

She leaned back in her boots. It took her a moment to decide. Her brown eyes softened. "All right." Then, getting back to business, she raised her arms and slipped a ribbon through her hair. He watched her weave her belt through her pants. She looked so damn good in his clothes, he had problems taking his eyes off her. And why did he have this strange feeling of pride looking at her? Proud that she was accompanying *him,* proud that she was wearing *his* things.

He didn't have time to think about it. All he could think about today was catching up to Cole. They closed the door and made their way down the hall.

They were the only guests up at five in the morning, but Belle, knowing how early they'd planned to rise, was busy in the kitchen. After a quick breakfast, Wyatt slid up to the front desk to speak with Harry. He had two things to negotiate.

Guns and money.

Sliding the derringer onto the counter as part of a trade, Wyatt was bargaining for a six-shooter when a man came through the front door. "This is my son, Clay," Harry said. Clay had shaved since Wyatt had seen him galloping past on the trail last night, and a neatly-pressed green shirt covered his bulk.

He slid his hat off his dusty blond head, nodding to Emma. He stared a little longer than necessary at her. Feeling suddenly tense and possessive, Wyatt circled an arm to her waist, one she couldn't see, but Clay could.

"Mornin' ma'am," Clay said. Nodding to Wyatt, he wiped his boots on the mat and tossed his hat to the rack by the door. A map of Montana was tacked to the log wall behind him. "Your horses are fed and watered."

"Much obliged," Wyatt thanked him. He already knew about the horses. He was keeping a close eye on the barn.

"You own a pair of fine horses, mister, branded with the Barlow ranch. You buy them off Wyatt Barlow?"

"I *am* Wyatt Barlow," Wyatt said in amusement.

Clay took a harder look at them, his gaze lingering on the B burnished into Wyatt's silver belt buckle.

The young man stepped closer, grinning. "Pleased to meet you, sir," he said with a firm handshake. "My brother and I just came back from Texas, drove some longhorns to the Sully ranch, east of Billings. They got a lot of cattle, but mister, you got a lot of horses."

Wyatt nodded. "How are things in Texas?"

"Busy. Hot."

As interested as he was in Texas, Wyatt didn't have a lot of time for talk. He was itching to get on the road. They had a long day ahead of them. But fortunately, it helped their cause that Clay had heard of Wyatt—he was able to negotiate credit at the desk, along with a wad of cash. Not to mention the decent rifle Clay passed on.

Emma kept her distance in the ring of conversation, gazing anxiously at the weapons, then seemed to come to terms with it. She stepped closer to his side as he said his thanks. "I'll send a man along to repay you as soon as I get home."

As Clay handed the rifle over at the door, his inquisitive eyes glanced at Wyatt's belt. "You any relation to a fellow named Jim? I didn't bother askin' him his last name, but he wears the same *B* on his belt."

Emma gasped and Wyatt's gut clenched. His boots rooted to the floor. Oh, hell, *Jim?* "He's a cousin. Why do you ask?"

Clay propped a hand on his hip. "A cousin? Well, then, I'm sorry I was so suspicious of them. I would've been friendlier, if I'd a' known he was your relation."

Wyatt felt the heat wash from his face. "What do you mean?"

"My brother and I met up with him and his friend, Abe, yesterday. They were worried that Abe's horse was goin' lame. They must have been drivin' them too hard. The way Jim looked at me and my brother when we stopped to help out, I could'a swore he was debatin' whether to steal my horse or not. I gotta admit, I wasn't too friendly. You'll apologize for me, when you meet up with them?"

With a pang in his heart, Wyatt glanced at Emma. She'd stiffened and the dread in her eyes loomed large and clear.

Wyatt's first reaction was to go along with Clay's assumption Jim and Abe were decent men. But on second consideration, he knew he had to warn them. "I'm not proud to say this of my own kin, but Jim's not a man to be trusted. Abe's no better." He swallowed. "They're dangerous men."

Harry grew sullen. Clay's eyes narrowed as he scanned Wyatt's face.

"If they come through here, carry your gun, Clay. And don't give 'em any liquor, for cripe's sake. There's no telling what they might do. How far behind are they?"

Clay turned to the map on the wall behind him, a three-foot square of Montana Territory and the bordering areas. He pressed his finger to the center of the faded paper. "Well, they decided to make camp somewhere around here, about six last night." He turned back to face them. "They figured by the morning, Abe's horse would recover. I'm not so sure, though. Can't push animals too hard."

Oh, God, thought Wyatt, studying the map. He gulped. The robbery had slowed them down last night. Jim and Abe might be just around the corner, if they rose early this morning. Wyatt scanned the names and places on the map. The Rocky Mountains, Idaho, Eagle's Pass… His gaze traveled north and the shock of what he saw numbed him to silence.

"What is it, Wyatt?" Emma dipped to his side, seeming to sense something was amiss. She glanced up at the map and frowned.

It was all tumbling through his mind. Dammit all to hell, Cole wasn't heading to Eagle's Pass. Wyatt shook his head, motioning to Emma, silently begging her to keep quiet. Her eyes acknowledged his request and she glanced away, darting an uncertain look at the other two men.

Wyatt had to keep it to himself for now. If he told these people where Cole was really headed, the information might get back to Jim. "It's not likely Jim will stop and bother you," he said to Clay. "Chances are they'll ride right past, trying to make up for lost time. They're looking to meet up with Melissa and Cole, same as we are."

Harry leaned forward across the desk. "You havin' some kind of family reunion?"

"Sort of."

Belle entered the room, and as Emma said goodbye to her, Wyatt pulled Clay aside. They had one last chance to send Jim in the wrong direction. "If Jim stops and asks about us, don't tell him right off we're headed to Eagle's Pass. Try to bluff him, then let it out real slow, like he pulled it out of you by mistake, that we're headed in that direction. You got it?"

"Yes, sir."

"Thanks kindly for helping us out. If there's anything I can ever do, or you and your brother are looking for work, come see me. I could always use a couple of honest, hardworking men." He meant every word.

With the heat of fear coursing through his veins, Wyatt cupped a hand around Emma's shoulder and they slipped out the door. No time to lose. His blood was rushing through his muscles so fast he tossed her swiftly on top of her horse.

In one fluid motion, he swung into his saddle and they bolted out of the barn. Hearts thumping madly, they raced into the dawn like two wildcats running from fire.

Chapter Fifteen

"They're heading north to Canada. To Alberta district." Wyatt's voice wavered in the quiet mountain air. The late morning mist had lifted.

He may never see Melissa again. His chest tightened and he moaned in distress, as if the ax that'd been lodged in his heart for the last six months had just twisted one more notch.

Emma swallowed hard and bit back her tears. Her face was bleak with sorrow. "Oh, Wyatt, are you sure?"

His broad shoulders heaved. He nodded.

She stood facing him in the middle of the wooded trail, with her mare's reins clutched between her fingers. They peered into the moist trail, searching for tracks. The sun glistened above her left shoulder, and the base of Mount Eagle formed a solid wall to her right.

Was there any sense in going on?

Wyatt sighed in resignation and tilted back his Stetson. Cole was taking his daughter across the border.

In a daze, he blinked and shook his head. Cole had won.

Wyatt motioned north with a slow nod. "The border's less than two days' ride from here, and folks up there lead a similar way of life. They got cattle, and horse ranches and the Rocky Mountains. I know drovers who took cattle all the way up to the town of Calgary. Said the land's as pure as gold. With lots of wild horses—''

"And freedom for Cole and Melissa." Emma bowed her head to the tracks and murmured. "They really do aim to disappear."

His horse nudged him. Wyatt took a deep breath and tried to think. Maybe it wasn't over yet. Maybe he'd still find a way to see Melissa again. "No border's going to stop me," he said in a rush of words.

Shielding her eyes from the sun, Emma cupped a hand to her face and peered at him intently. "Canada's out of the sheriff's jurisdiction."

Wyatt snorted and almost laughed. "I don't give a hoot about jurisdiction. She's my daughter, and Cole's not taking her anywhere." His arms tensed. "Maybe she doesn't even want to go to Canada. It might be purely Cole's idea."

Emma's eyes widened in astonishment and he stepped back, realizing how weak his excuses for Melissa sounded. "It's possible," he offered. Tracks in the mud caught his eye and he pointed under a spruce tree. "Those are their tracks."

They strode closer and Emma crouched to take a look. "How do you know?"

"They're the same prints we've been following since we left the ranch. And after the rain we got last night, they're a hell of a lot more visible. See here?" He pointed to the U-shaped wedge. "Cole takes care of his horses. The print's got crisp edges, like a newly shod horse, and the wheel rut is nice and straight, not wobbly." He gave that much to Cole. He was excellent with horses. Wyatt poked his finger into the print, dabbing at the cool mud. "It's moist."

"What does that mean? Can you tell how far ahead they are?"

"The tracks are dry on top, wet in the center. I'd say four, five hours at most." He squinted toward the sun and its warm rays heated his face. "We'll catch up with them late tonight or early tomorrow morning."

He watched her. Her face flickered with fear and she lowered her lashes, trying not to let him see it. He hesitated, measuring her for a moment, a cold knot forming in his stomach. She was caught in the middle, trapped between her love for her brother and Wyatt's need, his *lawful right* to haul them back.

A heavy weight seeped into him. What should he do? His mind spun with possible decisions and actions. Canada cast a whole new light on the situation. As Emma said, they really aimed to disappear. What if Melissa approved of the move to Alberta? Not only approved, but wanted to go?

God, did she really hate her life in Montana that much? The disquieting thought reeled through his mind.

Should he force her to come back?

It didn't seem right. The undeniable and gut-wrenching realization came out of nowhere and floored him.

How could he pry his daughter apart from the person she loved most? And he had no doubt now. Melissa did love Cole.

Wyatt's mouth ran dry and he swallowed. As he and Emma mounted their horses, he knew only one thing for certain. He intended on tracking the pair down. After that, he wasn't sure how he'd handle Cole, or what options he'd give Melissa.

For now, he just wanted to find them. And he pushed aside the other quaking thought tearing at his insides. The thought of Jim, lurking and threatening, just waiting to erupt.

In silence, he and Emma rode and reached the junction. West to Eagle's Pass or north to Alberta? He tugged the reins, his leather gear creaked, and he veered north. He hoped, with every quivering nerve in his body, Jim would veer west.

They rode steady for two hours, in a comfortable rhythm with each other, both of them drowned in their own thoughts. Emma never complained. She never looked at him with accusation in her eyes when he mentioned Jim, never brought it to his attention he should have dealt with Jim sooner than this.

Wiping a sweaty palm against his pant leg, he silently thanked her for keeping any blame she might be feeling, left unsaid.

He blamed himself enough for both of them. He *should* have dealt with Jim sooner. For over thirty years, Jim's black rage had simmered, sometimes visible, sometimes not, but always there, and always menacing. How long could a man burn angry?

Wyatt shook his head. Shifting in his saddle, he clenched his fists and vowed he wouldn't let Jim get anywhere near Cole or Melissa. He'd take the law into his own hands if he had to.

Their pounding hooves slowed as they barreled around a corner. And what about Emma? He stole a slanted look at her, galloping at his side. Her head held high with determination, her posture alert for danger, yet every curve and smile utterly female. His instinctive response to her was powerful. He stood in awe of her. The strong, resilient woman she'd become. A woman, it seemed, who could handle anything thrown her way.

A much stronger woman than Lillie had ever been.

The thought threw him off balance. It was another realization that wove around his heart and floored him.

Emma was a stronger woman than Lillie had ever been, he repeated in his mind. His pulse leaped at the implications.

What did that mean to *him?*

In thoughtful silence, he gazed ahead. The trail began to break in spots. Their climb slowed. Around each bend, the landscape rolled and changed, from leaf green to olive brown, to rich coppery barks. The dense aroma of damp earth and berries drifted with them in the warm, noon breeze. They removed their jackets, and Emma led the trail. She pointed through the branches when she spotted a grazing elk, and nodded in wonder when a startled family of white-tailed deer crossed their path.

Wyatt yearned to linger, to share this time with Emma, to search his heart about his new discoveries, but they pressed on, following the tracks. They stopped for lunch beside a rushing waterfall, and while it cascaded down the rocks, they ate biscuits and apples and marveled at the bit of heaven.

When he stood close to her, he stood close enough so he could feel the heat from her body. It sent his heart hammering to his ribs. Pink rushed to her cheeks every time he looked her way.

As the afternoon and evening wore on, their intimacy deepened. When they caught each other's private gaze, when he laced his fingers through hers and tugged her off her horse, even when, in the watery moonlight, they broke for camp and listened to the wolves howl.

Wyatt knew he was stalling for time. They could have forged on, caught up with Melissa and Cole sometime near midnight. But then the confrontation would take place in the dark, when Melissa and the baby were sleeping. So he told himself it was best to spend one more night alone with Emma.

He snared a rabbit and while they ate around the fire, he found himself burning with a hunger that couldn't be satisfied with food or drink. He hungered for Emma. His fingers ached to reach over and touch her.

For this evening, he took comfort she was his alone, and the rest of the world wouldn't invade their peace.

Tonight was theirs.

The fire spit and sizzled behind Emma. She bent over Wyatt's saddlebag, rooting for the soap tablet he said he'd packed, and her behind began to roast. Her fanny was getting downright hot, and she squirmed, enjoying the heated sensation. "You sure it's in here?"

Wyatt looked up from pouring the coffee. "It should be on the right side, toward the buckle."

Her fingers grazed a hard lump. "Got it." She pulled it out, the tablet wrapped in coarse paper, flicking her loose, tangled hair over her shoulder. She was determined to wash it tonight. Mud from yesterday's ride had dried at the back of her head, matting her hair into a nest.

She walked back to the fire and Wyatt extended a tinful of coffee. Reaching quickly for the handle, her fingers grazed his. Heat bolted through her body, and in a flash, she tilted her head back to peer into his eyes. A big mistake. His smoldering gaze sent shivers right down to her toes.

What had gotten into her tonight? She seemed to be all thumbs, and if she wasn't careful, she'd trip and fall into his lap before the night was over.

"Careful, it's hot," he said. The warning came too late. She pressed her lips to the tin of hot liquid and nearly scorched them. Lurching back clumsily, she dribbled coffee onto her britches.

"Whoa," he said, stumbling toward her, trying to help. "Did you burn yourself?"

"No." The tin wobbled in her hand, nearly spilling over the rim and Wyatt slid it from her grasp, placing it on a log beside them.

"Coffee can be a dangerous weapon in the wrong hands," he said. Then all he did was stand there, peering down at her, hands in his pockets, setting her pulse on fire. The partial moon shone down on his face, accentuating the planes of his cheek and jaw, illuminating the sparkle in his eyes. Her heart beat louder and louder and she wondered if he could hear it. If he looked at her much longer, she'd melt.

"Emma," he said in a tremulous whisper, flooding her with desire.

She clutched her soap tablet. "I have to…have to wash my hair." Was it wrong to want him? She swallowed hard and broke free of his gaze.

She could breathe again.

The empty cooking pot resting on a far log caught her eyes. She strode to it and scooped it up. "I need to get some water from the stream." She whirled around to explain and met with his dark mesmerizing gaze, which emptied her head of all reason. "To heat up," she stammered, "to heat up the water, watered pot…to pot my hair."

She was jabbering, but he didn't seem to notice. His Adam's apple rippled and his cheek twitched as he continued gazing at her. Lord, was she in trouble.

Must break free. Need air.

She swayed and wheeled around, staggering into the dark woods, stepping through a wall of cool air. Good. Cool air was good.

A branch cracked underfoot, right beside her, sending her

pulse careening with fright. A bear? She sprang in the other direction.

It was Wyatt. "It's dark, I'll help you." He slid the empty pot from her fingers.

No no no.

How would she be able to breathe if he was walking beside her?

She concentrated on putting one shaky boot in front of the other, trying to ignore the lithe, powerful man walking beside her. Moonlight softened the edge of his silhouette, and when she stole a glance at him, his eyes twinkled like the stars above, caught in a sea of charcoal.

They neared the stream, and he led them toward a curve in the bank where the water dipped. It formed a circular pocket, like a small lake, before veering off between the pines. A mound of broad leaves rustled in the damp earth beside them, stirring the scent of ferns and wildflowers.

Wyatt dipped the empty pot into the lake.

"Oh," he murmured in surprise. What was he surprised about? She watched him glance up at the stream as if studying the flow of water. Then he slid in his entire hand. The sound of his fingers gently swirling through the lake cascaded through the trees. "Touch the water, Emma."

Her eyes had finally grown accustomed to the darkness, and she glanced at the deep outline of his mouth and eyes. Perplexed, she looked to the water, scanning its border. It almost looked like steam was rising off the surface.

She dipped her fingers in. Oh, heavens, it was warm. The surprise sensation sent a wave of pleasure down her spine. She dipped her body lower, swirling her palm in the stillness. Very warm. The water was silk. Smooth, and beckoning.

"The water must be fed by underground hot springs."

His voice was husky, and he was almost whispering. Did he feel it, too? The awe of God's beauty?

"It's so warm," she said.

He searched her face in a shaft of golden moonlight. "Perfect for swimming."

Her breathing hitched and her stomach dipped. What was he implying? That they go swimming? Here, now? Together? *In the buff?*

Her wildly beating heart drummed through her body.

Surely she'd heard wrong. She marched toward him and reached for the pot in her most efficient manner. "Here, I'll take it now, thank you."

Grabbing the metal handle, she slid her fingers against his, but he didn't drop his hold.

A fuse of fire lit between them. She stood rooted, trapped in his sultry gaze, their wet, warm hands touching. Her pulse hammered beneath her skin, and she felt the heat envelop her.

Was it wrong to want him? Was it wrong to want the man she'd loved since time began?

Surrounded by the sweet night air, she felt him shiver. Desire smoldered in his eyes. Did he want her, too?

Could he sense what she wanted?

She didn't care anymore what would happen tomorrow. What she should or shouldn't do. They were alone, blissfully alone. All she knew was that she loved this man.

And their time had come.

They'd be together as it was always meant to be.

As they still held the handle together, he raised his other hand and slowly, steadily, reached for hers. With fingers entwined, he pressed her hand against his heart and looked into her eyes, the potent gaze of a lover. Her heart ached beneath her breast.

She could feel his heart pounding a thousand beats per

minute beneath her palm, and she could feel the effect of *them.* Their heat, their juice, their power, electrifying the air. It raced through her heart, her limbs, her breasts and nipples, and down her center, moistening the dark curls between her legs.

His smoky gaze raced over her parted lips, and she quaked at the rawness of his voice. "Emma, I'm afraid if I step closer, I'll never be able to let you go."

They stood together in moonlight.

And then his mouth crashed down on hers. Her hesitation faded and she responded, opening for him. His tongue circled gently, and she followed it with her own, shyly at first, then as hungrily as his. The pot of water dropped to the ground between them, splashing her boots. She didn't care how soaked she got. She wanted him. For however long it lasted.

Sliding his fingers through her hair, he kissed her throat and neck and up around her ear, and she laughed as it sent quivers through her stomach. She tried to kiss his face but he was devouring her throat again and making his way down to the button of her shirt, making her kiss impossible.

Burying her face in his dark locks, she laughed at his eagerness and tugged at his shirt. A button popped and his broad chest was revealed. She gazed at him slowly and seductively.

As he shrugged off his shirt and undershirt, he grinned boyishly, and she remembered him as he was when they'd shared their first kiss. Hungry and eager then, too.

His chest rippled in the dusky light as he tugged at her buttons, yanking off her shirt. He slid her see-through cotton undershirt, *his* undershirt, over her head, exposing her naked breasts. Grasping her by the shoulders, her hair spilling about, he stepped back to look at her. "I want to see you." He drank her in, his voice strained. "You're beautiful."

She jiggled and the crisp air rolled over her skin, yet she felt no shame at her nakedness. The sensations felt wondrous, the heat of her flesh, her nipples, thrusting into the cool night air. When he cupped her breast and suckled its rosy circle, she thought her body would explode.

She couldn't get enough of him. The sensual look in his eye, his muscles twitching, his biceps glistening in the streaky moonlight, the lazy smile on his lips.

He slid his bare chest against hers, skin touching skin, stroking her back with a smooth hard hand. What was he doing to her? Could always do to her? Every stroke along her spine echoed through her body and down between her thighs.

His breath raspy, he peeled himself away. "I want to savor every moment with you. I want to take my time and make you shriek my name with desire."

"I'd like that," she whispered with gentle humor, her body trembling with sensations she'd never felt before, "let's take our time."

"I've dreamed about this moment forever. Swimming with you." He motioned to the quiet lake. "Shall we?" He grinned that erotic smile that would always have the power to coax her into doing anything.

She met the smile and the gentle hand which was offered. "Yes. *Oh, yes.*" She wanted to jump into the warmth of the water, let his fingers glide over her body and fill every yearning pore. She craved to join with him the way wives did with their husbands.

In one smooth motion, his hand reached for the buttons at the crotch of her britches.

Her stomach fluttered and she grabbed his hand in midair. "Let me do it."

"I'd like to undress you."

A delicious chill ran through her, but she pulled back. She wasn't comfortable with him seeing her. *Her leg.* "You first. You jump in first."

"Don't be shy…not with me." He swallowed. The warmth in his eyes was intoxicating. "I've imagined you naked on more than one occasion, and I can't imagine any part of you that I wouldn't love to kiss."

Lord, he was sweet. She smiled shyly but couldn't bring herself to strip in front of him. "Please, I'm not used to this."

He laughed and kissed the hollow of her throat, sending tingles right through to her nipples. "I suppose you're not. Not yet. But I intend to change that." Her heart swelled with joy and anguish. "You promise you won't leave?" he asked.

"I promise."

"All right, then." He unhooked his belt and undid the fly of his pants. "I'll wait for you in the water with open arms."

She wasn't so shy that she turned away from observing him strip. With a bemused smile, she watched him take off his boots and socks, roll his pants off his muscled thighs, until he was naked, standing in front of her.

Passion flared through her. His muscles rippled, planes of light and shadow, smooth and lean over his shoulders, his upper arms, and tight stomach. A patch of dark hair matted his broad chest and down his abdomen, to the male hardness jutting proudly from his loins. His shaft was hard and smooth, and although she'd never seen an aroused man before, she ached to take him inside her, to take his seed.

He walked into the water and groaned in pleasure. She made him turn away while she removed her clothing, then she slid into the water. Warm, wet, protective, lapping against her skin, reaching to her shoulders and dipping around her hair. He met her halfway and circled her waist with a strong arm.

"You belong in my arms," he said in a silky voice.

She promised herself she wouldn't read more into what he said. She'd accept their time together for however long it was to last.

"Emma." He was nearly panting as he kissed her neck. She loved it when he kissed her neck. She loved it when he whispered her name. "Emma, are you...have you ever done this before?" He paused, struggling with the words. "Are you sure you want me to?"

"I may be inexperienced, but I know I want you."

He pulled his forehead away from hers and looked into her eyes. "Maybe I have no right. Maybe you should wait...."

"I've waited long enough. I want you, Wyatt. I love how I feel when you touch me. And wherever this leads us, I know I'll love that, too." She trusted him to lead her.

He groaned and melted against her, taking her lips and parting her mouth with his tongue. Circling, exploring. She knew instinctively her body was ready for him, flowing with desire. Her body and her soul. A part of her had always been ready for Wyatt.

She wanted to please him and pressed herself against his rock-hard body. Gingerly, she brought a hand to his hardness, exploring the silky feel.

He moaned into her mouth, then breaking their kiss, laughed gently. "If you do that for very long, it'll be over quickly. There's time for me," he said tenderly. "Let me please you first."

The lake shimmered in the moonlight. The warm water dripped down along her neck, between her breasts, rolling off the points of her nipples.

His hands were everywhere, around her shoulders, her waist, her breasts, her thighs. They found their perfect place, gently spreading her legs and weaving through her secret spot, where no one had ever touched her before. She trembled as he toyed with her, his fingers slick and tender. The sensation rolled through her. She couldn't believe anyone had ever done this before, that two people could share such exquisite pleasure.

He stroked her more, taking her to the brink of something wonderful. She arched against him, feeling as if she were falling, giving herself completely to him.

"Do you like that?" he whispered. His voice carried over the still lake.

"Mmm…"

"How about this?" As the pressure built inside her, pounding through her muscles, mounting to a frenzy, he bent his head, his hot mouth on her cold nipple. He tugged it with his lips.

She closed her eyes and let the feeling take her. "Wyatt," she moaned as her body exploded. Wave after wave spewed over her, every muscle releasing its tension, every need, every desire fulfilled. All she could think of was how much she loved him.

She opened her eyes and peered up at him, feeling so utterly complete. "Wyatt."

He smiled lazily and slid his hands around to grab her buttocks. "You're beautiful."

"I never knew it could be this good."

He lifted his ruffled gaze, and a muscle twitched in his cheek. "Neither did I."

She loved him more for saying it. Sighing with elation, she straightened her contorted body in the water. "You've twisted me like a noodle."

"I like noodles."

She laughed and drew him closer. Feeling bold again, she slid her hand down his chest and let her fingers explore the hair below his belly. She felt him tighten. He must like that.

She did it again, and he pulled away with an agonized expression. "Oh, what you do to me, woman...I want to make this moment last forever." He drew her closer. "Let me soap you. I'd like to wash your hair."

She let him, relaxing in a bliss of contentment, floating on her back. He soaped her arms and breasts, then her legs. Her eyes flew open. She forgot to shield her left leg. She held her breath and closed her eyes, hoping he'd pass it by. He didn't. He kept on soaping, treating every part of her equally.

When her eyes fluttered open, he was standing over her in the water, his voice swollen with tenderness. "Don't hide yourself from me, Emma. Every inch of you is beautiful. It's who you are. It made you strong." Dear sweet Wyatt, he kissed both legs before she stood up again.

With every breath, she knew she trusted him. Safe and protected in the warmth of the night, somehow, her leg didn't seem to matter.

It was her turn to lather him. Her hands followed the contours of his chiseled body, rising over the crests and dipping into the crevices. She felt the power in his muscles as his body arched and twisted.

When he rinsed her hair, every stroke at the nape of her neck felt like a wicked flame licking at her center. She moaned and felt the moist heat invade her again.

He rubbed her back. "I want to look at you—all of you. Let's go lie by the fire."

He pulled himself out of the water, splashing and yelping in the cool air, then yanked her out. Gooseflesh covered her body. Snatching their clothes and boots off the ground, he surprised her by scooping her into his arms. He did it with ease. With their clothing heaped on top of her middle, he raced through the woods, buck naked.

Laughter floated up from her throat as they dashed by the bewildered horses. "I think they're wondering why we're not wearing any clothes."

"They don't recognize us without our boots," he teased.

They tumbled onto his bedroll by the fire, the clothes flew out of her arms and her long, wet hair lashed their bodies. She'd never felt more alive, more wanted, more like a woman in all her life.

He rolled on top of her and pulled the soft blankets around them, tucking them right under her neck. Her body began to heat.

"Are you warming up?" he asked.

She nodded, then giggled at their situation.

"What's so funny?"

"I can't believe Wyatt Barlow is lying naked on top of me."

His grin was devastating. "And I can't believe Dr. Emma Sinclair is lying naked underneath me." Lifting his head, he howled in the darkness, like a hungry wolf, and her heart choked with emotion.

"I'm not bad for an assistant, wouldn't you say, Doctor?" He cupped her chin with his big hand. "You mean the world to me." She knew whatever happened, she would remember this moment forever.

His lips brushed her neck, her shoulder, her arm. The warmth of the fire settled in around them, and he loosened the blanket, enough to see her body. She watched him pull in a deep breath, then bury his head between her breasts, kissing his way down her belly, over her hips, along her thighs. Her blood pulsed and she wanted him again. Squirming with desire, she rolled her hips as he slid his hand between her legs. His fingers massaged along the moistness, the tiny pleasure spot.

"Are you ready?" he groaned.

She kissed his cheek. "Oh, yes."

With his knees bent on the ground between hers, he spread her legs and rubbed his hardness between her wet curls. Then slowly, he thrust forward. He filled her up, but she wasn't sure she liked it.

He gave a quick thrust and a jab of pain shot through her. She knew what to expect, it was nature's way, but now that it was happening, she pulled back, frightened.

"I'm sorry. We can stop."

She tried to keep the panic from her voice. "No, don't. Keep going." The pain would ease, she knew that.

Still inside her, instead of thrusting more, Wyatt slid his gentle fingers between her legs, sending waves of pleasure through her. Her muscles calmed and stretched, and she was able to take more of him.

She closed her eyes and let the feeling sweep her. He thrust in and out, and she clenched the blanket in her fists, riding the tide, feeling herself pulsate around his moving hardness. Her body and mind and soul exploded, crashing against the tide, her body nearly spent.

"You feel so good, Emma, wrapped around me."

He removed his hand and rocked deeper. Faster. The tension in her muscles mounted and she wondered how long this could last. How many times he could take her over the brink. She wanted him to fill her completely. She wrapped her legs around his waist and he understood her need. He pushed deeper, filling her to the brim, filling her womanly void with everything he could give.

His rhythm broke and his muscles tensed, a second before hers. "Emma," he called out. They'd finally become one.

As her body cascaded with pleasure, rippling over and over and over, she knew her heart would always belong to Wyatt.

Chapter Sixteen

From the waist up, they were still both naked.

Gripping the blanket around their shoulders, Emma turned on the hard ground and stared at Wyatt sleeping beside her. Dawn was breaking, and early-morning light flitted across his sharp, bronzed face. Touches of humor softened his mouth and eyes. She breathed in the wonderful musk of his body, telling herself she was the luckiest woman in the world.

Beside them, the fire glowed red-hot. Wyatt had kept it burning through the night. They'd made love once more, when he'd reached for her and whispered her name, stirring her from sleep. Oh, how she loved him.

She pressed her warm body closer, finding comfort in his heat, assuring herself she wasn't dreaming. They'd put their britches on during the night to protect themselves from the cold, but on top, their chests were still bare. And the sight of his smooth, square shoulders close to her naked nipples made her pulse hum.

He was real. He was here beside her, he'd called out her name last night and he'd touched her in places where only husbands touch wives.

She quivered with pleasure. Sighing heavily, she rolled

over, loose hair draping over her breasts, and gazed up at the sky. Through the layers of leaves, she caught glimmers of pale-blue sky, and streaks of white clouds.

High in the air, a line of geese soared past. She heard them honking, and in her exhilaration, felt like she could leap up and fly right along with them.

A fluttering arose in her stomach. She didn't want to face it. But taking a deep breath, she wondered if her happiness would be short-lived.

Because what now? Where did she and Wyatt go from here?

How could she go back to Philadelphia, after making love with him? What about the hospital and her hopes to practice surgery?

What she wanted most in the world was to spend every moment with Wyatt, share their lives, their dreams and aspirations. But in all their hours of passion, he hadn't said one word about loving her.

Why not? That's what her heart wanted to hear.

Why did his omission hurt so much?

Her eyes flickered at the sky. Why torture herself with questions she couldn't answer?

Because she couldn't control the questions, or her scattering thoughts. She braced herself and tried to force her confused emotions into order.

Last night, she'd told herself she'd enjoy the night for what it was, and not look to the future. But she'd never imagined Wyatt could take her to the heights he had, and that it would deepen what she felt for him.

The question was, what did he feel for her? Her head swirled with doubts, confused by the intensity of his response last night, unable to register the significance. Had it all been physical for him?

Why hadn't he said the words she longed to hear?

Could it be he hadn't declared his love because he didn't love her? Her heart ached thinking it was that simple, that empty. She knew he felt something, that much was obvious.

But he hadn't said he loved her.

She swallowed the anguish in her throat.

Where would they go from here? She wasn't the type of woman who'd be content to have only a part of him. She wanted a man who'd share everything, her life, her love, her dreams as a doctor. A man who'd understand her, who'd love her as a woman, who'd love her to the ends of the earth. She had to be honest with herself and admit it was what she needed. How could she pretend otherwise?

Last night had changed everything, yet in some ways, it had changed nothing.

Where would they go from here?

In his sleep, Wyatt sensed Emma stirring, and opened his eyes. As she stared up at the clear dawn sky, her smooth skin glowed, her beautiful soft lips parted open. Contentment wound through his body.

He didn't want to disturb her thoughts just yet. His gaze lingered on her golden features and dark lashes, the gloss of her chestnut hair. What a night they'd shared. His loins rippled, thinking of her lying in the moonlight, welcoming him. He hoped he'd pleased her. But more than that, much more, he hoped he'd shown her how much she meant to him. Their joining last night was more than physical. It was a union of soul mates.

His heart pealed out with joy. Emma, Emma, Emma.

She was everything to him. Right now, his mind was reeling, and at the same time, foggy with all sorts of dreams and hopes, promises of the future. But he wasn't sure he had the right to say it.

How did she feel about him? Was the pull in Philadelphia greater than the pull here?

Would she have him, even if he asked?

A tremor touched his lips. He was the type of man who took his time, thought before he spoke, controlled his emotions until he knew what they were, thought about a plan before suggesting one. And he was still sorting it out.

Uppermost in his mind was that he hadn't cleared the air about the past. And the guilt crawled up his spine.

It wasn't fair to Emma, for her not to know the truth. The real reason he'd left her, how much he'd actually loved her, not hated her. The reason he'd made her cry and kept her angry for sixteen years.

And when he told her, what then? Would she turn on her heel and say goodbye? Thanks for all the pain and heartache, I'll be seein' ya'?

He shuddered at the thought. His heart could no longer take the aching solitude of a world without Emma.

He watched her. The lines of concentration deepened along her brows and he wondered what she was thinking.

She was a gentle, loving person who deserved nothing but the truth, no matter what it cost him, he told himself. He knew in order to have a future with her, even the possibility of a future, he had a confession to make. And maybe, when it was all said and done, it might work out between them. His pulse rushed with a surge of confidence.

He took a deep breath. "What are you thinking, Emma?"

She spun her delicate face toward him, hesitated for a moment, then smiled. "I was enjoying the birds." She had a shy look in her eyes which he found amusing.

"You're not bashful, are you, after what you did to me last night?"

She blushed and he laughed softly, the tension in his

chest unwinding. Honesty was the best thing he could give her. He owed her that.

Under the blanket, he slipped a large hand over her naked breast, covering most of the delicious mound, claiming it like an early explorer claiming land. "I claim you as my woman."

She giggled, her breast shook under his palm, sending tingles down his body. She rolled closer and when they kissed, he filled with contented warmth. "How are you feeling this morning?" he asked. "Are you sore?"

"Not much. I think I was made for—" She blushed delightfully.

"I think you were made for me," he finished, filling with pride. "You were made for lovin'."

She held his eyes for a moment, and he wished their embrace could go on forever.

"I suppose we have to get up and get going," she said, "to catch up with Melissa and Cole." She shifted her head on the jacket she was using as a pillow, about to rise, but he stilled her with a strong arm.

He knew the clock was ticking and they should rise, but he was going to say what he needed to say. "I think we need to talk first. I need to tell you something. Something maybe I should have told you a long time ago."

Her arm dangled at the top of his shoulder. She paused to listen, her lips poised with a thoughtful smile.

He licked his dry mouth and swallowed the knot in his throat. "Do you remember that night on the ranch, before you left for Philadelphia the first time?"

Her brows drew together in confusion. "Yes. But that was so long ago," she said, shrugging, a faint pinkness staining her cheeks, "and so much has happened since then."

"I need to tell you something about that night. Will you

listen to everything I have to say before you judge me?''
His voice had lowered into a much serious tone and her
eyes flickered. He felt her shiver and his guilt mounted.

"Do you remember how you told me you loved me, and
what I said to you in return?"

She swallowed and averted her gaze. Pain flitted across
her expression. "I remember."

"I told you I didn't love you." His heart began to gallop
and his voice trembled. "Well, it wasn't true."

She started. Her gaze spun back to him, her eyes wide
in astonishment. The shock of his confession touched her
pale face. She merely stared, blank, amazed, tongue-tied.

He felt her hand pulling away from his shoulder and an
iciness seeped into his skin. *Oh, no.*

As she sat up on the bedroll, her hands shook, clutching
the top of the blanket around her nakedness. "What do you
mean? I don't understand. Explain it to me."

His stomach clenched tight as he watched her quake. Her
hair tumbled in knots over her pale shoulders.

He sat up and leaned closer. "I loved you, Emma. With
all my heart." His heart quivered as he said it. "That's
why I didn't want to stand in the way of your going to
Philadelphia, to study medicine."

Her heated eyes grew cold as they searched his. She
breathed in shallow, rough gasps as the unwelcome tension
stretched tighter between them. He shrank back at the
sound of her choked voice. "Wait a minute...we'd discussed that once before, remember? You promised me
you'd never talk about it again, me going to Philadelphia
without you."

"I know I did, but—"

"You ignored your promise. You ignored me."

"I didn't ignore you, you're all I thought about—"

"You told me you didn't love me hoping I would *dis-*

appear!'' She yanked her blanket tighter around her, like a shield to protect her.

"You make it sound awful!" He flung out his hands in exasperation. "It wasn't my intention to hurt you. You were meant to be a doctor. You have a gift."

"Help me to understand this." Her spine grew rigid as she glared at him. "You didn't trust me enough to tell me how you really felt? You thought it better to shred my heart to pieces, *for my own good?''*

"If I'd told you I loved you, you would have stayed in Montana." He shook his head over and over.

Her stifled gasp escaped. Her eyes darkened.

He had to *make* her understand. "Medicine was all you talked about. Your eyes danced when you talked about becoming a doctor. I couldn't stand in your way. And your family wasn't wealthy, neither was mine. The invitation your aunt and uncle extended, to help you through your schooling while you worked and studied along the way, was the only solution. Can't you see that?"

"You broke my heart." Her shoulders sagged, crumpled.

"It made you more determined to become a doctor." He reached out to reassure her, but she shrugged away his touch.

She smiled without humor. "You didn't wait for me. You married another woman."

That was what he felt most sorry for, and it tore his heart. How could he explain it to her? "I thought I'd never see you again." His throat squeezed, thinking of it. "In passing, maybe, on your visits home. And I was right, wasn't I? We never saw each other."

Her mouth trembled as she fought for control.

"I knew it'd take you years to finish," he continued in the brittle silence. "By then, you'd be settled in Philadelphia, not wanting to come back. And that's exactly how it's played out. Don't you see?''

"You didn't give me a choice," she said in a broken whisper. "It was *my* right to decide."

"You wouldn't have become a doctor."

She inclined her head. "I would have become your wife."

He lowered his gaze, grief spilling into his voice. "It wouldn't have been enough. You wouldn't have been happy."

"You don't know what I feel, and you shouldn't presume to tell me what *you* think is best for me." Clenching the blanket tightly around her, she rose to her feet.

Gooseflesh rippled on his arms. The air seemed suddenly cold. His heart seemed suddenly empty. He jumped up and towered above her. He had to convince her. "Listen, Emma, please, the last thing I wanted to do was hurt you."

"It was the first thing you did."

"I'm sorry."

Her mouth thinned. "How sorry are you? Would you do it again? If you had to choose, *tell me,* would you do it again?"

He sighed, not knowing what to say. He ran his fingers through his hair.

She squared her bare shoulders. "You would. I know you would. You want to control everyone. You're treating your daughter the same way."

Stepping back, he jarred at her rebuke. "What do you mean?"

"You robbed me of my choice, and now you're trying to rob Melissa of hers. For her own good," she sneered. "Who the hell do you think you are?" She turned on her heel and left him standing there, shivering, alone.

* * *

Hell, she was wrong.

Wyatt reminded himself of that an hour later as he kicked dirt onto the fire. He was still reminding himself as he saddled the horses.

He hadn't robbed anyone of anything. *Had he?*

As he dug deeper into his heart for answers, he wondered. What if he *had* let Emma choose between him and Philadelphia, as she'd gotten older, and in the end, she'd chosen the city anyway?

Was that what he'd been truly afraid of? Letting her *decide* to walk away? Was it easier for him to tell himself all these years that it was *he* who'd walked away from her? Did he have that much stubborn pride that he'd wanted to be the one to leave?

Hell. And was Emma right about how he was treating his daughter? He wanted Melissa to have the best, to be able to choose from the best. What father didn't?

His pulse thudded. Melissa *had* made her choice, and maybe he just wasn't willing to hear it.

Another thought hounded him. He'd lost his self-control with Emma last night and they'd made love. The one thing he'd been demanding from Cole all this time was self-control when it came to Melissa.

Seemed Wyatt had no more self-control than the boy did. How could he demand something of Cole that he wasn't capable of himself? Shaking his head, chiding himself, he tossed a pack over Emma's mare.

Wyatt tugged at the strap of the saddlebag, making sure it was secure. His crisp shadow, and that of his horse, fell on the hard dirt.

As he slid the rifle onto his gelding, Emma came to stand beside her horse, waiting impatiently for him finish. Her anger was still apparent at the way she crossed her arms and held her back straight.

He sighed. It was going to be a long day. The warm wind rustled the leaves beyond the stream. The hair at the back of his neck bristled. Slowly, Wyatt peered around. He had the uncomfortable feeling he was being watched.

That was impossible. He would have noticed something. Who'd be watching them?

Then again, he'd been so wrapped up in his thoughts, he might have missed something. He cursed himself for letting his mind slip. Strapping on his gun, he surveyed the woods. He stepped toward the clump of trees to his right, sliding out his six-shooter.

Emma tensed. "What is it?" She flung her braid over her shoulder and followed his gaze.

"I'm being cautious. Take out the rifle."

"I don't—"

"Don't argue, just take it out."

She stepped to his horse and slid out the rifle as he trained his gun around them. Nothing.

The horses were jittery, and he didn't like it. His pulse began to pound.

The trees behind Emma swished, Wyatt spun around and choked at the sight.

Jim stepped out of the woods, smiling with bloated arrogance, a gun raised in his hand. "I'm right over here."

Emma gasped at Wyatt's side and his heart stopped beating. "You found us."

"Sure did. I can track a man down as good as any Indian."

Remain calm, Wyatt told himself. He pulled in a shaky breath and took a good look at Jim, standing in the sun's glare. Dark and scruffy, half-grown beard, tired eyes and dirty clothes. He looked like he'd been camping for days, which he probably had.

"Where's Abe?" Wyatt asked cautiously, trying to sound as friendly as he could.

Jim tilted his head. The brim of his hat cast a shadow line across his face, obscuring his eyes. Wyatt couldn't read him. "How'd you know about Abe? Hell, you knew I'd come, didn't you? I knew Grandpa was bluffin'. Scared old man," he scoffed. "The man at the inn was better, he was real smooth, but I figured that one out, too." Jim displayed his crooked teeth.

They appraised each other slowly for a moment, guns drawn. Wyatt gently lowered his hand, hoping Jim would follow the lead. Wyatt didn't want a fight. He wanted the bastard to leave.

With a nervous shuffle, Jim lowered his gun. He coughed and gave a little laugh, as if he were laughing at himself for thinking Wyatt might use a gun on his own kin.

He just might.

Wyatt stepped toward Emma and she stepped beside and to the rear of him, accepting his silent offer of protection. God, it made his stomach heave to think he had to protect Emma from one of his own. Why hadn't he stopped this vengeful man years ago? Why had he given him all those chances to redeem himself? He'd never change.

The movement to protect Emma wasn't lost on Jim, and as he watched them inching closer, he frowned. Wyatt studied him, trying to figure out the best way to get the damn gun off him.

Wyatt could shoot his wrist and knock the gun out. It'd be fast and easy, but Jim would get maimed. No, no shooting. Or, he could dive for Jim's feet, surprise him. That would work, as long as Jim's gun wasn't pointing at anyone. With a heavy weight on his conscience, Wyatt knew he had to wait for just the right moment.

"Where's Abe?" Wyatt asked again. Tempering two

men would be more difficult, but Abe wasn't quite as vicious as Jim was.

Jim stiffened. "On his way to Eagle's Pass," he said bitterly, eyeing Wyatt with suspicion. A corner of his thin mouth twisted. "We had to split up. I had a hunch Cole was coming this way, and I came to help you find him. As a matter of fact, I wasn't sure when I spotted the smoke from your fire whether it was Cole's or yours. There's another campfire ahead, about an hour. It must be Cole's. Did you know that?"

"No," he said, "I didn't."

Jim stepped back and adjusted his hat. His eyes were still obscured. "That's not like you." He peered at Emma, then back to Wyatt. "What have you been doing that got you so distracted?"

"What are you doing here, Jim?"

"I came to help you get Cole."

Wyatt's stomach rolled into a tight ball. "I told you before, this isn't your fight. Stay out of it."

The color drained from Jim's face. His head turned in the sun and his cold dark eyes became visible, sending chills through Wyatt. "Ain't my fight? *Ain't my fight?* I came to give Cole Sinclair what he's got comin' to him."

Wyatt sucked in a breath, and calmly stroked the trigger of his gun. "It's about time you put your anger aside and go about your life. Turn around and go home, Jim."

Jim's shoulders twitched. "But I figured you changed your mind after Cole had the nerve to steal your daughter." He sneered at his cousin with contempt. "I know you ordered the sheriff, and I know you're chargin' Cole. He deserves what's comin' to him, and I intend to help you with the dirty work. We can hand over whatever's left of him to the law. If there *is* anything left—"

Emma lunged out, pounding the rifle like a vertical stick

at her feet, apparently unaware she was holding a weapon. "Stay the hell away from my brother! You've got no right—"

"Shut up, woman! You're a dog, just like your brother." Jim raised his gun at her.

Wyatt's heart rose to his throat. He lifted his arm to shield her, seething at Jim's insult. Emma stepped back anxiously, and Jim lowered his Colt. What the hell was Emma thinking? Wyatt wanted to shake her. Jim wouldn't care if he gunned down a woman. As long as she was a Sinclair.

Wyatt tried to temper his own rage. "There'll be no more fighting between Barlows and Sinclairs. It stops right now, here, with me. *Get the hell out of here!*"

Jim's eyes burned with fury and his face pulsed crimson. "What the hell are you talkin' about?" His hands shook on his gun. "You're not gonna stop me from gettin' even. The last card on the table was them killin' my Ma. It's my turn. I'm gonna play the next card!"

The dirt crunched behind Wyatt but it was too late to stop Emma from hurling out her words. "If you go near my brother you'll be hanged!"

Jim's mouth contorted. His neck bulged tight at his collar as he watched Emma butt the rifle at her feet.

Ever so slowly, with his heart pounding, Wyatt stepped in front of her and pried the rifle out of her hands.

Jim gazed from one to the other, his narrowed eyes dawning with recognition. "Oh, I see what's goin' on here." His gaze swept over her. "Can't say I blame ya. Sinclair or not, in the dark she must feel like any other woman."

Wyatt lurched forward. "You son of a bitch. Get out of here before I strangle you with my bare hands."

Jim balked. "Over her?" His filthy gaze slid over Emma.

"I know what it's like when a man needs a woman, and I don't blame ya for fornicatin' with her. You can always get yourself a real woman later, someone with two good legs."

"I'm ashamed to call you a Barlow!"

"Wyatt, don't!" Emma caught him by the back of his shirt, yanking him to a stop. "Leave us alone!" she screamed at Jim.

"Shut up! Quit talkin' to me!" In a flash, Jim side-stepped Wyatt and drew his gun at Emma, and in that one terrifying instant, Wyatt drained of blood. He knew Jim intended to shoot her down.

Wyatt dove straight into the line of fire, aiming his own shot at Jim's hand. He grazed Jim's wrist but not before Jim's gun exploded.

The bullet ripped through Wyatt's chest.

The blast echoed off the quiet trees. Wyatt had always heard a man's life flashes in front of him before he dies. As the bullet tore through him, an explosion of pain, all the important people in his life burst through his mind, beginning and ending with Emma.

All the lost years between them. How much he loved her.

And the utter shame and humiliation he felt at deserting her now. Leaving her behind to fend for herself, with this pitiful excuse for a man.

"Nooo...!" Emma reeled with the blast as if it'd shattered through her own heart. She shrieked and fell to Wyatt's side.

He groaned in agony, unconscious. She sobbed and screamed. She couldn't lose him.

A circle of blood seeped around the opening of his bullet-torn shirt on the left side of his chest, six inches below his heart. The entry wound was small, about a quarter inch diameter. By instinct, she bunched up his shirttail and clamped it on the bleeding, applying pressure. She mopped her tears with her sleeves, trying to keep up with the flow that blurred her vision.

Stop crying. Remain calm. Think.

Sliding her free hand to his throat, she felt for a pulse. Weak and thready, but thank God, there.

Jim paced above Wyatt's head, trembling and clamping his injured wrist. "Aw, hell, Wyatt, why'd you go and do that? Aw, hell. I meant to shoot her, not you."

The tears kept sliding down her cheeks, and Emma couldn't see. Mopping again, she got angry with herself.

Stop crying! Help Wyatt!

She gulped and steadied her breathing. Quickly, she slid a hand between the hard ground and his back, checking for an exit hole. She felt nothing. Her heart pounded with fear.

He had an entry wound but no exit hole. That meant the bullet was lodged inside and she had to get it out before he bled to death.

No medicine bag.

Deep sobs choked her.

She unclamped her hand to check the wound. The pressure had helped, the seeping had stopped. But as soon as she removed the pressure, it grew bigger. She flattened her hand against the cloth and bleeding, a hot, moist circle now as big as her palm. But at least the blood wasn't bright red, she told herself. An artery wasn't hit.

Jim's boots crunched on leaves and branches. Glancing up at him, the fear in her heart peaked, threatening to shatter her control.

In his confused state, Jim mumbled to himself, oblivious to her. "Aw, hell, Wyatt, what now?" He rubbed his scruffy chin, his lips swollen. He stopped pacing and turned to her with tight, black eyes. They watered and suddenly focused. "This happened because of you. You came between Wyatt and me. We never had no problems before you showed up in town."

"Help me, please!" she begged him. "Wyatt needs help."

"Looks to me like he's a dead man, and I'm gonna be facin' charges." His eyes got glossy. "You should be facin' the charges. It's your damn fault." He slid his gun up to her head.

"We need to help Wyatt," Emma pleaded with everything she had. "I don't have my medicine bag but the bullet's got to come out. We have to stop the bleeding. Please!"

His voice lowered and he stopped shaking. "Take your stinkin' hand off my kin."

Terror, stark and vivid, quaked through every cell in her body. She gasped for air. "If I let go, he'll bleed to death."

Jim cocked his gun, real calm. "It's your touch that killed him. We never would have been fightin', if it weren't for you and your bastard brother. Take your hands off him."

Her throat was raw with silent protest. She raised her head with dignity. "No, I'm not letting go." She slid her gaze to Wyatt's serene face, and braced herself for the bullet.

"If you don't leave my sister alone, I'll blow your head off." Cole's voice surprised them both. Jim's head jerked back, he whirled to the trees and fired.

With a moan, Emma closed her eyes. Two gunshots rang out.

When she opened her eyes, Jim stumbled to the ground, dead on impact.

Chapter Seventeen

Emma didn't know where she found the strength. She just pulled her shoulders tight and rode with the powerful current as Cole, then Melissa, came to her aid. While she knelt at Wyatt's side, pressing the wound with her palm, she ignored the tortured sob at the back of her throat and called out orders. Start a fire. Haul some water and boil it.

"Do you have any whiskey?" she asked Cole.

"No," he said, shaken and distraught.

Her pulse raced. She needed antiseptic. Wyatt groaned. His face twisted in agony. She saw Cole's eyes flash, his lips tremble as he witnessed it.

"Focus on me, Cole, I need you."

He gulped and looked to her for direction. Minutes before, he'd traded places with her, applying pressure to the wound while she'd examined Jim. Jim was dead, and there was nothing she could do.

But for the grace of God, Wyatt would be too, except the bullet had missed his heart. And by the symmetrical rise and fall of his chest, she knew it'd also missed his lungs.

Melissa vented her sobs and Cole went to her. She dipped her head on his shoulder, clutching Billy in her arms. The sleeping baby didn't look any worse for wear, but Melissa was in a state. Emma was shocked how ragged and weary she looked. She could barely speak, gazing at her Pa, and Emma's eyes filled with tears, listening to her.

"Oh, Pa, I'm so sorry, I'm so sorry," she wept. Her voice grew to a fevered pitch. Cole swung both arms around her to comfort her. She raised her sleeve and wiped her wet nose against it. "We shouldn't have run off, Pa. I've been cryin' about it for four days, and I'm sorry. We realized our mistake. We were already turned back when we heard the gunshots."

Emma desperately needed the girl to remain in one piece. If she collapsed, who would help her? "Honey, be strong for your pa."

Melissa looked at her with tortured eyes. "He's not gonna die, is he?"

"No." Emma lifted her chin. She wished she had time to comfort Melissa, but she had a job to do. "Listen, Cole. Jim's horse must be nearby. Find it. See if Jim packed any whiskey. I need to clean the wound before I go in for the bullet."

While Cole ran off, Emma glanced at the fire, several feet away. The water was close to boiling, gentle steam rising from the pots. As soon as Cole returned, she'd have him switch her places and she'd sterilize her makeshift instruments in the boiling water. So far, precious little—her pocketknife, Cole's knife, a ball of fencing wire, and a small teaspoon.

"Melissa, did you pack a sewing kit? Do you have needle and thread?"

"Yes, I do," the girl said, her face brightening, her freckles regaining color.

Emma's pulse rushed. "Go get it. All the sewing supplies you have. Quickly now."

Melissa placed Billy into the basket beside Emma and ran. The baby cooed, half-asleep.

Turning back to Wyatt, Emma swallowed hard at his paleness, how thready his pulse was becoming. Her insides tore at how helpless he looked. "Don't leave me, my love." The last time they'd spoken, they'd argued. She clenched her jaw to kill the hot tears in her throat.

Melissa returned with more than Emma had hoped for. A small pair of scissors, two sewing needles, one long, one short, five buttons of assorted colors and a wad of cotton thread.

Blast it all. Cotton thread. Emma couldn't keep the disappointment from her voice. "You wouldn't happen to have silk thread, would you?"

Melissa's face shrank. "No, I—I don't." She held up the spool of white cotton. "What's wrong with this?"

"It's not strong enough. Cotton will disintegrate and the stitching will melt open." *Think.*

She concentrated on the options. *Yes.* Her pulse surged. "Doc Brady used to tell me stories about being stranded in the lumber camps. He used to use horsehair for stitching. I need you to pluck some hairs from your horse's tail. Half a dozen. Can you do it, or should we wait for Cole?"

Melissa jumped to her feet. "I can do it."

"Good girl."

Cole hollered fifty yards behind her. "Got it!"

Emma twisted around, being careful to maintain pressure, and her heart lurched at the sight. Cole was waving half a bottle of golden liquid in the air, leading a palomino. "Good old Irish whiskey!" He tethered the horse to the nearest tree.

Emma gulped with delight. "Oh, thank you. Bring it over here with the rest of the supplies. Melissa's over there.'' She motioned to the horses. ''She needs your help.''

When everything was collected, after Melissa and Cole had ripped two of Melissa's skirts into strips, Wyatt began to stir.

''Oh, no, he's coming to.'' Emma pulled back, her breathing shaky. ''I can't dig for a bullet while he's looking on, feeling every cut.''

''Knock him out,'' Cole said.

''With what? I don't have any chloroform.''

''I'll clip him in the chin.''

She gasped. ''We can't do that.''

''Why not?''

Wyatt moaned and turned his head. His lids fluttered, about to open. Emma shook her head, her heart beating faster, her mind racing. What choice did she have? ''All right, do it quickly.''

Cole raised his fist just as Wyatt opened his eyes. ''What the hell?'' muttered Wyatt. In a stupor, he swaggered as he tried to duck and swing back at Cole, but Cole got in a good shot and knocked him cold. Emma had temporarily lost her grip on the wound, but she swiftly applied her pressure again.

Melissa turned away. Sobs racking her body, she snatched the baby into her arms and rocked him.

''It's all right, Melissa, he's out again. Cole, switch me places. Wash your hands first and come back.''

He did as he was told and then Emma sprang to her feet, collecting her supplies. Flinging her braid over her shoulder, she slipped the metal things into boiling water.

Melissa followed, trembling, her eyelids red and swollen, shuffling Billy from one arm to the other. ''What can I do for my pa? I want to help. I can't just sit around.''

As horrible as it was for Melissa to see her pa laid out

like this, Emma knew the baby needed her more than Wyatt did, and the baby was bound to wake up crying soon, needing to be fed. "We need you to do the most important thing of all. Take Billy to the buggy, under the shade of that tree, and recite the Lord's prayer nice and loud for your pa."

Smothering a sob, Melissa swung around gracefully. She pressed Billy to her cheek and began. "Our Father, who art in heaven…"

Emma raced like a mountain wind.

Cole was her assistant. He held Wyatt's arm out of the surgical field as Emma soaked the surrounding skin with whiskey. Wyatt jerked in pain and even though she expected it, she jolted along with him. It must have stung.

Cole unrolled the fencing wire, cut it into strips and propped the ends directly into the fire. After wrapping the other ends with rags so their hands wouldn't burn, he heated them up like cattle brands, and Emma used them to cauterize blood vessels that were too ragged or too small to sew up with the needle.

If she had a suction bulb, she would have been able to suction out the seeping blood which obscured her vision. Instead, she used the strips of cloth from Melissa's skirts and soaked it up. She discovered the bullet was lodged in a rib. It'd cracked three ribs along its path. When Wyatt woke up, she told herself with a pang, he'd be sore.

With her unfolded pocketknife, she tried to grab for the bullet. Wyatt winced and she steeled herself, going deeper to try to snag it. When it loosened, in place of forceps she took the sterilized teaspoon and scooped the bullet out of the wound. The slug was dented on one side, the side that'd grazed the ribs, but hallelujah, it came out in one piece.

She cauterized the remaining vessels and began stitching with the horsehair. Pliable and strong, she felt confident the sutures would hold. But her fingers were getting slippery in the blood, working through his leathery skin. She grabbed the largest button from the pile, a shiny white one, and used it like a thimble to push the needle through. Glancing up at Wyatt in between the stitching, relief began to wash through her and her breathing ran easier. His color had remained pink and his pulse had strengthened.

"You're going to make it," she whispered to him, her heart swelling with joy. From the corner of her eye, she saw Cole give an encouraging wave to Melissa, and she was grateful her brother was by her side.

Emma lost track of time, but when she finished, she was drenched in sweat—a combination of the midmorning heat, and her emotions.

She glanced up at Cole and smiled in weary relief. "All done," she said.

"You're amazing," was all he said.

Wyatt tried to dig out from underneath the heaviness, but no matter how hard he pushed, the weight clung to his chest. Where was he?

When the darkness came, he shuddered in the cold, but with every flash of light, his body rushed with heat. He struggled to rise to the surface, to the heat and light and sound.

Why wouldn't his eyes open? He tried to move his body and pain shot through his left side.

He lay still. Wheels rolled in soft earth. Hooves pounded. Voices in the wind... Did he recognize any of them?

The inn, the innkeeper.

"Emma..." he called out.

The voices murmured. "He's askin' for her an awful lot."

"The marshal's here."

Darkness found him. Then light again, intensifying, the warmth rising to the surface.

He called out.

"Shhh…Emma's ridin' right behind us, Pa, it's my turn to tend to you."

Melissa. Was she all right?

She laid something on his chest, a heavy, warm bundle of softness. It wriggled and pulled his hair. He laughed, understanding.

She continued talking to him, then to someone else. He tried to listen, he tried to lean closer.

"He's out of it again."

Wyatt's eyes jarred open.

He didn't recognize any of it, not the simple curtains, not the bare, utilitarian room, not the steel bed. Shirtless, his chest bandaged tightly, he stretched to look out the window. His left side quaked with so much pain he rolled back on the mattress. He'd seen enough out the window to know the room was situated on the main floor of a house, across the corner from the bank.

Doc Brady's spare room.

Swinging his legs over the side of the bed, his head rolled with dizziness. His tongue felt fuzzy and dry. He thought better of standing up, and heaved against the pillow in a sitting position.

"Oh, my heavens! Cole, everyone, he's awake!" Melissa swung around the door, and her tray nearly dropped to the floor. The glass of water on it slid against the flower vase, and the clink echoed in the room.

He grinned and his lips cracked. He licked them moist. "Sure could use that water. It'd be a shame if it got spilled onto my lap."

Lord, his daughter looked good, good for his soul. He

grinned wide. Dropping the tray on the dresser, she ran to him and hugged him. He winced in pain, but he didn't want her to let go. She kept on hugging, fresh and brightly dressed in a white blouse and purple skirt. He wondered how she came to be here, and was about to ask when footsteps skidded down the hall. In his grogginess, Wyatt fully expected to see Cole.

It was Emma.

The heartrending tenderness of her gaze made his breath stop.

Her braid swung around her chest. She wore a pretty blue dress. Her cheeks flushed looking at him, and her soft brown eyes shimmered, all warm and feminine.

Then he remembered. "You got away from Jim."

Before she could respond, Cole, Doc Brady and his wife came barreling around the corner, asking him how he felt.

His head started to swim, the pain overtook him, and he sagged into the pillow. Working quickly, Emma drew up a needle and Doc Brady shoved it into his arm. It took a few hushed moments before the stabbing in his chest began to subside.

"How is everyone?" he asked weakly. "How are Tommy and Grandpa and the baby?"

Melissa fluffed up his pillow. "They're fine. We're all worried about you."

Then they all started talking at once, telling him how he'd been out for five days. Finally, he turned to Emma, who was standing shyly in the background. His throat felt awfully dry and he suddenly felt self-conscious. "How'd you get away from Jim?"

Her expression clouded and she stammered. "I tried...he wouldn't let me...Cole showed up, he—he had to shoot him. I'm sorry, we never wanted to hurt anyone, but Jim wouldn't listen."

"He's dead," Cole added.

Wyatt slumped back into the pillow. His mind tumbled with the horrible memory of that final scene.

Cole stepped forward, not afraid to look him in the eye, Wyatt noticed. Cole stood tall and proud, wearing a shiny leather vest and crisp white shirt. He spoke with calm authority. "When I showed up, Jim had a gun pointed to Emma's head, demandin' she remove her hand from your chest. He didn't care if you bled to death."

Wyatt's eyes misted. So it'd come to that, had it? He gazed at Emma. Her eyes glistened with sorrow, then her gaze faltered. She looked down at her hands and twisted her fingers. Wyatt turned back to Cole. "What happened when she took her hand away?"

Cole shook his head. "She didn't."

Wyatt's heart clenched as he slowly turned back to Emma. To think what she must have suffered for him.

Doc Brady slid a stethoscope off the dresser and listened to his chest. "How you feelin'?"

"Whatever you just gave me in the needle is working, but overall, I've seen better days." He slid a hand over his bandaged ribs. "I remember getting shot."

The old man nodded, his muttonchop whiskers moving up and down. "Yup, you did. Bullet was lodged in your ribs."

Wyatt had figured as much. He'd cracked his ribs before, falling off a horse, and the pain was similar, every time he pulled in a breath. "Thanks for taking the bullet out, Doc."

"Oh, I didn't do it," the old man said.

Wyatt blinked and frowned. When he looked to Emma, she was breaking out into a pretty smile. "Who did?" he asked, suspecting he already knew the answer.

"I did." Her eyes twinkled and he felt his skin getting warm.

"How?"

"Oh, I found a few things around the campfire."

The group laughed. "Buttons," said Melissa.

"Fencin' wire," said Cole.

"Horsehair," said Doc Brady proudly.

"What on earth...?" asked Wyatt. Then he realized it didn't matter how, but that she'd done it. On her own. He inclined his dark head and felt a lock of his hair spill onto his forehead. "I hope you're proud, Emma, of what you managed to do without your magic bag."

"I am." She said it with such confidence, and he was so damn proud of her, they just kept staring at each other, grinning.

"It's gonna be hard when you go," Doc Brady told her, "we're gonna miss you around here."

The room grew uncomfortably quiet. Emma and Wyatt both sobered. She was still thinking of leaving? After all they'd been through together? No. She couldn't leave now. *Oh, hell.*

Well, he decided, setting his jaw, it wasn't going to stop him. Not this time. Before she left for Philadelphia, he'd lay it all out before her.

He noticed the others were watching and he bent his head and cleared his throat. What he was itching to do was throw them all out of the room, everyone except Emma, and lock the door. He had a few things to say to the woman.

God, they'd wasted so much time.

But looking around at the group of people who'd resumed their chattering, telling him the details of what happened, he could see that time alone with Emma would have to wait.

An hour later, while eating a bowl of chicken soup that Mrs. Brady had fussed over, he sat listening to Melissa. Life was good. Tommy sat on one side of him, Grandpa on the rocker in the corner, and Melissa sat curled up at the foot of his bed, the baby sleeping in her arms. "...and then she took out the bullet with a teaspoon."

He'd heard the story twice now, and he was still in awe of Emma. She was one hell of a woman, wasn't she?

"Tell us the part again about branding Pa like a horse," Tommy said.

"Well, he's not branded on the outside...." Melissa continued.

Wyatt looked above her head at Grandpa, who in his own way was dealing with all the news. He was hard hit by Jim's death, but it seemed he was more hit by the news that Jim had actually shot *him.* Abe, apparently, had been just as bewildered at the horrible turn of events. He'd already been by to apologize to Wyatt, and Wyatt and the marshal were satisfied Abe was telling the truth.

"...and then the marshal showed up...."

"Mmm..." Wyatt's hand shook bringing the spoon of soup to his mouth, but he insisted on feeding himself. He'd rather starve than be spoon-fed like an invalid. A wave of tiredness washed over him. He fought the dopey feeling.

Where was Emma? She and Doc Brady weren't back yet from the call down the street. Wyatt knew he was being selfish, wanting her for himself, but if he couldn't have time alone to talk with her, the least she could do was have the decency to stand in the room so he could gawk at her.

She was beautiful. Every time he thought about the night they'd spent together swimming, his pulse dipped and his confidence grew. An idea was brewing in his mind, a surprise. And if he worked hard, he knew he could pull it off....

He heard footsteps in the hall, people approaching, and he waited in anticipation, gaze glued to the door. Emma stepped through, followed by Cole.

Her big green-brown eyes flew straight to Wyatt, and his pulse tingled. He'd managed to tug a shirt around his shoulders, but his face was still unshaven, and he imagined he didn't look too good.

She smiled and sighed, and he felt his chest rise. His energy was returning. Why, if she lay down with him, here on the bed, there was no telling what he'd be capable of.

Grandpa stood up, his red suspenders twisting. "Would you like a chair?" he offered Emma.

Stumped by the offer, Emma shook her head. "No, thank you, please sit." She stared at the quiet old man for a long moment. The friendly gesture wasn't lost on Wyatt, either. It was the first time Grandpa had shown her a sign of respect, and silently, Wyatt applauded him.

"Now don't go gettin' all teary-eyed on me, woman, I'm just offerin' you a seat," Grandpa mumbled.

Emma laughed out loud, walked over to him, and planted a kiss on his cheek. He turned beet red, the top of his head, his ears, his neck. He grumbled and shuffled. "You still don't look like a doctor. Don't kiss like one, either."

When the laughter died down, Wyatt turned to Cole. "Melissa told me how miserable she was on the ride through the mountains. What made *you* change your mind, and turn around?"

"I did it for Melissa."

There was more to it. Wyatt sensed it. The boy ran deeper than he looked, he just wasn't good with words. Not around Wyatt, anyway. He had a lot to learn about the boy. "But why, though, Cole?"

Cole gazed down at his boots. "I lost my pa six months ago, and I still miss him. When Melissa didn't stop cryin', I got to thinkin' it was a lot like her pa had died, too. That by takin' her away from her family, I was makin' it like all of you were dead. It didn't seem fair to do to her."

A muscle in Wyatt's jaw flickered. His respect for Cole shot up. "You came back to face me, when you were only miles away from the border, close to your own freedom?"

"Four days gave me a long time to think. Billy's a big responsibility, I saw that clearly on our journey. I made some mistakes, and I'd like to work them out."

Cole *was* becoming a man.

Wyatt extended his hand. "I made some mistakes, too." Cole's eyes grew wide, and he eagerly accepted the hand-shake.

"Maybe this is askin' too soon, sir, but I gotta say what's in my heart. I love Melissa and Billy with all my heart, and I'm askin' you again if you'll allow us to marry."

Wyatt's gaze slid from Cole to Melissa. This time she didn't plead. She just stared at him with respect in her eyes. Emma, standing next to her, slid her arm around her, easing the tension. Emma's tender eyes were full of hope.

"This time," added Cole, "if you say no, I'll work harder until I prove to you I can take care of them."

Wyatt's voice grew husky. "I'd be proud to have you as a son-in-law."

Chapter Eighteen

Alone.

Doc Brady was making his rounds in the valley, and Wyatt was recuperating at home. Emma slid the clean instruments from the basin of disinfecting water and placed them on a fluffy towel. She wiped them dry. Her movements, and the sound of metal against metal, echoed through the room. Unable to bear the quiet and the loneliness, she stepped to the overcast window and flung it open, grateful for the breeze and the sound of passing voices in the street.

She winced, remembering how eager Wyatt had been to leave days earlier. As soon as he was able to stand on his feet, he was gone, as if the most important thing in the world was waiting for him on the ranch.

Wasn't she important to him?

Didn't he want to spend time with her?

Apparently not, and that's what hurt. He hadn't said one word about the possibility of her staying in Pine Creek, or even the possibility of him packing up and moving with her to the city. Granted, they hadn't had much time alone. And the time they did have, he'd slept through, weary from the medicine.

She knew he was still recovering, but even so, he hadn't given her any hope of a future together. Not a word.

Didn't their one night together mean more to him than just one night?

Sighing, she opened aged cupboard doors and began folding the towels and putting them on the shelves.

A cold, familiar feeling wove its lonely path around her heart. Where did she belong? In Philadelphia? In Montana?

Sliding a hand into her skirt pocket, she pulled out the stagecoach ticket and studied it again. A sharp black stamp. One Adult, One-way to Philadelphia.

Why did the ticket fill her with such gloom? She *wanted* to go back to the city, didn't she? Wasn't it what she wanted all along?

The date on the ticket was stamped for next week, ten days away. Only five days after Melissa and Cole's wedding.

She shoved the ticket back into her pocket and continued with her work. At least she had the wedding to cheer her up.

And it did. As soon as she got thinking about Cole and Ma, and their enthusiasm, she started to smile.

Emma was elated for Melissa, and the whole town was captured by the news. The church wedding would be followed by a reception at the schoolhouse, which often doubled as a community hall, and everyone was helping out with food and preparations.

Rose insisted on supplying the silk for Melissa's gown, Ma was busy baking cakes and promising more of her cucumber sandwiches, and Cole, well, Cole couldn't stop grinning.

Wyatt had offered him a job at the ranch, and Cole had jumped at the opportunity. Of his own accord, he'd gone to Mr. Wolf and apologized for leaving his job they way he had. In amends, he offered Mr. Wolf two weeks of his free time before starting his new job with Wyatt.

Emma was proud of her brother, the man he was becoming. And despite Wyatt's lack of affection toward her, she was grateful he was treating her brother so kindly.

A knock at the door startled her.

"Hel-looo?" Mrs. McCullough peered around the door and Emma's stomach dipped.

"Afternoon," Emma replied.

The old woman stepped inside, brushing her faded country dress, smoothing her tightly pinned white bun. Gazing around the fresh, tidy office in approval, she settled her sights on Emma.

Emma bristled under the scrutiny. The woman wanted something. Gossip, news, *something*.

"Ready for the weddin' day? Wyatt's standin' in for Cole, I hear."

Emma nodded. "Cole wants to show his respect."

"Wyatt sure is a busy man. I bumped into him at the telegraph office this mornin'."

Wyatt was in town this morning and didn't drop by to say hello? Emma shrugged to hide her confusion. She turned away and began folding towels so Mrs. McCullough couldn't see the hurt in her expression. That's why the woman was here, to get her digs in about Wyatt.

"It's turned out fine for everyone, it seems. I'm glad." The older woman nodded awkwardly and took a hesitant step.

Emma frowned. Why wasn't Mrs. McCullough throwing in her usual barbs? "Are you feeling well, Mrs. McCullough?"

"Well, actually…"

Emma's lashes flew up. The woman's face looked drawn and pinched, with dark rings circling her eyes. She'd lost weight, too. Emma felt terrible for not noticing earlier. Stepping closer, she clasped the woman's hands and led her to the examination table.

"I'm sorry, but Doc Brady won't be back till four." While she held the woman's hands, she unobtrusively slid her finger against the woman's pulse. It felt fairly strong. A little fast, but strong.

"I—I came to see *you.*"

Emma reared back in surprise. Mrs. McCullough had never confided in her before. *"Me?"*

The older woman's cheeks grew red. "It's so difficult to talk about, that's why I came to a woman. I saw Dr. Pendleton in Levi Valley about it, that is, I talked to him. Lord knows I'd never let him examine me *down there.* Oh, and heavens, talking to Russell Brady about it, well, we went to grade school together, and I just couldn't— "

It took Emma thirty minutes, two cups of tea, a hand-drawn sketch of the dress Rose was sewing for her for the wedding and a promise to never tell anyone, before Mrs. McCullough explained her problem.

With a quick examination, Emma confirmed it. "You have a prolapsed uterus, Mrs. McCullough. It often happens to women who've given birth to as many children as you have, nine if I recall. That would explain your symptoms, the bladder problems, the discomfort."

The woman trembled as she did up the final button of her dress. "Do you have medicine you can give me?"

"Medicine won't help. In your case, the problem will get worse unless you have surgery."

Mrs. McCullough paled. "Surgery?"

Emma put a hand around the shaking shoulders and led the woman to a chair. "Do you know what a hysterectomy is?"

The older woman nodded. "But who'll do it for me?"

she said in a weak voice. With a sudden new spark in her eyes, she tilted her head up at Emma. "Will you do it?"

Emma's fingers fluttered to her throat. She stepped back uneasily. "I can't."

"I heard how good you were with Wyatt, removing his bullet with a fork."

"A spoon."

"Please do it for me," Mrs. McCullough pleaded. "It would be a big relief to know I'm being looked after by another woman. Someone who understands."

While the older woman insisted, Emma's resolve began to melt. Other women in town felt the same as Mrs. McCullough, wishing they had a woman doctor to open up to. They'd told Emma outright during these past few days. Even some of the men were taking to her.

Pine Creek was full of really fine folks, people who cared about her a great deal. Emma's skin tingled with the satisfying realization.

Mrs. McCullough started weeping, and Emma, sliding her hand into her pocket for a handkerchief, accidentally yanked the stagecoach ticket out with it.

Taking a deep breath, she stared at it long and hard. The right decision finally came to her.

It was a beautiful day for a wedding. The clear Montana sky shimmered deep blue, and the warm August sun danced across her cheeks. Emma clutched her bouquet of red wildflowers, picked up the hem of her lavender dress and walked up the church stairs.

She stood proudly beside the young couple as they said their vows, and stole a glance at the man who possessed her heart, Wyatt, smiling on the other side.

With his broad shoulders and muscular frame handsomely dressed in a navy suit, his black hair slicked at the sides, he looked as if his health and power had returned.

And his strong, dark looks made her heart pound and her knees quiver. Standing this close to him was bittersweet torture.

He was happy. She could see it in his smile, the way he looked at his daughter. And, in the captivating smile he sent her way. His sparkle filled her up, and Lord, she tried to smile back, not wanting to show him how badly her heart had cracked, but she couldn't gaze at him for long without trembling.

To protect herself, she had to stay her distance. She'd cried enough tears and soaked enough pillows. They'd be friends, nothing more. She'd learn to accept it in time. And his kindness and companionship as a friend were precious to her, something she held dear.

It was all she had.

Besides, she wouldn't dwell on herself any longer. Her problems were trivial compared to problems others had to face. She saw it every day in medicine. She thanked the Lord for what she did have, and promised to be the best doctor she could be. Her new decision about her medical career filled her senses with fresh hope and excitement.

Today was Melissa's day. She looked bewitching in her cream silk gown. Three real pearls were sewn into her neckline, and her lace veil flowed behind her, dipping to her hips. Her auburn hair, done in ringlets around her face, set off her deep, dark eyes, and her freckly nose kept scrunching up all day, she was doing so much smiling.

Cole, dressed in a gentleman's charcoal jacket with black trousers and black satin tie, couldn't keep his eyes, or his hands, off his bride. Every time Emma caught them whispering happily to each other, her own heart gushed.

Billy, of course, was the delight of the ceremony. Rose

had taken a piece of Melissa's extra lace, and the black satin from Cole's tie, and sewn the baby a little black vest and a lace-covered diaper cloth. Combined with the tiny cowboy hat Wyatt had bought for him, the baby was irresistible. Ma wouldn't put him down.

For Emma, staying away from Wyatt at the ceremony was a lot easier than staying away from him at the reception.

Outdoors, she found herself walking right next to him, mingling with the crowd as they headed to the schoolhouse. She tried not to step too close.

With her hair swirling loose and long, they accidentally brushed shoulders and Wyatt's hand dipped close to hers. A hot current shot through her skin, and she pulled her hand away. The quick movement jarred the beaded purse on her wrist. Did he notice her sudden jerk?

His deep black eyes sparkled, making her knees wobble. "Are you enjoying yourself today?"

"Very much. Melissa and Cole seem so happy together, and I'm glad for them, after what they've been through."

His breathing grew shaky and his body swayed.

Concern shot through her. "Do you feel all right?"

He nodded, swallowing. "I'm fine."

Since he was walking straight, and he looked fine, she decided not to press him.

A lazy grin tugged at his lips. "Are you worried about me?"

"Of course I'm worried."

"How much?"

"As much as any doctor would be."

The smile faded. "Doctor, huh?" He kept walking, thinking, as his boots crunched on gravel. His eyes flashed with mischief. "You know, I enjoyed our…*swim,* the other day, Doc."

Emma gasped and felt her cheeks heat. How could he bring up the topic, here in front of everyone! Why the baker and his wife were walking only three feet away, Mrs. McCullough was practically behind them and the reverend himself was just up ahead, talking to Cole and Melissa.

She couldn't contain her frustration. "I should have let you drown."

He stared at her, grinning wider, laughter in every line on his handsome face.

"What are you staring at now?" she demanded.

"It's that jiggle."

She snorted and ducked into the crowd ahead, pretending she had something important to say to Rose. She could hear him laughing softly behind her, and when her heart stopped pounding and she felt safe again, she let her guard down. Honestly, the man had no manners.

She gave him an icy shoulder and stepped through the doors of the schoolhouse.

It was as if she'd stepped back into her school days. The shiny polished plank floor, the rows of windows along the side wall, the memories of the days when they were forbidden to speak to each other.

Except this time, their families, the Barlows and Sinclairs, had joined together to decorate the schoolhouse with streamers, flowers, wedding cake and wine. And she was proud of all of them. Wyatt mirrored her thoughts in a moving speech.

Fortunately, Emma was protected from him by talkative family members during the meal, and the coffee and pastry afterward. But when the tables were cleared for dancing, and his sensual gaze turned her way, she scurried for a route of escape.

Straight out the door.

The night breeze rustled over her warm skin, and the

rich scent of pines and cedars and cottonwoods filled her lungs.

She sighed. She lived in heaven. There was no place like Montana.

The musicians started playing softly in the background, and she smiled, recognizing the waltz. She slipped back inside to watch Melissa and Cole dance their first dance.

Standing near the back, lost in the crowd, she gazed warmly at the two young people in love. Candles flickered on tables lined up against the walls. Pale moonlight filtered through the window squares. It all combined to shimmer magically over Melissa's gown, and as the couple passed by Emma, Melissa's gaze held her own for a gentle, lingering moment.

"Thank you," Melissa mouthed softly.

Emma smiled tenderly, her eyes spilling over. It'd all worked out so well.

"Everyone join in," called the musicians.

A hand grazed her shoulder. She looked up at Wyatt just as she was wiping her eyes.

"Dance with me," he asked.

"Oh, Wyatt, I don't know...."

His hand on her shoulder tightened and his voice grew husky. "Please, just one. We've never danced."

His gaze was so gentle and tender, her resistance faded and she dissolved. He was her friend. Would always be her friend.

She smiled. "I'd love to dance with you."

He slid his warm fingers into hers, making her quiver, and led her through the crowd to the edge of the dance floor.

Turning to face her, he held her close, a large firm hand pressed at the back of her waist, his mouth inches from hers. Her body tingled from the contact.

Looking into his dark passionate eyes, she began to tremble. She would remember this moment for an eternity. How long had she waited for it? How many years? Her whole life? Was it really happening? Yes, he was staring at her, waiting for her answer.

"Oh, yes, I'll marry you."

The families cheered.

Wyatt hooted and yanked her tight, standing a breath away, dipping his face to hers. When they kissed, the music started again.

"I'm not going back to Philadelphia," she whispered against his ear.

"You're not *what?*"

His obvious pleasure made her melt against him.

"I'm not going back, I've already wired the hospital. I've decided to stay, right here where I belong. If the trip through the mountains taught me anything, it's how badly Montana needs doctors. And how badly I need Montana."

He crushed her in his arms and nuzzled her neck. "I need you. I love you, sweetheart. Tell me you love me."

She shivered with joy. "I love you. I've always loved you and I'll never stop."

He moaned, sending wicked pleasure cascading right through to her bones.

Laughing softly, she looked down at the envelope in her hand. "Where are we headed?"

His eyes shone brightly. "London, then on to Paris for our honeymoon." He stroked the nape of her neck and her shivers began again.

"Paris, how perfect. Our honeymoon," she sighed, rising on tiptoe to kiss him.

"It'll be an adventure," he murmured, "you can tell our children...."

* * * * *

Lookin' for some spicy Westerns seasoned
with just the right amount of sizzling
romance and rollicking adventure? Then help
yourselves to these Harlequin Historicals novels

ON SALE MARCH 2002

A MARRIAGE BY CHANCE
by **Carolyn Davidson**
(Wyoming, 1894)

SHADES OF GRAY
by **Wendy Douglas**
(Texas, 1868)

ON SALE APRIL 2002

THE BRIDE FAIR
by **Cheryl Reavis**
(North Carolina, 1868)

THE DRIFTER
by **Lisa Plumley**
(Arizona, 1887)

 Harlequin Historicals®

Take a jaunt to Merry Old England with these timeless stories from Harlequin Historicals

On sale March 2002

THE LOVE MATCH
by Deborah Simmons
Deborah Hale
Nicola Cornick

Don't miss this captivating bridal collection filled with three breathtaking Regency tales!

MARRYING MISCHIEF
by Lyn Stone

Will a quarantine spark romance between a determined earl and his convenient bride?

On sale April 2002

MISS VEREY'S PROPOSAL
by Nicola Cornick

A matchmaking duke causes a smitten London debutante to realize she's betrothed to the wrong brother!

DRAGON'S KNIGHT
by Catherine Archer

When a powerful knight rushes to the aid of a beautiful noblewoman, will he finally conquer his darkest demons?

 Harlequin Historicals®

HHMED23

This Mother's Day Give Your Mom A Royal Treat

Win a fabulous one-week vacation in Puerto Rico for you and your mother at the luxurious Inter-Continental San Juan Resort & Casino. The prize includes round trip airfare for two, breakfast daily and a mother and daughter day of beauty at the beachfront hotel's spa.

INTER·CONTINENTAL
San Juan
RESORT & CASINO

Here's all you have to do:

Tell us in 100 words or less how your mother helped with the romance in your life. It may be a story about your engagement, wedding or those boyfriends when you were a teenager or any other romantic advice from your mother. The entry will be judged based on its originality, emotionally compelling nature and sincerity. See official rules on following page.

Send your entry to:
Mother's Day Contest

In Canada	**In U.S.A.**
P.O. Box 637	P.O. Box 9076
Fort Erie, Ontario	3010 Walden Ave.
L2A 5X3	Buffalo, NY
	14269-9076

Or enter online at www.eHarlequin.com

PRROY

HARLEQUIN MOTHER'S DAY CONTEST 2216
OFFICIAL RULES
NO PURCHASE NECESSARY TO ENTER

Two ways to enter:

• **Via The Internet:** Log on to the Harlequin romance website (www.eHarlequin.com) anytime beginning 12:01 a.m. E.S.T., January 1, 2002 through 11:59 p.m. E.S.T., April 1, 2002 and follow the directions displayed on-line to enter your name, address (including zip code), e-mail address and in 100 words or fewer, describe how your mother helped with the romance in your life.

• **Via Mail:** Handprint (or type) on an 8 1/2" x 11" plain piece of paper, your name, address (including zip code) and e-mail address (if you have one), and in 100 words or fewer, describe how your mother helped with the romance in your life. Mail your entry via first-class mail to: Harlequin Mother's Day Contest 2216, (in the U.S.) P.O. Box 9076, Buffalo, NY 14269-9076; (in Canada) P.O. Box 637, Fort Erie, Ontario, Canada L2A 5X3.

For eligibility, entries must be submitted either through a completed Internet transmission or postmarked no later than 11:59 p.m. E.S.T., April 1, 2002 (mail-in entries must be received by April 9, 2002). Limit one entry per person, household address and e-mail address. On-line and/or mailed entries received from persons residing in geographic areas in which entry is not permissible will be disqualified.

Entries will be judged by a panel of judges, consisting of members of the Harlequin editorial, marketing and public relations staff using the following criteria:
• Originality - 50%
• Emotional Appeal - 25%
• Sincerity - 25%

In the event of a tie, duplicate prizes will be awarded. Decisions of the judges are final.

Prize: A 6-night/7-day stay for two at the Inter-Continental San Juan Resort & Casino, including round-trip coach air transportation from gateway airport nearest winner's home (approximate retail value: $4,000). Prize includes breakfast daily and a mother and daughter day of beauty at the beachfront hotel's spa. Prize consists of only those items listed as part of the prize. Prize is valued in U.S. currency.

All entries become the property of Torstar Corp. and will not be returned. No responsibility is assumed for lost, late, illegible, incomplete, inaccurate, non-delivered or misdirected mail or misdirected e-mail, for technical, hardware or software failures of any kind, lost or unavailable network connections, or failed, incomplete, garbled or delayed computer transmission or any human error which may occur in the receipt or processing of the entries in this Contest.

Contest open only to residents of the U.S. (except Colorado) and Canada, who are 18 years of age or older and is void wherever prohibited by law; all applicable laws and regulations apply. Any litigation within the Province of Quebec respecting the conduct or organization of a publicity contest may be submitted to the Régie des alcools, des courses et des jeux for a ruling. Any litigation respecting the awarding of a prize may be submitted to the Régie des alcools, des courses et des jeux only for the purpose of helping the parties reach a settlement. Employees and immediate family members of Torstar Corp. and D.L. Blair, Inc., their affiliates, subsidiaries and all other agencies, entities and persons connected with the use, marketing or conduct of this Contest are not eligible to enter. Taxes on prize are the sole responsibility of winner. Acceptance of any prize offered constitutes permission to use winner's name, photograph or other likeness for the purposes of advertising, trade and promotion on behalf of Torstar Corp., its affiliates and subsidiaries without further compensation to the winner, unless prohibited by law.

Winner will be determined no later than April 15, 2002 and be notified by mail. Winner will be required to sign and return an Affidavit of Eligibility form within 15 days after winner notification. Non-compliance within that time period may result in disqualification and an alternate winner may be selected. Winner of trip must execute a Release of Liability prior to ticketing and must possess required travel documents (e.g. Passport, photo ID) where applicable. Travel must be completed within 12 months of selection and is subject to traveling companion completing and returning a Release of Liability prior to travel; and hotel and flight accommodations availability. Certain restrictions and blackout dates may apply. No substitution of prize permitted by winner. Torstar Corp. and D.L. Blair, Inc., their parents, affiliates, and subsidiaries are not responsible for errors in printing or electronic presentation of Contest, or entries. In the event of printing or other errors which may result in unintended prize values or duplication of prizes, all affected entries shall be null and void. If for any reason the Internet portion of the Contest is not capable of running as planned, including infection by computer virus, bugs, tampering, unauthorized intervention, fraud, technical failures, or any other causes beyond the control of Torstar Corp. which corrupt or affect the administration, secrecy, fairness, integrity or proper conduct of the Contest, Torstar Corp. reserves the right, at its sole discretion, to disqualify any individual who tampers with the entry process and to cancel, terminate, modify or suspend the Contest or the Internet portion thereof. In the event the Internet portion must be terminated a notice will be posted on the website and all entries received prior to termination will be judged in accordance with these rules. In the event of a dispute regarding an on-line entry, the entry will be deemed submitted by the authorized holder of the e-mail account submitted at the time of entry. Authorized account holder is defined as the natural person who is assigned to an e-mail address by an Internet access provider, on-line service provider or other organization that is responsible for arranging e-mail address for the domain associated with the submitted e-mail address. Torstar Corp. and/or D.L. Blair Inc. assumes no responsibility for any computer injury or damage related to or resulting from accessing and/or downloading any sweepstakes material. Rules are subject to any requirements/limitations imposed by the FCC. **Purchase or acceptance of a product offer does not improve your chances of winning.**

For winner's name (available after May 1, 2002), send a self-addressed, stamped envelope to: Harlequin Mother's Day Contest Winners 2216, P.O. Box 4200 Blair, NE 68009-4200 or you may access the www.eHarlequin.com Web site through June 3, 2002.

Contest sponsored by Torstar Corp., P.O. Box 9042, Buffalo, NY 14269-9042.

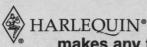